Rainy Day Dreams

RAINY DAY DREAMS

LORI COPELAND
VIRGINIA SMITH

THORNDIKE PRESS
A part of Gale, Cengage Learning

GALE
CENGAGE Learning·

Farmington Hills, Mich • San Francisco • New York • Waterville, Maine
Meriden, Conn • Mason, Ohio • Chicago

Copyright © 2014 by Copeland Inc. and Virginia Smith.
Seattle Brides Series #2.
Thorndike Press, a part of Gale, Cengage Learning.

LIBRARY OF CONGRESS CATALOGING-IN-PUBLICATION DATA

Copeland, Lori.
  Rainy day dreams / by Lori Copeland and Virginia Smith.
    pages ; cm. — (Seattle brides series ; #2) (Thorndike Press large print Christian historical fiction)
  ISBN 978-1-4104-6574-0 (hardcover) — ISBN 1-4104-6574-8 (hardcover)
  1. Brides—Fiction. 2. Seattle (Wash.)—History—19th century—Fiction.
I. Smith, Virginia, 1960- II. Title.
PS3553.O6336R35 2014b
813'.54—dc23   2014002778

Published in 2014 by arrangement with Books & Such Literary Agency, Inc.

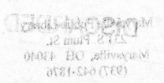

He that dwelleth in the secret place of
the most High
shall abide under the shadow of the
Almighty.
I will say of the LORD,
He is my refuge and my fortress:
my God; in him will I trust.

PSALM 91:1-2

ONE

Seattle, Washington Territory
Monday, January 7, 1856

An unkempt sailor, scraggly and reeking of fish, pitched the steamer trunk from the ship's gangway to the pier as though tossing a salmon onto the deck. Instead of flopping wetly on the wood, Kathryn's trunk landed on the platform with a sickening thud that did not bode well for the contents.

"Here!" She charged down the sloping plank, skirts swishing around her cloth-topped boots, and fixed the man with an outraged glare. "What do you mean, heaving my things about like that? There are breakables inside."

Footsteps pounded the wooden dock from behind and the captain drew up beside her. "Is there a problem, ma'am?"

She whirled to face him. "The problem is my mother's fine porcelain basin and pitcher, which are packed inside my trunk and probably in shards due to careless handling."

The sailor snatched the cap off his head and ducked to reveal a pink, balding scalp. "Sorry, ma'am. That's a heavy trunk, that is. It slipped plumb out of my hands." His gaze slid upward toward his skipper, as though to test the reception of his explanation.

"Hmm." Kathryn didn't believe him. With her own eyes she'd watched him pitch the trunk rather than carry it the extra ten steps down the gangway. On the other hand, the large number of books with which she'd lined the bottom no doubt made her portmanteau heavier than most.

"Accidents do happen, ma'am." The captain offered the explanation with a hopeful smile.

An answering retort rose to her lips, but she bit it back. What benefit would come of arguing? If the washbasin had been broken, the deed was done. She'd have no recourse, regardless of the exorbitant price her father had paid for her passage. Nor would she seek redress and risk offending the captain. She needed to remain in his good graces in order to ensure her place on a return voyage to San Francisco the next time the *Fair Lady* put into port in Seattle. Besides, she cared little for the breakable items inside the sturdy chest. Her library and art supplies were of far more import, especially here in this forsaken wilderness. And they could withstand a fair amount of rough handling.

She forced a smile and shone it on both captain and crewman. "I'm sure there has been no harm done."

Relieved, the sailor planted the cap back on his head and stepped lightly up the plank, presumably to manhandle another passenger's luggage. Having seen the exchange, a middle-aged woman stood on the gently swaying deck near a pile of trunks, clutching a valise in both hands and watching anxiously as the man headed her way.

The captain returned to his conversation with a handsome young man to whom she had been introduced during the voyage and whose name she had promptly forgotten.

She scanned the shore. The pier where the *Fair Lady* was moored extended into the water from a wide wooden dock. From there a muddy street stretched inland, lined with buildings made of rough-cut timber. Signs suspended above doorways identified a variety of businesses including a livery, a laundry, and even a dentist. The thick forest she had seen from the ship's deck as they glided parallel to the shoreline this afternoon grew right up to the structures, leafy heights towering high above. In fact, trees surrounded the dock area on two sides, so thick she could barely see a few feet beyond the tall trunks of the first few. The forest ended abruptly to her right in a clearing that laid bare the shoreline all the way to a riverhead and beyond. A building sat on the shore at the mouth of the river, white clouds billowing from a tall smokestack. Ah, the famous steam mill. Before she left San Francisco, Papa had insisted on describing it in enthusiastic detail.

"Imagine, Kathryn! You'll live near the only steam-powered sawmill in the northwest. That mill was the making of Seattle, you know. Without it, the town would be nothing but a handful of pioneers trying to scratch out a life in the forest. Mr. Yesler is a forward-thinking gentleman, to be sure. And his vision has made him rich." Admiration had gleamed in Papa's eyes, and then his gaze turned speculative. "A shame he is married. Perhaps you'll meet someone like him in Seattle."

Kathryn had lowered her eyes in what may have been interpreted as meekness. In reality she hoped to mask the scorn that his ill-concealed enthusiasm stirred. Truthfully,

Papa cared little for the bankroll of her prospective beaux, so long as they weren't destitute. Actually, he probably wouldn't mind a penniless son-in-law either, so long as the young man relieved him of the responsibility of his unmarried daughter. His insistence that she find a husband was downright insulting, as though a grown woman of modern times was incapable of surviving on her own.

I'm surprised he hasn't placed an advertisement in the Chronicle *offering a sizable dowry so he can be rid of me quickly.*

The thought drew a bitter smile. What need had he in placing an advertisement when he could send her to Seattle and accomplish the same end with much less expense? She scanned the area, taking note of the people who scurried down the covered walkways or stomped through the wide, muddy avenue. Men, every one of them. Not a woman in sight, except her and the few female passengers who had accompanied her on the *Fair Lady*. The rumor circulating among the patrons at the San Francisco Center for Fine Arts must be true. Imagine, one woman to every hundred men.

And several of them openly staring at her at this very moment. She returned the direct and curious gaze of a man standing in the doorway of an establishment halfway up the street, beneath a sign identifying the place as Hop Sing Washing Ironing. With a prim look in his direction, she turned her back.

"Excuse me, ma'am." A nearby voice drew her attention to a wiry man with threadbare clothing and an eager expression. "Can I tote your bags for you?"

She hesitated only a moment. She couldn't very well lug her own trunk through the mud, could she?

"Yes, I think so." She cocked her head and fixed a narrow-eyed stare on him. "Do you know the Faulkner House?"

"I know the place." His gaze became speculative and roved over her from head to toe. "You planning on working there, are you?"

With a hot flush, she thrust her nose into the air. Was the question a judgment on her apparel, as if she didn't look wealthy enough to board there? "The proprietress, Mrs. Garritson, is my cousin."

"You don't say." His lips pursed as he studied her a second more, and then his expression cleared. "Twenty-five cents. And I'll treat your trunk like it was made of glass too."

Obviously he'd overheard her exchange

with the captain.

"Done." She jerked a nod to seal the deal, and then went on with a concerned glance around the area. None of the buildings in the vicinity looked like proper hotels. "Is it far?"

"Just up the hill a ways." The man grabbed a handle of her trunk, tested the weight, and then hefted it up onto his back as though the heavy case were packed with feather pillows. "Foller me, miss."

Kathryn started out after him, her heels pounding soundly on the plank walkway. She'd gone no more than three steps when a deep voice from behind halted her progress.

"Pardon me, but did I hear you mention the Faulkner House?"

She turned to find the young man with whom the captain had been speaking standing at her elbow. He wore an expression of polite inquiry, his square jaw set. Something about his expression put Kathryn off. Perhaps it was the way he slanted his shoulders away from her, or the way his gaze darted in her direction and then away. His bearing shouted of arrogance while the inexpertly sewn patches on the sleeves of his suit coat denied the unspoken claim.

She tilted her chin upward. "That is correct."

A smile emerged on the serious face, its charm lost when it faded just as quickly. "I am headed there myself, as chance would have it." His gaze sought the lackey who was placing her trunk into the bed of a small wagon while a mournful mule hitched to the front turned its head to watch. "Have you room for my luggage as well?"

"If you have twenty-five cents, I have room."

"That's fine then. Shouldn't be but a few minutes." He awarded her a distracted nod and then turned to watch the crewmen unloading trunks and crates from the cargo hold. Then his eyebrows drew together and he lifted his voice toward the ship. "You there, take care with that!" With three long-legged strides he was up the gangway and onto the ship's deck, his finger stabbing toward the crew.

The captain stepped up to the dock's edge beside Kathryn, the lady with the valise at his side. "Miss Bergert, I expect you'll have met Miss Everett?"

They had been formally introduced before the *Fair Lady* set sail in San Francisco and had shared a cabin, though the older woman kept to herself throughout the week-long

14

voyage. Dark hair with a few streaks of silver had been pulled back from her face in a severe knot at the base of her skull, and she hid her expression beneath the deep brim of a plain and sensible travel bonnet. An air of sadness surrounded the woman, creating an invisible barrier that the other passengers had respected and not broached. Kathryn nodded a silent greeting, which she returned.

"Miss Everett has also booked lodging at the Faulkner House." He raised his voice. "Carter, you'll take her along with Miss Bergert and Mr. Gates."

Had the commanding tone been directed toward her, Kathryn would have bristled. The wagoner merely grinned and snapped to attention with an impudent salute. "Aye-aye, Cap'n."

The captain paid him no attention but strode away, his boots connecting with the dock in a confident *thud-thud-thud*. Kathryn watched his retreat while pulling her cloak tighter around her throat with a gloved hand. A constant breeze blew across the water and brought with it a chill that had not been present in San Francisco. She glanced toward the sky. Somewhere behind that thick ceiling of gray the sun lay in hiding, its absence fitting on this day of what

15

she could only think of as her exile.

Susan would not have accepted this fate meekly. She would have recruited Mama to her side and then pitched a fit until she got her way.

A sniffle threatened, but she straightened her shoulders against such a piteous gesture. Her sister's very nature, so different from her own, would have prevented her being placed in such an undignified position to begin with. That's why Susan ran away from home, to escape Papa's attempts to manipulate her life. Her leaving had bought Kathryn almost five years of peace. After their initial shock at Susan's farewell letter, her parents feared they might lose Kathryn too if they tried to force her into a life she did not choose. If Papa had spent a single moment considering the difference in his daughters' personalities he would have known he had nothing to fear. She would never act in such a headstrong manner.

With a stomp of her heel against the wooden dock she pushed such thoughts to the back of her mind. Adventure had been thrust upon her by Papa, and she might as well make the most of it. Better that than become morose. Besides, she didn't intend to stay in this primitive town one day longer than necessary.

The other passenger — Mr. Gates, the captain had called him — returned with a carpetbag slung over one shoulder and a leather satchel in the other hand. A crewman followed, carrying a narrow wooden crate awkwardly before him.

"Load it there." He pointed toward the mule cart. "And take care, if you please."

When the luggage had been positioned in the wagon bed to everyone's satisfaction, Carter approached the edge of the dock and, with a two-handed flourish, gestured toward the narrow bench. "This way, ladies."

Miss Everett threw a startled glance toward Kathryn. The wooden platform ended a few inches above the dirt-packed shore, a matter of one shallow downward step. Recent rains had softened the soil into mud, and apparently they were expected to walk through it in complete disregard for their footwear. Though Kathryn cared little for fashion, she had no desire to ruin her shoes. Judging by the handful of rustic buildings within sight, she doubted if Seattle offered much in the way of ladies' clothiers. Replacements would be hard to come by.

"Can you draw your mule nearer?" She drew aside her skirts to reveal the stylish boots Mama had insisted on purchasing before she left. "We're hardly dressed for tromping through the mud."

Carter eyed her feet and indulged in an impolite chortle. "I hope you packed something sturdier. Them dainties ain't gonna last long here."

Still, he obliged by grabbing the mule's harness and angling the cart near enough to the wharf that a long step would see them safely aboard. When he made no move to offer assistance but stood holding the mule's bit, apparently ready to watch them leap for the bench, Kathryn opened her mouth to deliver a sharp word. She shut it again when Mr. Gates stepped to Miss Everett's side and extended a hand.

"Allow me."

With a grateful smile, the older woman grasped his arm and climbed safely aboard. She scooted across to the opposite end of the bench and began arranging her cloak around her while Mr. Gates turned to assist Kathryn.

"It's nice to see that someone in Seattle has manners." She spoke loud enough for Carter to hear. "Though obviously they're not native to the locals."

Rather than taking offense, Carter's chortle returned with increased volume. "They's some gentlemen here. A few anyway. We're plain folk, mostly."

Kathryn accepted Mr. Gates's extended hand and climbed onto the wagon with one long step. He released her the moment she had her balance and hopped off the wharf. His boots hit the wet soil with a muddy splat. As she settled her skirts, a pair of sailors sauntered by and one of them let out an admiring whistle. She pretended to ignore them, though heat rose into her face.

Carter dropped the mule's lead rope, hands clenched into fists, and fixed a glare on the passing soldiers. "You watch yourself, y'hear? These here are ladies."

Kathryn exchanged a grin with Miss Everett. Carter may disregard the need for manners personally, but he clearly held others to a different standard. Or perhaps he simply disliked sailors. Her gaze slid to Elliott Bay, where a military ship lay in anchor. They had passed closely by her on their way to the pier. The name stenciled on the ship's side read *U.S.S. Decatur.*

"Mr. Carter, what is the purpose of that vessel?"

As she asked the question, the man urged the mule forward and the wagon lurched. She grasped the edge of the bench to keep her balance.

"Been here for months." The answer was

tossed over his shoulder. "Matter of fact, they hauled her out and cleaned her up not long ago. In a terrible state, so folks say."

Kathryn glanced over her shoulder. The *Fair Lady* and the *Decatur* were the only ships in sight. "Seems an odd place to go for repairs. Doesn't the Navy have shipyards or similar places?"

"Oh, she didn't come here to be fixed up. She came a few months ago on account of the Injuns, and stuck around."

Beside her, Miss Everett gave a little gasp and her wide eyes snapped to Kathryn's face. "Is there trouble with the Indians?"

The mule stepped sideways when the wagon wheels slid and then tossed its head in an attempt to dislodge his handler's hold. Kathryn tightened her grip on the bench. Carter became preoccupied in keeping the animal moving forward.

Mr. Gates, who had been walking beside the wagon, answered in his stead. "Captain Baker and I discussed the same thing. Apparently there was a scare some months ago, along with a few random attacks on lone travelers. But he assured me those were isolated events and nothing to worry about."

Kathryn turned her head to address his profile. "Then why has the Navy not recalled its ship?"

"The former captain was relieved of command not long ago, and the new captain found the ship in a state of disrepair." He shrugged, his tone matter-of-fact. "They decided to repair her here."

Miss Everett leaned forward to see around Kathryn. "So there's no conflict with the Indians?"

"Not according to Captain Baker. A few panicky settlers raised a fuss, but the authorities have investigated and found no cause for concern."

A smile flickered onto his face, and his eyes warmed. For an instant he looked quite handsome, and Kathryn found herself smiling in response. Unfortunately, his features didn't appear accustomed to the arrangement and returned to their serious state after mere moments.

"Hmph." At the mule's head, Carter's stiff posture shouted disagreement as he tugged on his animal's rope.

"You don't agree, Mr. Carter?" Kathryn leaped on the question, eager to turn away from Mr. Gates.

"There's good Injuns and bad ones, that's all I'm sayin'."

"That's true of all men." She went on in a teasing tone. "Some have manners, and some don't."

Instead of smiling at her good-natured jab, he jerked his head around and fixed her with a tight-lipped stare. "Jest so."

The response stirred feelings of disquiet. She exchanged a troubled glance with Miss Everett, and then fell silent.

Buildings lined the wide avenue on either side and a covered walkway ran along in front of them. They met another wagon heading in the direction of the pier, this one pulled by a sturdy horse. The driver nodded at Carter as they passed and lifted an eager gaze toward Kathryn and Miss Everett, who both kept their gazes modestly averted. In fact, it was hard to find any place to look without encountering a staring man. They came out of the buildings to line the walkway and watch their progress. Some shouted greetings like, "Howdy, ladies," and "Welcome to Seattle," while others snatched caps off their heads and bobbed them eagerly. The weight of dozens of eyes pressed against her on both sides. They seemed starved for the sight of a woman. Some ladies of her acquaintance would revel in such attention, but these men's expressions left her distinctly uncomfortable. Would it be safe to traverse the streets of Seattle without hiring a guard?

"It appears you have created a stir."

She glanced down at Mr. Gates. An amused grin curved his lips as he trudged along beside the wagon. A moment ago she had found his smile comforting, but this one rubbed against nerves made touchy by being the unaccustomed object of so much male scrutiny.

"And it seems you are enjoying our discomfiture."

His eyebrows arched, and the grin twisted enough to become sardonic. "Surely you aren't surprised by the attention."

Kathryn's spine stiffened at his tone. "What are you implying, sir?"

"Only that a woman traveling to a town where men make up an overwhelming majority of the population must realize she is certain to become an immediate focus." He cocked his head slightly and narrowed his eyes, as though evaluating her. "In fact, most men would assume such a woman chose the town for that reason."

Why, the nerve! He practically accused her of being a coquette. She bristled, a sharp denial rising to her tongue. In the next instant the words died unspoken. That was exactly the reason Papa had sent her to Seattle. Against her wishes.

But she certainly wasn't inclined to reveal her personal trials to a stranger. With a flounce she turned away from him and faced forward, her posture rigidly correct.

What an infuriating man.

Jason regretted the words the instant they left his mouth. As usual, he'd spoken without fully considering what he said. Women always took a man's words personally. He'd learned that from Beth early on. He didn't intend to insult Miss Bergert, merely to make an observation that was perfectly obvious to everyone. Seattle was a man's town, a place where brute strength and ingenuity won the day. Thousands of men agreed with him, proven by the fact that they came in droves to work the forest and the lumber mill that was quickly making a name for the fledgling town. Why else would a single woman journey here, if not to find a husband? That was a perfectly acceptable reason, as far as he was concerned. As long as she left him alone, Miss Bergert could have her pick.

Beside the girl on the bench, the older woman sat with her head lowered, staring at the gloved hands folded in her lap. With a start he realized she'd taken his comment as directed at her as well. During the voyage from San Francisco, Captain Baker had confided that she was looking to start a new life away from the painful memories of the city. Jason had identified with her as a fellow escapee, and took care to treat her kindly the few times she emerged from her bunk. Cursing himself for a thoughtless idiot, he opened his mouth to apologize, but then snapped it closed. The look on Miss Bergert's averted face still held a frosty fury. No doubt whatever he said to the older lady would be misinterpreted as another insult to her.

Instead, he lengthened his stride and overtook Carter at the front of the wagon, where he was coaxing his beast forward. He'd feel more comfortable talking to the mule than to the women.

The line of buildings ended abruptly. On the right lay a wide clearing, the ground still littered with knee-high stumps and a pile of felled trees, their sawed-off branches scattered untidily about. A new building site, perhaps? Beyond that the street sloped upward and the surrounding forest pressed in on both sides. The cart tilted as the mule trudged up the hill, and one of the bags in the wagon bed slid backward and slapped into the rear gate. He shot a quick glance over his shoulder. Ah, good. It was one of the smaller bags. The crate holding his painting was still wedged securely between the side rail and the heaviest of the trunks.

The wagon lurched sideways and Miss Bergert grabbed at the bench to brace herself. He averted his gaze from her startled expression. When her dark green eyes were rounded like that, they held a loveliness he had not noticed at first. Though he certainly had not examined her closely, he'd formed a vague opinion of plain, rather severe looks. But perhaps that was only because of the square-brimmed bonnet and unflattering cloak that hung from her shoulders more like a bag than a fitted garment. And the fact that he had rarely seen a real smile on the lips that were perpetually tightened in an expression of disdain. This young woman was a picture of arrogance, a quality for which he'd never had any patience in men or women.

Beth was the opposite of arrogant. Her sweet temperament had won her many an admirer back home in Michigan.

Thoughts of Beth sent a wave of homesickness washing through his soul. How he missed her! Sometimes his arms felt so empty they ached.

I can't dwell on thoughts of Beth, or I'll go crazy.

With an effort that threatened to exhaust him, he forced himself to focus on the here and now. They were traveling uphill on a wide road that had been carved out of the forest some years past. Mud sucked at his boots with every step and a raindrop splashed onto his head. It was quickly followed by another, and then another. He glanced up. Was the darkening sky due to the setting of the invisible sun or an approaching rainstorm? Impossible to tell. His pocket watch was buried beneath the layers of his heavy overcoat.

They rounded a curve in the road, and once again the forest gave way to a clearing on the right. More buildings stood here, forming another area of town that extended up the hill. Some neat, white-washed structures were clearly public establishments. Beyond and behind them lay a row of houses both large and small. Here, then, was the proper town, tucked halfway up the mountain, away from the wharf and the mill. Not a bad plan, to keep the two separate. Though judging by the clearing work occurring down by the bay, it wouldn't be long before that area expanded up the hill and joined this charming little collection of stores and homes.

As Carter led the mule down the street, a door opened in the building to the right and a figure appeared. A tall woman with a generous figure cloaked inside a merchant's apron stepped onto the plank walkway beneath a sign that read Coffinger's Dry Goods.

"Yoo-hoo, Mr. Carter!" She waggled her fingers in his direction. "Is the ship in, then?"

Carter halted his mule and ducked his head. "Yes'm, Miz Coffinger."

She turned her head and shouted over her shoulder in a commanding tone that could surely be heard down on the deck of the *Fair Lady.* "Boy, the ship's finally here. Get down to the pier and see to those supplies." She turned back to them and fixed a wide smile on the ladies seated on the wagon bench. "Welcome to Seattle, my dears. When you get settled, I'll pay you a call and we'll become acquainted."

When her gaze switched to Jason, an appreciative smile widened her lips, the only thing that could be described as thin on this woman's entire body. "You too, dearie."

Without waiting for an answer, she looked at Carter and barked, "Well, what are you waiting for? Can't you see it's about to pour?" And with that dire prediction, she retreated into the store.

Carter stood staring after her, scratching at his chin beneath his scraggly beard. "If you want my advice, watch yourself around that one. That woman'll have you begging to pay half a month's wages for a pail of dirt if you let your guard down." He shook his head and tugged the mule forward, but his grin held a touch of admiration.

With a final glance toward the dry goods store, Jason fell in step beside him. "I'll keep that in mind."

As they rolled past the store, Kathryn cast a wary eye skyward. One needn't be a weather predictor to know the store owner had spoken truthfully. There had been no need to carry her parasol ashore since the sun was nowhere in evidence, but she may have been wise to take it out of her trunk. Though it wouldn't provide much in the way of shelter, it would be better than nothing if the rain started in earnest before they reached their destination.

Her eyes were drawn to a tall, straight pole situated halfway down the avenue. How odd that the builders would leave a single tree stripped of its branches standing in the middle of town. When she looked again, she realized it was not a tree at all, but a tall post, as though someone had planted a ship's mast in the ground.

As they neared, she saw that its surface

had been carved and painted. The pole stood in front of a wide building that sat back from the others, fronted by a grassy area. Evangeline's Café, the sign said. She barely gave the place a glance, intent instead on studying the painted carvings as the wagon rolled past. They were nicely done, though somewhat primitive. Images of a bear and howling wolf were detailed and beautifully proportioned. The wood had been furrowed to look like animal fur. The people, though, were inexpertly carved. Disappointment dampened her momentary enthusiasm. No DaVinci did this. Certainly the work of an amateur, though a talented one. Ah, well. What did she expect in a backwater town like Seattle?

Carter brought the wagon to a halt in front of the building beyond the restaurant. The placard suspended from a post beside the door read FAULKNER HOUSE, ROOMS FOR LET. At last. With approval she inspected the wide porch, chairs placed to one side in an inviting display. Two stories tall, topped with a steeply pitched roof and rows of double windows with frilled curtains visible behind the multipaned glass. The immediate surroundings looked a bit austere, especially compared to the restaurant next door, which had no glass in the single wide window but boasted planters overflowing with colorful winter blooms on each side of the doorway. The paint on the Faulkner House could use refreshing too. In a few places the whitewash had worn thin on the porch posts. Perhaps she could suggest the idea to her cousin.

After she had settled in, that is. She certainly couldn't go suggesting changes the moment she met her relative for the first time. A rush of nerves invaded her stomach. What if she and Cousin Mary Ann didn't get along? They may not be compatible. After all, what kind of woman would voluntarily move to a remote and backward town like Seattle? Mr. Gates had rudely pointed out one kind. Papa had known little more than the bare facts about his distant cousin — that she had married an older, ailing man and spent her youth caring for him in a small town in Kansas Territory. With her husband's passing she had moved West to manage a boardinghouse for one of her father's friends, Captain Faulkner, in order to support herself. That sounded like a determined woman, one who knew what she wanted and set out to accomplish her goals. A woman Kathryn could admire.

Carter secured the mule's lead rope around a post in front of the porch. "This here's it," he announced as though they couldn't read the sign for themselves. "The Faulkner House."

He rounded the wagon and approached the bench, arms extended to assist Miss Everett in climbing down. Mr. Gates went round the opposite side and lifted his oddly shaped carton from the bed. He shot a worried glance toward the sky and strode quickly to the protection of the covered porch, where he took great care in leaning the crate against the wall beside the lodging house's entrance.

Fat raindrops fell with increasing speed to splat against her thick black cloak. Kathryn waited while Miss Everett turned to retrieve her valise from the bench and then hurried toward the porch, clutching Carter's supporting arm. A breeze kicked up and whipped a smattering of rain beneath the brim of Kathryn's bonnet. She froze, momentarily stunned at the sensation of being slapped in the face with cold water.

And then the downpour began in earnest.

Water dumped from the heavens as though a divine dam had burst directly overhead. Within seconds her cloak was drenched, her thin gloves sopping wet, and the ends of her hair, not protected by her sturdy bonnet, clung to her neck in dripping ringlets. The wind whipped water into her face with a hundred shocking, chilly slaps.

"Oh!" She stood paralyzed while buckets poured from the sky.

The others watched from the shelter of the porch, their expressions as startled as hers. Miss Everett's hand rose to cover her opened mouth, and even Mr. Gates's eyes bulged as he stood frozen, seemingly transfixed by the sight of her standing in the deluge.

Only Carter displayed any emotion at her predicament. He bent double, clutched his stomach, and laughed uproariously. "Why, wouldja look at that? We hardly ever get a gully-washer like this one here. Seems the good Lord has decided to give you a proper greeting, missy," he called over the roar of the rain. "Welcome to Seattle."

He guffawed at his own joke while Kathryn stood stranded on the wagon, too surprised to be angry at his ill-mannered humor. If this is how the good Lord chose to welcome her to Seattle, things did not bode well for her stay here.

Mr. Gates sprang into action. He leaped into the weather and waded the few steps through the quickly thickening mud, his arms outstretched to her. She didn't spare the time to think but tumbled forward, trusting that he would catch her. He did, and carried her to the porch with no more effort than if he were toting a bucket of goose down.

The minute her stylish boots, which were only partially soaked by virtue of being shielded beneath her heavy skirt and petticoats, touched down on the wooden porch, he released her. She wavered on her heels for a moment, grateful for the shelter. Within seconds, the deluge lightened and the rain returned to its previous steady drizzle. Never in all her days had she seen a rainstorm arrive and leave so quickly. The weather in San Francisco was far more predictable.

Before she had recovered her composure enough to thank Mr. Gates for rescuing her or to deliver a scornful reprimand to Carter for laughing at her predicament, the door was flung open. The voluminous form of a woman filled the doorway. Kathryn had the impression of pudgy red cheeks, steel gray hair, and a truly impressive bosom that strained a row of pearly buttons on the bodice of a cotton blouse. In the next instant, a coarse voice assaulted her ears.

"Finally here, are you? That Captain Baker will be late for his own funeral, mark my words." Beady eyes peered at them from sweaty folds of flesh. They fixed on Miss Everett. "You've paid in advance, so I'll see you to your room first." She switched to Mr. Gates. "If you're Jason Gates, Yesler was looking for you yesterday. He'll have seen the ship, so I expect he'll be around shortly."

In the few seconds it took for the piercing gaze to roam in her direction, Kathryn's stomach tightened. Surely this loud, forward woman could not be Papa's cousin. But the beady eyes fixed on her and swept her from bonnet to boots.

"You'll be Philip's daughter, then." The fleshy lips curled upward. "Not much to look at, are you? Still, maybe when you're dry and cleaned up you'll show some improvement."

The insult jolted through Kathryn like a spear. Her mouth gaped open, and her chest heaved with outraged breath in search of words on which to explode. "I beg your pardon!"

The woman waved a dismissive hand. "Don't go getting huffy right off the bat. You'll find I'm a woman who speaks her mind. No use taking offense at plain truth."

Miss Everett and Mr. Gates averted their gazes politely, but Carter seemed unfazed by the woman's blatant rudeness.

"I'll jest get them bags." He hopped off

35

the porch and sloshed five muddy paces toward the wagon.

Cousin Mary Ann cupped a hand aside her mouth and shouted at Carter. "Leave them on the porch. I don't want puddles inside." She turned a stern look on her guests. "See those hooks?" Her gesture indicated a row of pegs lining the wall to the right of the door. "Those are for your coats so you don't drip all over the entry hall."

With that, she disappeared inside without a backward glance.

Kathryn stood staring after the woman, her jaw slack. Imagine demanding that her guests disrobe and leave their things outside. Had she no inkling of hospitality, of common courtesy even?

Well that, at least, was a quality Kathryn could offer. Since she was temporarily forced to stay here and "help out around the place," as per Papa's arrangement, at least she could lend an air of gentility that was desperately needed.

Kathryn extended a hand toward Miss Everett, who had already obeyed the command to shed her cloak, though of the three of them, hers was by far the driest. "I'll take that," she offered. "You go on inside and get settled."

With a quick smile and a quiet "Thank you," the lady handed over the garment. When she had followed Cousin Mary Ann through the doorway, Kathryn hung the garment on one of the pegs and then shrugged out of her own. Rivulets ran from her saturated cloak to pool on the wooden slats. She turned to take Mr. Gates's coat, but he had left the shelter of the porch to help Carter unload the baggage. Good. Offering courtesy to a quietly dignified woman like Miss Everett was one thing, but a man who flung insults at women? Let him hang his own coat.

Two

The inside of the hotel was as austere as the outside, though at least it was dry. Kathryn stepped into a long room, bare but for a few hard wooden chairs lining the plank walls and a writing desk situated beside a closed door against the far wall. The only windows were the two in the front, and the deep porch outside them would prevent much sunlight from penetrating the room. She tested the rough wooden slats beneath her boots with a toe. This was the floor that must be protected from puddles?

To her right a narrow stairway led upward, and she heard signs of movement from above. The harsh tones of Papa's cousin seeped through the ceiling in short, staccato blasts, the words unintelligible from the distance. At least a fire crackled in a stone fireplace to her right, the flickering flames lending a bit of light to the otherwise gloomy interior. She crossed the room and stood before it, hands extended in an attempt to chase the chill from her sodden fingers. This room would benefit greatly from the addition of a few nice pieces of artwork on the walls, and perhaps a table where fresh flowers might be displayed. And a bright woven rug — not to mention some comfortable chairs — would add warmth.

Heavy footsteps on the stairs behind her alerted her to Cousin Mary Ann's descent. At the same moment the door opened. She whirled as Mr. Gates entered the hotel without his heavy overcoat. In his hands he carried his narrow rectangular crate, which he set on the floor at his side and kept upright with one hand.

"There you are." Cousin Mary Ann's crass voice filled every corner of the nearly bare room as she heaved herself down the stairs. "I've saved you a room upstairs." She drew to a halt at the bottom and tilted her head sideways to peer at him. "The charge is double the normal rate, since your letter said you want to be private."

He straightened. "I insist on it."

She shook her head, unruly wisps of wiry dark hair floating around her scalp like the halo on a deranged angel. "That's two of you asking for private accommodations. Waste of a couple of beds, I say, but it's all the same to me. I'll have two weeks' in advance, though."

"That's fine."

Eyes narrowed, she thrust out a hand, empty palm upward. Certainly payment in advance was an acceptable arrangement for a place of lodging, but Kathryn found the woman's brash manner embarrassing. Surely the business of collecting rents could be conducted with a bit more finesse. She averted her eyes so as not to appear to stare while he extracted a thick wallet from an inside pocket of his suit coat.

When the money had changed hands and been secreted in the pocket of her skirt, the woman turned again toward the stairs. "This way. You'll have the corner room in the back. I can't be responsible for noise. There's a woman who lives nearby with a couple of brats who squall half the night. I suggest you keep the windows shut till they quiet down." She hauled her bulky body upward, breath coming heavily after a few steps. "I don't serve meals, but Evangeline's next door has decent food and doesn't overcharge for what you get. If you want a tray brought up, I can arrange that for a small fee."

"I wouldn't want to put you out." Mr. Gates picked up his crate and, holding it before him in two hands, followed her up the stairs at a distance.

"Not putting me out at all," puffed the woman. She stopped halfway up to lean heavily on her knees. "My hired girl can do it."

She looked toward Kathryn with a grin. Kathryn's answer was a hesitant smile. She certainly didn't expect to be waited on while she was here, even if she *was* a relative. The distance between here and the restaurant next door wasn't much farther than the walk from her upstairs room at home to the formal dining room on the main floor. The inconvenience of having to go outside was minor. Unless the rain persisted.

Mr. Gates's gaze scanned the empty room and came to rest on Kathryn. His eyebrows arched high on his forehead. "Your hired girl?"

"That's right." She turned her smile on the young man. "If you want her to take care of your laundry or other personal concerns, we'll work out the details. That's one of the reasons I've hired a strong young woman, so I can offer good service to my customers."

When she gave Kathryn a disturbingly proprietary glance, the meaning of her words struck with force.

"I?" She rested a hand on her chest. "I am to be a . . . a maid?"

Pudgy fingers waved in the air in her direction. "We'll work out the details in a bit. Let me see my guest settled first."

She continued upward and disappeared through the doorway at the top. Kathryn stared after her, jaw slack. This was Papa's arrangement? Not that she assist in the management of the hotel, but that she become a servant? Then she realized she was the object of close scrutiny. Mr. Gates's gaze connected with hers for a moment. Was there more than curiosity in his stare? Did she detect a superior smirk? Heat flooded her cheeks. She whirled around and made a show of splaying her hands to warm them before the fire. The sound of creaking steps told her of his departure.

She forced a long, even breath from her lungs. A mistake had been made. She would write to Papa immediately.

No — on second thought, there was no need to write. She didn't intend to be here long enough for her letter to reach him and his reply to arrive. First thing in the morning she would speak with Captain Baker and book passage on the *Fair Lady* for the return voyage home.

■ ■ ■ ■

The room was bare, but sufficient. Jason stood in the open doorway to inspect the interior. A pair of narrow beds, little more than cots, really, lined two walls and took up most of the space. Between them stood a nightstand with a lamp on its surface, and very little room for much else. The area between the beds was hardly big enough for two men to stand side by side, but that wouldn't present a problem since he did not intend to share his lodgings. He had money enough to ensure his privacy for the duration of his stay in the Faulkner House. As soon as he had settled into a routine at the mill, he would arrange for permanent lodgings.

"There's plenty of light in this room." The proprietress peered over his shoulder. "Two windows, you'll notice. Good breeze when they're open."

Since the room was situated on a corner, windows graced two of the four walls and gave the impression of more space than was actually available. The curtains had been tied back, though the dark sky outside shed little light at the moment. Rain drizzled down the glass on the rear-facing wall and turned the trees behind the hotel into mirages. The other two walls were as bare as the ones downstairs. He would take care of that shortly.

He stepped through the doorway and set the crate containing his painting down on the floor. "This will be fine for my needs. Would you arrange to have the spare bed removed?"

"It'll be morning before my hired man comes, but I'll have him see to it." A gleam flickered in her eyes as she looked at the second bed. "I can move it across the hall and turn that room into a triple."

Unless the other room was significantly larger than this one, Jason couldn't imagine how three beds would fit. But that was not his concern.

He dipped his head in a courteous farewell. "Thank you, Mrs. Garritson." Hopefully he'd gotten the name right. Her correspondence had been nearly illegible, and she had not introduced herself since his arrival.

"Madame Garritson's what everybody in these parts calls me." She smiled, a somewhat gruesome gesture considering two of her teeth were charcoal gray and the rest yellow. "Or Mother Garritson, if you prefer."

An image of his mother, genteel and

educated and exquisitely groomed at all times, rose in his mind. If he were given the task of selecting a complete opposite to Mother, the woman before him would be his top candidate.

Arranging his lips into a polite smile, he said, "Thank you, Madame Garritson."

An unladylike cackle issued from deep inside her ample bosom. "Madame it is." She started to leave, and then stopped and turned back with a sly grin. "Forgot to ask. Did you want to hire my girl to see to your needs?"

While inspecting his room he'd forgotten about Miss Bergert. Her shocked expression upon discovering that she was being hired as a maid had wrung an unexpected response from him. For a moment he'd felt sorry for her. What position had she expected to take when she arrived? He didn't know, but clearly it was something different. Taking a servant's role would no doubt be hard for one so arrogant, though a lesson in humility might soften the sharp edges of her personality a bit.

But that was not a task he wished to undertake. The very reason he had agreed to come to Seattle was because there would be few females to distract him from the business of managing a successful steam mill operation. Why put himself directly in contact with one? His heart belonged to Beth, and he intended to remain true to her for as long as it continued to beat.

"Thank you, but I believe I can manage without any assistance."

Madame Garritson shrugged. "If you change your mind, let me know."

She waddled down the narrow hallway toward the stairs. Jason closed the door with a soft *whisk* and turned to rest his back against it. His gaze was drawn to the crate. The painting inside begged to be released and allowed to breathe, to spread oil-and-canvas sunshine into this gloomy room. Into his lonely heart.

When the proprietress descended the stairs once again, Kathryn crossed the floor to meet her head-on, heels echoing on the unfinished plank floor.

"Cousin Mary Ann, there has been a mistake."

The woman stepped off the bottom step with an *umph* and continued without a pause toward the closed door next to the desk. "Call me Madame Garritson, like everybody else. Wouldn't want to give the impression of favoritism, would we?"

"Certainly not." Actually, she preferred

not to advertise her kinship with this crass person, however distant it may be. She followed close on the woman's heels. "My father arranged for me to help with the management of this hotel, not to become a maid."

"Management?" She made an impolite sound halfway between a grunt and a snort. "No mistake, missy. Except I thought you'd be" — she paused with her hand on the knob and sent an appraising glance the length of Kathryn's body — "different."

Kathryn drew herself upright. How offensive! "What do you mean?"

A hand reached out to finger a bedraggled lock of hair that had begun to dry in the warmth of the fire. "Fancier, you know? Being from San Francisco and all, I figured you'd dress nicer, fix your hair up, maybe use a bit of rouge to give your face some color. Philip described you as an attractive girl." She pursed her lips. "*Accomplished* was how he put it."

Papa had called her *accomplished*? Kathryn indulged in a moment of satisfaction. He'd never encouraged her pursuit of art. Why, she'd come to believe he thought her without talent. "I am an accomplished *artist.*" She lifted her nose in the air. "I paint landscapes."

Madame gave a rude snort of laughter. "What use is a painter to me? Help emptying chamber pots and straightening bed linens, that's what I need." With a smirk, she pushed open the door, gesturing for Kathryn to follow.

The idea! "I most certainly will do no such thing."

They entered a generously sized room fitted with a few mismatched pieces of plain, block-style furniture. A large window looked out onto a stand of trees so dense that shadows dark as night filled the spaces between them. The glass had been left open and rain had blown in, leaving puddles on the floor.

Madame Garritson appeared not to notice. She stopped in the center of the room and turned. "What do you think the manager of a hotel does?"

"Well . . ." Kathryn stopped, taken aback. In the weeks prior to the journey, her efforts had been focused on convincing Papa not to send her away. When he remained stubborn, she'd comforted herself with a single recurring thought — that she would come, spend a few weeks here, and then return home with the tale that things had not worked out as he hoped. As to the actual duties she might be asked to perform, she had given them no thought at all.

She cleared her throat. "I suppose a manager collects rents, and sees to guests' inquiries, and ensures they are comfortable."

"Rents don't touch a single hand but this one." She extended her palm and slapped it with the fingers of her other hand. "And if someone has an inquiry, what help could you offer? You don't even know where the privy is."

"Of course there will be an initial adjustment period."

Her answer went unnoticed as Madame's lips formed a cynical twist. "And just what do you think guests need for their comfort?"

"Well, I . . ." She swallowed. The only time she had stayed in a hotel was last year, when she and Mama traveled to Sacramento with Papa on business. Her needs were seen to by Mrs. Lassiter, owner of the Lassiter House. While Papa worked, she and Mama toured the city and discovered a delightful little art gallery. When they returned for the evening, their rooms were neat and orderly. Now that Kathryn thought about it, she'd seen no maids or anyone else about the place. Had their clean rooms been due to the efforts of the proprietress?

"You see?" Excess flesh on Madame's

neck jiggled with the force of her nod. "I'm not as young as I used to be, and steps are proving a challenge to these old joints. I want someone younger to see to the work upstairs. Rents and inquiries I can handle down here."

She turned her back and waddled toward a closed door, leaving Kathryn standing in the center of the room, searching for an argument. The problem was, she saw the woman's point. Well, except for the fact that the weakened state of her joints was probably due to overload more than advancing age. Still, managing a hotel of this size no doubt included the unpleasant tasks of keeping the rooms clean and, therefore, the guests comfortable. And if one was incapable of handling those tasks, one would need to hire someone to help. Hence, the arrangement with Papa.

It made sense. If she were going to stay, that is. Which she most certainly was not. But she had overheard Captain Baker mention to a crewman that the *Fair Lady* would be in port for four days. Though Papa had not sent her away penniless, her travel allowance was by no means generous. And unbeknownst to Papa, she had spent quite a bit on the painting supplies that were packed carefully in her trunk, for who knew how hard they would be to find here? Between that and the donation she had managed to make the day they sailed, of which Papa would certainly *not* approve, her ready cash had been severely depleted. If she had to pay for room and board, she may not have enough left to purchase passage on the return trip to San Francisco.

It appeared she had no option but to accept Madame's offer of employment, distasteful though it may be.

Well, and why not? If a woman were to make her way in this world, she couldn't be afraid to work even menial jobs. She was a grown, capable woman, and certainly wasn't unaccustomed to household duties. At home she tidied her own art room. Papa and Mama employed a cook and a housekeeper to take care of the other chores, but she did not trust anyone to enter the sanctity of her studio, especially when she was working on a painting.

She would not call herself a maid, though, even for four days. A girl had her pride, after all. "I accept the offer to become your assistant manager."

"My assistant, eh?" Madame's blast of laughter ended in a snort. From the surface of a small table in the corner she took up a match, struck it, and lit a candle. "Call yourself what you will, as long as those rooms get cleaned every day and the guests are happy."

A minor victory, but one that would have to do. A thought occurred to her. "How much will I be paid?"

Scraggly eyebrows shot upward. "Paid? You'll get a bed, a blanket, and a roof over your head. That was my arrangement with Philip." A smile that looked more like a taunt leaped onto her face. "And the honor of calling yourself my assistant, of course. Here's your room."

She threw open a door in the far wall and gestured for Kathryn to enter. When she did, she blinked to adjust her eyes to the darkness. Behind her Madame held the candle high and details emerged from shadows. No wonder the woman stopped in the doorway. Her rotund figure would have filled the tiny space without an inch to spare. The only furnishing was a narrow bunk, not even as wide as Kathryn's berth on the *Fair Lady*. There was no chest of drawers, no writing desk, not even a chair to sit and read.

She whirled, her mouth gaping open. "Why, this is not a room! This is a closet."

"I used it for storage until they got me a shed built out back." She moved the candle in a circle as though to shed light into the corners, an unnecessary gesture since the room was so small there was not enough room for shadows to hide from the candle's glow. "Once you start earning your keep, I figure you can move upstairs. Only now we're full up with paying guests so this is the best I can do."

Kathryn opened her mouth, but no words would come. The idea of spending even a single night in this, this *cell,* was unthinkable. Why, there was no room for her easel, her palette. Not that there was a breath of inspiration in this cramped alcove.

It's only for four days. Then I'll put this place and Madame behind me.

She forced a long, slow breath through pursed lips before she trusted her voice. "I suppose my trunk can serve as a nightstand temporarily." Provided it would fit in the narrow space between the bunk and the wall.

"I'll get one of the boarders to fetch it in as soon as it's dried out."

Taking the light, Madame turned away. Kathryn hurried out after her. The first order of business would be to take possession of that candle. She feared the odor from a lamp would choke her in the confines of her new room.

"Speaking of drying out," Madame said as she blew the candle out with a puff, "looks like the rain has let up. Downpours like that are rare in these parts. There's a stack of scrap linens in the shed out back. Fetch some and clean up that mess, would you?" She pointed toward the standing water beneath the open window, and then pressed a hand into the small of her back. "Lumbago's acting up lately."

Kathryn opened her mouth, but then closed it again. No doubt any protest she made would receive a tart rejoinder concerning the duties of an assistant hotel manager. Clamping her teeth together, she managed a nod.

When she got home, she would give Papa a blistering earful. She had four days and the length of a sea voyage to plan what she would say.

Merely walking through the door of the café eased the tension in Kathryn's shoulders. The smell of savory stewed spices filled the room, along with the tuneful humming of a male voice from somewhere on the floor above. The cheery atmosphere, so different from the Faulkner House, greeted her before a single word had been spoken. A collection of square and rectangular tables, their surfaces covered with white linen cloth that shone brightly in the light of a dozen or so lamps, filled the room in neat, almost military-like rows. With an artistic eye she mentally angled them into a different arrangement, one more aesthetically appealing. Yet this utilitarian organization gave the immediate impression of being full and busy, something the main room at the hotel next door lacked and needed desperately. Of course, this restaurant was as empty of patrons as the Faulkner House was full. Not a single chair bore a customer.

"Welcome." A cheery voice from across the long room called a greeting as she stopped in the doorway. "I'm just mixing up the dough for the dumplings, so it'll be a minute or two before they're ready. Help yourself to tea. The kettle's just started whistling."

A woman in the far corner spoke over her shoulder, her flour-covered hands absorbed in the task of kneading dough on the surface of a long table. Kathryn hesitated. Was she expected to fill a servant's role here too? But she dismissed the thought as soon as it occurred. The invitation to make tea was nothing more than expedient, given that she was the only guest and the cook was elbow-deep in dumplings. She untied the laces of her still-wet cloak and bonnet and hung them from one of a row of pegs on the inside wall.

When she approached the stove, upon which a huge pot bubbled and produced ribbons of fragrant steam, the woman at the table started.

"Oh!" She jerked around, leaving a slab of dough on the work surface. Sticky hands flew to her cheeks. "I beg your pardon. I thought you were Louisa."

Wisps of dark hair escaped a clasp at the back of her neck to dance around a heart-shaped face. Her lips formed a hesitant smile that Kathryn could not help but answer. The young woman, who looked to be about her age, snatched a towel from her waistband and wiped her hands.

"I'm Evie Hughes, and I'm so sorry to bark an order as if you were a hired hand. Please accept my apology."

Coming so soon off of the episode with Madame, the apology soothed Kathryn's raw feelings like a balm. Evie. That must be short for Evangeline, the inspiration for the restaurant's name. Probably the owner and, judging by the flour-covered hands, the cook as well.

"Kathryn Bergert, newly arrived from San Francisco. No apology is necessary." She

56

poured warmth into her smile. "I'm happy to make tea, though if you asked me to cook anything I fear you would not be pleased with the result."

Evie hesitated and bit down on her lower lip. White flour smudged cheeks made rosy with equal amounts of heat and good humor. "I feel terrible putting you to work, but if you want tea right away, I'm afraid you'll have to serve yourself." She held up her sticky hands and shrugged.

Kathryn laughed off her discomfort and headed toward a huge iron stove situated near the back door. Several teapots lined the surface of a high worktable, along with a burlap bag filled with tea leaves. She measured leaves into a porcelain pot, and then retrieved a steaming kettle from the stove.

Evie returned to her dough. "I take it you arrived today on the *Fair Lady.* Staying at the Faulkner House next door, then?"

"That's right." She poured water over the tea leaves, leaning well back to avoid getting a faceful of tea-scented steam. Pride urged her to keep her silence concerning the details of her lodging at the Faulkner House, but what good would that do? Since she was forced to spend the next four days in Seattle, word would quickly spread about her employment. Though she had barely known Evie two minutes, she felt an immediate affinity with the young woman. She would enjoy having a friend in this male-dominated wilderness town, even for such a brief time. "Actually, I've come to help Madame Garritson."

"Oh?" Evie once again stopped her kneading and turned with a searching gaze. "How so?"

"I'm to be her assistant." The pot filled, Kathryn returned the kettle to its place on the stove, thereby avoiding eye contact. "I'll help with some of the day-to-day details of management."

Evie considered that for a moment, and then gave a nod and returned to the dumplings. "I'm not surprised, now that I think about it. There hasn't been an empty bed in that hotel in months." Her tone became devoid of emotion as she continued. "I'm sure Madame Garritson will appreciate having someone to help."

Her activity with the dough sped up ever so slightly, a fact Kathryn did not miss, though she watched only from the corner of her eye. Interesting. Evie did not like Madame and was too polite to say so. They had that, at least, in common.

"If you're to live next door, that means

58

we'll be seeing a lot of each other." She turned toward Kathryn with a charming grin. "There aren't many women in Seattle, so we tend to spend as much time together as we can. I hope you'll feel free to visit with me here at the café often."

Her smile was infectious, and a little more of Kathryn's tension seeped away as she returned it. It was almost a pity that she wouldn't be here long enough to get to know this lady. Given the opportunity, they might become fast friends.

"Thank you, I shall. But I won't be here long. In fact, I intend to leave when the *Fair Lady* sets sail later this week."

"Really?" Surprise showed on Evie's face, and once again she turned from the dough. "Arrangements at the Faulkner House aren't what you expected?"

"Definitely not."

An understanding look passed between them, and they shared a smile before returning to their tasks. A shelf on the wall held several stacks of cups and saucers, and Kathryn selected one that matched the teapot she had just filled. An intricate ivy leaf design circled just below the rim, and the handle ended in a delicate curve at the bottom.

"How pretty," she remarked, holding it up

to inspect the detail on a leaf.

Evie glanced over her shoulder. "Thank you. That set came all the way from Tennessee. I hope you got one that isn't chipped. Several didn't fare well on the journey, but I can't bear to throw them away. They belonged to my grandmother."

The sugar bowl had been filled, and Evie directed her toward a jug of cream keeping cool on the back windowsill. Kathryn took a seat at the table nearest the stove so she could watch the process of dumplings being produced while she sipped her tea. When the giant mound of dough resting on the floured surface looked like a sticky lump, Evie reached for a spoon. She plunged it into the mass and scooped out an uneven dollop, which she plopped into the huge, simmering pot. She repeated the process quickly, pausing every so often to give the liquid a gentle stir.

The sound of humming above had blended into the background, forgotten until it stopped. A pair of boots appeared at the top of a ladder in the corner and started the descent, followed by trousers, a flannel shirt, and finally, a man. Once on the floor he glanced her way, and then smiled a greeting.

"Hello!"

Evie didn't pause in her work, but spoke over her shoulder. "This is Miss Bergert from San Francisco. Kathryn, this is my husband, Noah Hughes."

He was a handsome man with dark, curly hair and a ready smile, a suitable match for the pretty Evie.

"Welcome to Seattle, Miss Bergert. I hope you'll find our town to your liking."

"Thank you." She set the cup in its saucer. The way he said *our town* indicated a sense of pride. Of course, he would have to like the place since he and his wife owned a business here. A lot of people did prefer small towns over bigger cities, even though the smaller population meant less in the way of entertainment and culture. Granted, she had not seen much, only what had been visible from the wagon on the short trip from the pier, but she very much doubted that Seattle could compare to San Francisco in any way that mattered to her.

"I'm sure it's a . . ." She grasped for a word. "A lovely town. Though a bit wet for my tastes."

He laughed, not at all offended. "The area really is beautiful, especially when the sun is shining. Unfortunately, that doesn't happen as often as we'd like. Still, if you stay long enough you get used to the rain."

From the stove, Evie answered. "Kathryn won't be here long enough to see our beautiful summers. She came to help out at the Faulkner House, but once here has had a change of heart."

Husband and wife exchanged a glance, and when Noah turned back to Kathryn, his face bore a knowing look. "I see. Well, in that case we'll say a prayer that we get a break from the rain while you're here."

Judging by his carefully arranged expression, Noah shared his wife's opinion of Madame. More evidence that her decision to leave was a good one. She would be able to report to Papa that the owners of the neighboring businesses did not hold his distant cousin in high regard, and, therefore, having his daughter in the woman's employ would be entirely unsuitable. She picked up her teacup and sipped from the milky liquid.

The door opened and within the space of a few seconds, the restaurant filled. A string of men filed in noisily, talking and laughing with each other and shaking rain out of their hair. Their deep male voices combined to form a cheerful roar, a pleasant sound that Kathryn enjoyed. One man, a redhead, seemed to be the recipient of much good-natured kidding regarding something that had happened earlier in the day. She caught mentions of a grinding wheel and bark, and someone mentioned the foreman. They must be employees of the steam mill, then, and their shift had just ended. Apparently Evie expected their arrival, which explained the timing of her dumplings. They approached the tables without pausing to make a selection, which spoke of a familiar routine.

When one of the men caught sight of her, he halted in the process of winding his way between two tables. He was a huge man of near-giant proportions, with powerfully muscular arms bigger around than either of Kathryn's thighs.

"It's a *wo*man."

He pronounced the word *woe-man,* and stared at her through eyes so wide she might have chuckled if she had not then found herself the focus of every soul in the crowded room. The easy chatter fell silent. Every face turned her way, most of them covered with thick beards. No one moved.

After a second that seemed an eternity, Noah came to stand beside her chair. "Men, this is Miss Bergert. She's just arrived today."

In the next instant, Kathryn's table was surrounded with an unbroken wall of flannel and cotton. Greetings of "Welcome to

Seattle, Miss Bergert" and "Glad you're here" flew at her with such a rapid pace that she could not answer them all. Instead she fixed a smile on her face and tried to nod toward each man. But there were so many! Wet sawdust clung to many of their shoulders, and the smell of raw wood vied with the odors wafting from Evie's stew pot. Everywhere she looked an eager face greeted her, and they pressed around, towering above her until she began to feel out of breath.

From somewhere behind the crowd came Evie's voice. "Let's everyone take a seat, shall we? Give Miss Bergert some breathing space."

A minor tussle occurred over the chairs at her table. A man with a thick thatch of bright red hair scooted out the one on her right, only to have it jerked out of his hand by the giant.

"Hey, what's the idea, Big Dog? I was fixing to sit there."

"Well, now you can sit somewheres else."

The man appropriately named Big Dog lowered himself into the seat with a sideways grin at Kathryn. At first she thought the redhead might put up a fuss, but then he dove for the chair directly across from her, the only remaining unclaimed seat at the rectangular table, and slid into it a moment before someone else. He rested his folded arms on the surface in front of him and leaned forward, his gaze fixed on her. His friends up and down the table did the same, and Big Dog actually turned sideways in his chair to face her. Those left standing backed away, disappointment clear on their faces, but as they claimed their chairs most angled themselves to be able to see her. Kathryn scooted to the left side of her seat, away from Big Dog's hulking form, as unobtrusively as possible. Thank goodness she had selected a place at the corner of a table against the wall. Otherwise she would be boxed in on all sides. How could she possibly manage to eat a bite beneath the weight of all those stares?

Did Papa have any idea that Seattle would be like this when he blithely made the decision to send her here? She may as well have been a ripe tomato at a vegetable stand on market day. Yet another item to add to her list when she next spoke with him.

Noah, who had disappeared into a back room, reappeared carrying an armload of plates. He placed a stack on the end of each table and, without being instructed to do so, the men passed them out. Big Dog set one before her with exaggerated care and a

65

huge grin.

"Thank you," Kathryn mumbled.

Evie began serving food, moving back and forth between her huge stove and the tables with laden hands. Loaves of bread with lumps of soft white butter, tubs of strawberry jam, bowls of cooked apples and green beans, and ears of yellow corn drenched in butter and piled in pyramids on platters. And dumplings, plump and steaming and nestled amid huge chunks of stewed chicken. Noah helped deliver the bountiful meal to the tables, both of them working quickly.

The arrival of dinner gave Kathryn a welcome respite from the attention as the men fell on the food as if they had not eaten in weeks. The only sounds were the scraping of forks on plates. She took modest helpings and tried not to stare at the huge mounds they piled before them, nor the speed with which it was consumed.

The door opened and a familiar face appeared. A wave of relief washed over her. Finally, someone she knew. She nearly raised her hand and called a greeting to Jason, but caught herself at the last minute. Familiar, perhaps, but definitely not friendly. He stood just inside the door, his head turning as he took in the room. When

66

he caught sight of her, recognition flashed in his eyes and he inclined his head in a greeting, but did not speak.

Evie turned from the stove. "Hello. Take a seat wherever you like."

He nodded and made his way toward an empty seat on the opposite side of the room from Kathryn. She focused on cutting a bite-sized piece of dumpling when he passed. Though she found him highly irritating, she wouldn't have minded having someone at least vaguely familiar seated nearby. At least she need not fear seeing the hungry glint in his eyes that the rest displayed as they watched her. Now, though, they seemed to have found a new object for their attention, and many a glance was cast his way.

Noah entered from the storeroom carrying three more loaves and, catching sight of the stranger, made his way across the room. He set down the bread and extended a hand. "Noah Hughes."

Mr. Gates rose and shook the hand. "Jason Gates."

The introduction accomplished, he reseated himself while Noah grabbed an empty plate from a nearby table. He set it in front of the newcomer, and sounds of eating resumed while they engaged in a quiet conversation.

"Hey, Red," whispered Big Dog across the table. "Think that's him?"

His fork full of apple, Red studied Jason. "Might be. Do you recollect the name Yesler mentioned?"

The dark-haired man next to him answered. "I do. It was Gates. That's him, all right."

Kathryn followed their gazes toward Jason. She'd never thought to ask what brought him to Seattle. He was to be a mill-worker, then, like these men. Could mill-workers afford Madame's rates for a private room at the Faulkner House?

Evie left the stove, hands once again full, and headed toward Jason's table. When she arrived, Noah took a bowl of dumplings from her.

"This is my wife, the best cook in all of Seattle, as you'll soon discover. Evie, this is Jason Gates, Henry Yesler's new mill manager."

Jason rose from his chair to greet her while Red and Big Dog exchanged nods.

"We've been expecting you, Mr. Gates." Evie set down a bowl of stewed apples. "Please sit down and help yourself."

When Jason had lowered himself once again, Evie wiped her hands on her apron.

"How funny. The *Fair Lady* delivered two new managers to Seattle today. One for the mill and one for the Faulkner House." She turned a wide smile toward Kathryn.

Jason's eyebrows shot upward, and he leveled a piercing gaze on her. "Oh?"

Kathryn busied herself with her plate. She and Madame may have reached an uneasy truce regarding her title, but that had not yet been communicated to the guests. Would he correct their hostess and name her a common hotel maid? If he embarrassed her here, in front of all these people, she would die of humiliation.

"I suppose you two met on board?" Evie's sharp-eyed glance volleyed between them.

A long silence, and then Jason answered. "Yes. Yes, we did."

Kathryn released a pent-up breath. Apparently he had decided to display some of those gentlemanly manners for which she had praised him earlier.

The door opened once again. More customers? Goodness, this restaurant certainly enjoyed a brisk trade.

Evie called a greeting. "Captain Baker! I hoped we would have the pleasure of seeing you this evening."

Kathryn straightened to attention. Sure enough, the captain and his first mate

69

entered the restaurant. Excellent. No need to wait until morning to arrange for her return trip.

"You know I won't miss an opportunity to enjoy a meal at Evangeline's." His gaze circled the room and came to rest on Kathryn. "I see some of my passengers have already found their way here."

He gave a courtly half-bow in her direction and then took a chair across from Jason. Kathryn finished her meal as quickly as propriety allowed and excused herself to the disappointment of the men seated around her. Once again she became the focus of every pair of eyes in the room as she made her way across the aisle. When she approached the captain's table, all three men rose politely.

"Pardon the interruption, Captain. Might I have a word with you?"

"Of course, my dear." He waved toward an empty chair. "Won't you be seated?"

Not exactly what she had in mind. She'd hoped to speak to the captain in private, but she couldn't very well expect him to leave his dinner to grow cold, could she? She glanced at Jason, who didn't quite meet her eye.

"Thank you."

She sat, smoothing her skirts as the men

70

returned to their chairs.

"Would it be possible to book a return passage to San Francisco when the *Fair Lady* leaves on Friday?"

What she really wanted to ask was how much the voyage would cost. If the price were too high, she hoped he would agree to defer payment until after their arrival in San Francisco. His answer took her aback.

"I'm afraid not." Captain Baker picked up his fork and speared a gooey apple slice. "Every bunk is spoken for this trip."

"What?" Disbelief stiffened her spine. "Surely you have room for one more."

"Not on this voyage. I've got a ship full of lumberjacks heading south, eager to spend their hard-earned pay."

"But . . ." She cast about in her mind, her thoughts whipping into a desperate pace. "Can't one of them wait until the next ship?"

The skipper and his mate exchanged a smile. "It wouldn't just be one of them, now, would it? Not unless you intend to bunk with a cabin full of lumberjacks. We have no private accommodations on the *Fair Lady,* as you well know."

On the trip here there had been six empty bunks in the cabin Kathryn had shared with Miss Everett. Jason had given up the pretense of eating to watch the exchange. She ignored him.

"Eight men, then. I'm sure my father will make it worth your while."

"I gave my word to your father to see you safely to Seattle. I've done that." Captain Baker awarded her a paternalistic smile. "I doubt if he intended for you to turn around and go home immediately."

She was still trying to come up with a persuasive argument when the door opened yet again. This time it burst inward and slammed into the wall with a loud *crack*. A man rushed into the restaurant, his eyes wild and his breath coming in ragged gulps. His head whipped back and forth as he searched the room.

Noah, who had been standing near one of the tables talking with the men while they ate, straightened. "What is it, Lawson? Is something wrong?"

Laying eyes on him, Lawson ran across the room and grabbed Noah by the arm. "It's the Indians! They're attacking!"

Chair legs scraped on wood as half the occupants in the room leaped to their feet. Kathryn joined them, her heart thudding in her throat. An Indian attack?

The room began to whirl and her vision darkened. A last thought shouted in her mind before she collapsed. Here was yet another item to add to the list of complaints for Papa. If, of course, she lived to present them.

THREE

Jason lurched sideways in time to catch Kathryn as she crumpled. He scooped up her still form, her weight no more than a satchel full of feathers.

"She's fainted," shouted a deep voice.

"Quick, get some smelling salts," instructed someone else.

A few men rushed toward him, pressing close to stare at the drooping figure in his arms while the man who'd rushed into the room collected his own audience near the door. Someone pulled out a chair and he collapsed into it, panting heavily.

Jason shifted his weight from one boot to the other. What in the world was he to do with a fainting woman? Stand there and hold her until she came to? Lay her out on the table? The floor? He was just about to deposit her into the arms of the big man who hovered anxiously over him when Mrs.

Hughes's voice cut through the worried chatter.

"Get back, everyone. Give her room." She shoved her way between two men as if they were tall stalks of river grass, pulling the stopper from a bottle. "Here. It's just vinegar, but it ought to do the trick."

Actually, Kathryn's eyelids were already fluttering. When Mrs. Hughes held the bottle beneath her nose, her head jerked away and her skull cracked against his chin.

"Ow!" He couldn't even rub his stinging jaw.

"She's awake," announced the proprietress, and a collective sigh sounded around the room. She laid a hand across Kathryn's forehead. "Kathryn, dear, are you all right?"

"Yes, I — I'm fine." Her voice trembled on the last word, but otherwise sounded strong enough. When she looked into his face, her eyes went wide and her body stiffened in his arms. "Please put me down immediately."

"Here." Evie scooted out a chair, and Jason wasted no time in depositing Kathryn in it. He whirled on his heel and pushed his way through the hovering men to join those circled around the messenger, watching him gulp down a cup of water. She was in capable hands, many pairs of them.

■ ■ ■ ■

"That's right, drink it all and catch your breath." Noah spoke through a clenched jaw, tension obvious in the cords standing out on his neck.

"Hurry up," urged one of the men watching. "Tell us what's happened."

Lawson drained the water and lowered the cup, his chest heaving. "There's been another attack, up near Holmes Harbor. Fella from over in Alki disappeared, and a posse set out to track him. Didn't find him, but they was attacked by a group of Indians. Killed a couple, and one of them was killed too. Shot clean through."

Alki Point. Jason knew the place. The *Fair Lady* had passed the settlement on the way here, on the exposed side of the Sound. Word had it that was the place where the founders of Seattle landed first before coming here in search of a site with shelter from the harsh seas during rough weather.

While Lawson talked, the men surrounding Kathryn had joined them, and now they mumbled to one another. Their voices contained equal tones of anger and fear.

Noah pointed toward the man nearest the door. "Go get David. He needs to hear this."

The messenger left at a run.

Jason shot a glance behind him, where Evie stood with a hand on Kathryn's shoulder looking his way. "Look here, Hughes." He spoke quietly. "I thought the natives in these parts were peaceable."

"They are." Captain Baker, who stood nearby with a coffee mug in his hand, inserted himself into the conversation. "I had a word with Captain Sterrett before he left, and he assures me there is no threat of conflict with the natives. Frankly, I'm surprised at your reaction. You people have lived practically side by side with them for years."

Noah didn't answer at first, his jaw working as he stared at the man. Then he nodded slowly. "That's true enough. The Duwamish tribesmen are our friends and have been since we settled here. But Chief Seattle moved the bulk of his people to a reservation some time ago. A few stayed, but most left with him. These are new tribes coming in from the north, and they aren't as tolerant of white settlers who've moved in and taken possession of what have traditionally been tribal lands."

"Unhappy with the arrangements, perhaps, but not violent." The captain's posture straightened and he rocked back on his heels. "No doubt they'll come to see reason after a while. In the meantime, we mustn't be alarmists."

Lawson rounded on the man. "You sayin' the report about the fight over at Holmes Harbor is wrong? 'Cause I'll bet there's a widow lady in Alki who might have something to say about them folks not being violent."

One of the millworkers spoke up. "We all know there's a few Indians who'd just as soon kill us as look at us, but most of them are as friendly as you or me."

The man standing next to him shook his head. "Maybe so, but it only takes a handful to start shooting. Before you know it we've got a war on our hands."

A man in dingy red-striped suspenders rounded on him. "Why'd you have to mention war? That kind of talk is what's causing folks around here to panic."

The other's fists clenched, and Jason noted that his was not the only reddened face in the circle. Obviously emotions on this topic ran high, as well they should. Given the reports in years past of the savage slaughter of westward-bound pioneers on wagon trails through the plains, people were prone to panic at the mere hint of conflict between red men and white.

A pair of men entered the restaurant followed closely by Noah's messenger, whose breath came hard.

Noah's tension visibly relaxed. "David, glad you could come so quickly. There's been another attack." He jerked a nod toward Lawson, who launched into his tale for the second time.

Jason studied the newcomer. David Denny, one of the founders of Seattle. Along with his older brother and a handful of others, this man had established the timber trade that attracted the attention of Henry Yesler, who then built the first steam mill in this part of the country. Since that time, Seattle had thrived and grown beyond anyone's expectations. David was younger than Jason expected, probably not more than twenty-five or six, which would make him around ten years younger than Jason. But intelligence gleamed in the dark eyes that focused intently on Lawson.

When the man finished, David and Noah exchanged a loaded glance. Seeing it, Jason felt the stirrings of unease deep in his gut. He may not know them well, but his years managing crews of millworkers back East had taught him a thing or two about judging men's character. These two were no alarmists, no matter what the captain said.

If they shared a concern about hostilities between white men and Indians, there was a valid reason for caution.

The heavy silence that descended on the men as they waited for David's reply spoke of their high opinion of him. When he did speak, he looked around the group, his gaze connecting with as many as possible. Jason's opinion of the man's leadership rose another few notches. That the men looked up to him was obvious in the attention they afforded him.

"We can't ignore this latest episode. We need to take steps to protect our families, our town."

A snort of disgust sounded from someone, and several men left the group to return to their plates. The one wearing suspenders folded his arms across his chest with a jerk and fixed a glare on David.

"Of all the people in this town who'd give in to panic-stricken ravings, I never thought *you'd* be one, Denny. Why, you were friends with the Duwamish before anyone else."

His tone fairly dripped scorn, so much that Jason had a hard time keeping his tongue silent. If that attitude were directed toward him, he would be hard-pressed to hold his temper. But he was new here, and his job at the mill would be to lead these

80

men regardless of their opinions or attitudes. To start out by entering into a local conflict would be inviting trouble.

"I still am," David answered in a level tone. "But I've told you before about Chief Seattle's last words to me before he moved his tribe. Northern tribes like the Nisqually and Klickitats are angry at the loss of their lands. He told me point-blank that war is coming."

The facts couldn't be stated more clearly, as far as Jason was concerned. Several heads nodded, and Noah's wasn't the only face that grew solemn with the pronouncement. Unbelievably, others still scoffed openly.

Captain Baker set his coffee down on a nearby table, folded his arms across his chest, and rocked on his boot heels, his upper lip curled. "They've received payment for their lands. The treaty at the Tulalip agency —"

Noah rounded on him, emotion giving his voice volume. "You mean the one where the Indians were given torn blankets, mouth harps, and a couple of barrels of blackstrap molasses?" He scowled. "Oh, *that* was fair trade for tribal lands that they'd lived and hunted on for centuries."

The captain's eyes narrowed. "Why, Mr. Hughes, I had no idea you leaned toward the Indian cause."

Noah drew himself up, eyes blazing. "I lean toward any cause that is righteous, and disdain unfair treatment of any man, white or red."

In other circumstances, Jason would have applauded. Here was a man who could command his respect.

David laid a restraining hand on Noah's arm. "Gentlemen, let's keep our heads about us, shall we? The question of the fairness of the treaty is not our purpose this evening. We're faced with far more pressing concerns." His gaze became solemn. "Like keeping our women and children safe in the event of an attack on Seattle."

A frigid chill settled over the captain's smile. "Well, then, I'll leave you to discuss the matter." He crossed to the pegs on the wall to retrieve his coat. Digging in the pocket of his trousers, he extracted a few coins and tossed them on the table next to his abandoned mug. "Mrs. Hughes, thank you for a delicious meal, as always."

Across the room, Evie still stood beside Kathryn's chair. She nodded an acknowledgment, her expression gracious but strained. Kathryn's eyes had widened to the size of saucers, and her face was a pasty white, whether due to her fainting spell or the conversation, Jason didn't know. When the captain left the room, a good third of the men followed, leaving their meals half-eaten.

When they had gone, David heaved a pent-up breath. His chest deflated and he rubbed a hand across his eyes. "That didn't go well, did it?"

The man who had arrived with him agreed with a nod. "Could have been better."

"Oh, I don't know." Noah swept the room with an openhanded gesture. "At least now we know who's in agreement with us." His gaze fell on Jason. "Sorry you had to witness a conflict on your first night in our fair city. And I haven't even introduced you. Jason Gates, meet David Denny and William Townsend. Jason is the new manager down at the mill."

"Welcome." David's grip was firm, his smile slow but open. "I know Henry's been looking forward to having you here."

The other man was older by a couple of decades, his clean, dark hair liberally sprinkled with silver. He clasped Jason's hand and searched his face with keen eyes. "We'll be seeing a lot of each other. I'm the daytime foreman."

Jason kept rigid control of his expression, though his eyebrows nearly rose when the man identified himself. In his correspondence Yesler mentioned daytime and nighttime foremen, and Jason had wondered about them. Yesler had managed the mill himself since he built it four years before, and now that the operation was running smoothly, he wanted to devote himself to other pursuits. Why, then, hadn't he made one of his foremen the new mill manager? More importantly, had either of them expected to step into the role? If so, he'd have a conflict on his hands before he even started work.

"Good to meet you, Townsend. I look forward to working with you."

The eyes narrowed slightly, as if weighing the sincerity of his words, and then he dipped his head.

"Oh, and another manager arrived today as well, or at least an assistant manager." Noah's tone became lighter as he turned and looked toward the ladies. "This is Miss Kathryn Bergert, who's come to help with the management of the Faulkner House."

Had Jason possessed fewer manners he would have snorted a laugh. The girl had plenty of nerve, he'd give her that.

Actually, if he were honest with himself, he had to admit a grudging respect. She'd managed to turn an unpleasant situation into one that sounded enviable. Unpleasant to her, at least. As far as he was concerned there was absolutely nothing wrong with plain hard work in any capacity. He fully intended to roll up his shirtsleeves and put in some long hours alongside the men he managed. But not everyone shared his opinion. If calling herself an assistant manager made her job more palatable, what was it to him?

A surprising change had come over Townsend's features. What began as a pleasant enough glance across the room became a wide-eyed stare. He jerked upright, his lips parted, and his mouth gaped open. Jason followed his glance toward Kathryn. Did the two know each other? Judging by the polite inquiry in her expression, she didn't seem aware of any prior acquaintance with the man.

"I —" Townsend took a backward step. "I must go. I have to —" He tore his gaze away, his mouth snapping shut and his throat constricting in a convulsive swallow. "I'll see you tomorrow, Gates."

"Yes, in the morning." Jason's reply was directed toward the man's back as he beat a hasty retreat through the door.

What curious behavior. An awkward silence settled over the room, with many glances cast toward Kathryn. She stared after him, eyebrows drawn together, looking as perplexed as everyone else.

Kathryn watched the man leave. What astoundingly bad manners, to leave that way in the middle of an introduction.

Noah shook his head. "I wonder what made him rush off like that?"

"No idea." David shrugged, and then dismissed the matter by turning his back on the door. "We've got a decision to make. What are we going to do about this latest attack?"

Nods all around and mumbles of "That's right," and "We can't ignore this one."

This one? They'd suffered previous Indian attacks, then? Startled, Kathryn glanced up at Evie, who still stood at her side, hand resting on her shoulder. She gave a comforting squeeze.

"Why don't you all sit down?" Evie crossed the room, her long skirts swishing smoothly around her ankles, and placed a hand on her husband's arm. "Supper's getting cold, and there's nothing worse than cold dumplings. You can talk while you eat."

The men returned to their plates. Noah and David made their way to the back table where Jason had been seated across from

Captain Baker. Jason followed, and gave Kathryn a searching look as he slid into his chair.

A warm flush crept up her neck. How embarrassing to faint as though she were one of those ridiculous females whose behavior she had always found so annoying. They pretended a fragility they did not feel merely to appear weak and helpless before the men they hoped to entice. She had no patience for women like that.

On the other hand, the pronouncement of an impending attack by savage Indians directly after the shock of learning that she was stranded here until the arrival of the next ship was enough to make anyone's head spin.

With a smooth gesture, Evie scooped up the captain's and mate's half-eaten dinners and whisked them away. "Noah, you sit there with David. I'll fetch some plates."

David gave her a grateful nod. "Louisa and the children will be along any minute. When the word came, she sent me ahead."

The smile Evie turned on Kathryn held a touch of strain, understandable given the circumstances. "You'll get to meet my friend."

When she bustled toward the stove, Kathryn rose. She couldn't sit there like a pampered lady and watch Evie work.

Beside her, Jason looked up with an expression of polite concern. "Are you sure you shouldn't sit a while and rest?"

She found his conciliatory manner irritating. "I'm fine," she answered pertly, and turned away with her head high. From the corner of her eye she saw him shrug and focus his attention on the men seated across from him.

Evie answered her offer of assistance with a grateful nod. "If you don't mind, fetch clean plates and forks from that storage room." She gestured with a tilt of her head while she scraped food scraps into a bucket. "Might as well grab a dozen or so. When word gets around, I expect people will start showing up to find out what's happening."

Kathryn headed for the doorway. "So your restaurant is a kind of public meeting hall or something?"

"It was the first business in town, so I guess people got used to gathering here." She gave a delicate shrug. "And we have plenty of seating."

That made sense. Kathryn stepped into the storage room and took a minute to get her bearings. The room was a lot bigger than she expected, and judging by the freshly-cut look of the floor slats, a recent addition to the original building. A lamp burned on a table by the door, and she picked it up to shed light on the deep shelves that stood against all four walls. Most were piled high with jars, bulging bags, and containers covered in oiled cloth. She found dishes stacked on a low shelf and retrieved a dozen or so along with a handful of utensils. The aroma of freshly baked bread permeated the room, and she discovered the source beneath a white linen cloth on the table beside the lamp. Another dozen loaves lay waiting to be served.

She arrived back in the dining room at the same time a woman closed the main door, one hand clutching that of a little girl perhaps three or four years old. Several of the men called a greeting to "Miz Louisa." When she turned, Kathryn saw Evie's friend was well along in pregnancy.

David leaped up from his seat and dashed toward her to take her arm and help her to a seat. A smile curved her lips, and her eyes sparkled above round cheeks.

"I've just walked all the way down the street with a child at each side, and you act as if I can't make my way safely across the room." Teasing laughter tinged her tone, but she indulgently allowed him to guide her toward a chair and hold her arm as she lowered herself into it.

Had Kathryn not glanced at Evie at that moment, she would have missed a look of intense longing that flashed across her face. Not jealousy of the attention her friend received from her husband. She had seen an equal amount of love in Noah's eyes when he looked at her. Desire for a child, then?

"Auntie Evie!"

The little girl flew across the room, arms opened wide, and threw herself at Evie's skirt. Evie immediately set down the plate she'd been scraping and knelt to gather the child in a tender embrace. Her eyes closed, and she buried her face in dark brown curls and breathed in slowly as though the scent were heavenly. When she opened her eyes, she sought out Noah. Her expression affirmed Kathryn's guess. Evie longed for a child of her own.

The embrace ended, and Evie held the child at arm's length. "But where's John William?"

"His grandpa took him home. He said he wanted to come here to see you, but he was not allowed." She lowered her voice and leaned forward as though confiding a secret. "His grandpa was cross with him."

"Was he now?"

The child gave a solemn nod.

"Well, perhaps he was in a hurry. Go and sit down by Mama, and I'll bring your dinner."

She ran off, and Evie smiled at Kathryn as she straightened. "John William is Will Townsend's grandson," she explained. "His parents died when he was an infant, and Will is raising him. He stays with Louisa during the day while his grandfather works at the mill."

Kathryn worked under Evie's direction by fetching half-full bowls from the tables and returning them full from the stove. The men who remained mumbled their thanks and she was the object of many bashful glances, though on the whole they seemed to have gotten over their initial enthusiasm at her presence and retreated into a communal shyness. Thank goodness for that. A quick smile or two was easy enough, and much preferable to the weighty stares of before.

When she set the final bowl on the corner table in front of Noah, Louisa aimed an entreaty at her. "Won't you join us? You too, Evie," she called across the room. "This table needs a stronger female presence. I feel like a trout in a salmon stream."

Kathryn couldn't help but return the infectious grin. She had already eaten and probably should return to the Faulkner House with the tray she promised to bring Miss Everett, but when Evie arrived at the table with the teapot and the cup she'd emptied earlier, what could she do but accept? Besides, the two men seated here, Noah and David Denny, were clearly leaders in Seattle. What they had to say about the possibility of an Indian attack would no doubt be vital information.

Evie slid into the chair beside her husband, and Louisa had already been seated at the opposite end of that side of the table with the little girl stationed between her and David. That left only the chairs on either side of Jason empty. Not a place she would have selected, had there been another choice. Embarrassment for fainting still itched beneath the calm surface she projected, and bordered on humiliation at the realization that she had come to in his arms. A distinctly uncomfortable position in which to awaken. Judging by the speed with which he had deposited her in the chair, he enjoyed the situation as little as she. Before sitting, she slid her chair slightly away from him to create a satisfactory distance between them.

This position placed her directly across the table from Louisa, whose smile became warm. "We haven't been introduced. I am Louisa Denny, and this is Emily Inez. We just call her Inez."

The child, who barely sat tall enough to see over her plate, paused with a dumpling on a miniature fork to flash a pair of appealing dimples. "Pleased to meet you."

Kathryn returned the little girl's smile. "And you, Inez." She looked up. "I am —"

"Kathryn Bergert, lately from San Francisco, and cousin to Madame Garritson." Louisa displayed a set of dimples that matched her daughter's. "I know all about you."

"Madame is a distant cousin of my father's," Kathryn hurried to say, and then added, "By marriage."

A look of understanding arose in the woman's eyes. "I see."

From the other end of the table, Evie gave her an astonished look. "How could you possibly know all that? I met her barely an hour ago."

Louisa answered while spreading butter on a piece of bread. "Letitia."

"Ah."

The two women nodded at one another.

"Who is Letitia?" Kathryn asked. Since her arrival she had met no one but Madame.

"Letitia Coffinger." She set down the butter knife. "She and her husband own the dry goods store next door. She saw Carter bringing you up from the docks, and as soon as she could, paid a visit to the Faulkner House. When she'd learned all she could from Madame, she came straight to my kitchen to relay what she'd heard. She'd barely been gone ten minutes before the messenger arrived bidding us to come here." Her gaze slid to Jason. "I know a bit about you too, Mr. Gates, though not as much."

"Small towns are the same the world over." Though Kathryn did not turn her head, she spied a good-humored grin on his face out of the corner of her eye. "A good thing I haven't been free with information to Madame."

"Wise on your part, but extremely frustrating for those of us who rely on clothesline chatter for our news."

"Clothesline chatter?" Noah snorted. "Gossip, you mean."

She inclined her head. "If you insist."

"Speaking of news." He glanced over his shoulder at the nearest table, where the men were focused on their plates, and then went on in a lowered voice. "What do you make of this latest attack?"

David's expression became grave. "It's

alarming, but not really surprising. If the report we heard is factual, those men over in Alki were tromping through the woods, exposed. They should have taken greater care."

"But they had a man missing. They couldn't sit back and do nothing."

"Maybe if they'd taken a bigger posse they would have presented a more intimidating presence." David shook his head, worry forming crevices on his brow. "After what we learned from Salmon Bay Curley, they should have been more cautious. We all should."

Beside her, Jason posed the question she wanted to ask. "Who is Salmon Bay Curley?"

Balancing his fork on the rim of his plate, Noah provided the answer. "A Duwamish Indian friend of ours. Last year he told us he overheard some of the newcomers bragging about killing a white man and dumping his body in the forest over near Lake Union. We put together a search party and found the remains, or what was left of them. They apparently waylaid him in the woods, robbed, and murdered him. His skull was —"

His glance slid sideways to connect with Kathryn's, whose horror had blossomed as

95

the tale unfolded. Whatever he had been planning to say remained unvoiced.

He cleared his throat before continuing. "Anyway, we never found out who the fellow was. Probably a seaman from one of the San Francisco sailing vessels. Here in Seattle we've taken care not to venture too far alone since then."

Louisa tore her bread in half and laid part on Inez's plate. "That's why we live in town now. We used to have a cabin in a peaceful clearing, but with David working all day long, Inez and I were alone most of the time."

Kathryn didn't bother to suppress a shudder. What kind of place had Papa sent her to?

"Are we safe here?" She glanced around the cabin, suddenly fearful. Would ferocious Indians attack them while they ate?

Evie leaned across the table to rest a hand on her arm. "Of course we are. We've never had any trouble in this vicinity. Why, we have Indian friends who live right here in town."

"We do." Though he agreed in words, David's expression remained troubled. "But even those friends are starting to worry. I think we need to do something."

Beside her, Jason leaned back in his chair.

"What do you propose?"

"Yeah, Denny, what are you thinking?"

The voice came from the next table over. David turned his head to see who had spoken. Kathryn glanced around the room. Every eye was once again aimed in her direction, but this time she was not the focus of the men's attention. They were all looking at David, waiting for his answer.

He twisted around in his chair to face the room. "A couple of us have been talking, tossing out ideas."

A burly man seated near Big Dog slammed a fist on the table. "I say we strike first."

"Yeah." A flannel-clad blond near the door nodded. "Can't stand the thought of sitting around waiting for one of their raiding parties to swarm the streets. We ought to go after 'em and show 'em we aren't afraid."

"Are you nuts?" Noah shook his head, disbelief etched on his features. "Didn't you hear what happened to the posse from Alki? A man's dead because they stormed into the forest looking for trouble."

"They weren't prepared like we'd be," the blond answered.

Red stood and turned to look at the man. "They were armed, according to Lawson. Sounds pretty prepared."

"Seems to me that's what the Navy's here

for," commented Big Dog. "If there's any attacking to be done, shouldn't they do it?"

Kathryn had been watching a battle play across Louisa's face. Now she snapped upright. "I don't believe what I'm hearing. How can you even consider attacking anyone? We've spent five years assuring our Indian friends that we are peaceful." Her eyes flashed around the room, the fury in them belying her words. "And we are."

David cleared his throat, and a respectful silence fell over the men. "I was thinking of something a little more defensive. Like building a blockhouse."

Big Dog straightened. "You mean a fort?"

"A small one, yes, but big enough to shelter the townspeople, and sturdy enough to stand up to an attack. Something we can build quickly."

"Where would we put it?" asked Red, settling back into his chair.

"Somewhere near enough for everyone to get to quickly," said Noah. "What about the knoll at the foot of Cherry Street?"

Thoughtful nods around the room. Kathryn wanted to ask about the location, specifically how far it was from the Faulkner House, but she couldn't bring herself to enter the conversation. This, after all, was a Seattle matter, and she was merely a visitor.

Nor did she have any intention of being here long enough to see the completion of whatever fort they decided to build, unless they intended to have it finished by the time the next ship left for San Francisco.

"We'll need a load of timber for that. It'll take time to cut and mill that much." Big Dog cast a cautious look at Jason. "That's time away from our jobs."

A quick glance over her shoulder revealed a carefully composed blank expression on the face of the mill's new manager. Whatever thoughts lurked behind those taciturn eyes remained unknown except to him.

When she turned back toward the room, she intercepted a silent communication between Louisa and David. Louisa gave a nearly imperceptible nod, and her husband addressed the room.

"I have a large consignment of timber rafted down on the beach, waiting for transport to San Francisco. I think it'll be enough."

Noah leaned toward his friend. "But you've put in weeks of hard labor cutting that wood. Not to mention losing the sale means several hundred dollars of cash money out of your pocket."

David rested an arm across the back of little Inez's chair. A tender smile hovered around the corners of his mouth as he looked down on her silky curls. "What's money compared to the safety of our families?" His glance swept the room. "Of our town?"

Admiration flared within Kathryn. What a magnanimous gesture. If she were ever to find a man as unselfish and honorable as this one, she could actually see herself giving up her independence to marry him. Louisa was a lucky woman.

Lawson, the man who had brought the message that prompted this conversation, spoke from near the door. "When can we get started?"

Noah answered. "How about first thing in the morning?"

"What about our shifts down at the mill?" Red asked.

Big Dog shook his head, his expression solemn. "Yesler won't like us slacking off there, even if the reason's important."

As one, the men turned toward Jason. Kathryn leaned slightly away from him so as not to get caught in the intensity of their stares. She could almost feel sorry for the poor man. He had not yet set foot inside the sawmill and already he was at the center of a potential controversy between his

100

employer and the men he had been hired to lead.

"We'll have to work around our other responsibilities, of course," David said smoothly. "With all of us pitching in during our free time, we'll make good progress." He aimed an assuring nod at Jason.

Jason maintained his stoic expression for a long moment. The room grew quiet while he studied the man across from him. Finally, he dipped his head in a sign of agreement.

"I'm in," he announced. "If someone will tell me where Cherry Street is, I'll be there when I leave the mill tomorrow."

A measure of tension evaporated from the room, and the men murmured approvingly to one another as they returned to their meals. Noah and David turned relieved smiles toward him, which let Kathryn know that they'd been concerned. Were they afraid he would oppose them?

A companionable silence fell over the table as everyone returned to their meals. She picked up her teacup and sipped the now-cool liquid. By throwing his lot in with the men in this room, Jason had been accepted into their company. Beyond that, he had apparently joined the ranks of the acknowledged leaders, David and Noah. Though she sat at the table beside them,

Kathryn felt like an outsider, and was surprised to realize the feeling stung.

Nonsense. I don't want to be a part of this town, especially when it is surrounded by savages.

Still, she couldn't help feeling a twinge of envy. These were good people, and their care for one another was fully apparent. It would be nice to be counted among their friends.

The rain still fell in a steady drizzle by the time she tied the laces of her bonnet beneath her chin, ready to leave the restaurant. The sun had fully set, and the moon and stars were obscured behind a ceiling of clouds. Though she was not normally fearful of the dark, she couldn't help but wonder if there might be hostile eyes watching her from within the black shadows that lined the opposite side of the muddy avenue. Dim lights shone in several windows of Faulkner House. Clutching the tray Evie had prepared for Miss Everett, she paused in the doorway of the restaurant and peered in that direction, trying to gauge the distance between her and those flickering beacons.

"Can I help you carry that, ma'am?"

The question came from directly behind her. She turned to find a handful of men standing shoulder to shoulder in a semi-circle, watching her. Big Dog stood in the center, his lumbering height drawing her attention to his eager face.

"I can mana—" She closed her mouth on the automatic refusal. The tray wasn't heavy, but the darkness outside would certainly be less frightening with a couple of strong men at her side. She arranged a smile on her face. "I hate to impose on your time . . ." She let the sentence trail into an inviting pause.

Six voices instantly assured her that it was no imposition, and that they were happy to be of assistance. Red took the tray from her hands, and several muscular arms were offered for her to choose from. She awarded a smile all around before slipping her hand in the crook of Big Dog's elbow. His chest puffed importantly while the others' deflated.

"Thank you, gentlemen. I do appreciate your kindness."

As she turned toward the door, her gaze snagged on a pair of eyes across the room. Having just shrugged on his overcoat, Jason stood behind his chair watching her. His lips tightened into a scornful line, and he shook his head slightly, as though in disgust. Irritated, Kathryn turned away with a toss of her head. One minute he made an endearing offer of help for the blockhouse project, and the next he stood in judgment of her for accepting help across a dark alley in an unknown and possibly hostile street. Had he been a true gentleman, he would have offered to escort her himself since they were both going in that direction anyway. Not that she would have accepted.

She stepped through the doorway, Big Dog beside her and her entourage close behind. Was it her imagination, or did that insolent stare remain fixed on her? By sheer force of will, she did not cast a backward glance.

Jason watched Kathryn leave the restaurant with a company of attentive men trailing behind her. Not three hours past she had vehemently denied the suggestion that she was a coquette, though he hadn't accused her of such. Not openly, anyway.

"She has certainly entranced them."

He turned to find Evie staring at the doorway through which the party had just exited, a stack of empty plates in her hands. Noah had left a few moments before to accompany David and his family up the street so they could discuss some logistics concerning their blockhouse. With Kathryn's departure, that left Jason alone with Evie. Something about her open, calming manner invited an uninhibited response.

"No doubt they'd be entranced by any female," he commented.

Delicate eyebrows arched on her smooth brow. "You don't find Kathryn attractive?"

"I didn't say that." The answer sounded like an affirmation, which he hurried to correct. "Not that I do. I haven't considered the matter one way or another. I merely meant that females are notoriously scarce here."

An amused grin arose on her lips. "That is true enough." She took the plates to the long worktable beside the stove and put them with the other dishes.

"No doubt they'll be disappointed to learn that this female doesn't plan to stay." He'd seen the consternation on Kathryn's face when Captain Baker delivered the news that there was no room aboard the *Fair Lady*. "How long will it be before the next ship arrives?"

Evie answered over her shoulder, her hands occupied in scraping the remains of her customers' dinners into a bucket. "I think the *Leonesa* is scheduled to arrive next week."

"Miss Bergert won't have too long a wait, then."

"A lot can happen in a week." Her tone became light. "Seattle has a way of growing on a girl."

He found her words faintly disquieting. The sooner Kathryn was installed on a ship and sailing for home, the better. He found her annoying, denying that she was a flirt one minute and commanding the attention of a roomful of millworkers the next. Over the years of working with timber crews, he'd learned that the biggest enemies of a tight schedule were distractions. This blockhouse would be diverting enough. Adding a woman into the mix was a complication he would prefer not to deal with, especially during his first month on the job.

Evie finished scraping one stack of dirty plates and started on the next. He glanced toward the doorway and the Faulkner House beyond. He had letters to write, having promised to let his family back home know when he arrived. Starting tomorrow, his free time for tasks like correspondence would be limited. And yet, with the evening's talk about Indian attacks, he hesitated to leave a woman alone.

Though he had just donned his coat, he unfastened the top button. "Can I help you clean up? I'm a fair hand at washing dishes."

She paused in her work to turn a surprised look on him. "Are you? That's not a skill most men would lay claim to."

"My wife trained me well."

"You're married?" Her eyes went round with interest. "I had no idea."

Pain erupted in his chest. Not the knife-sharp grief that tortured him for the first few months after Beth's death, but the familiar suffering that had since become his constant companion. Sometimes it was no more than a dull ache and at others, like now, it pounded against his heart with the force of a lumberjack's ax.

"Not anymore." He clipped the words.

Compassion flooded her eyes. "I'm sorry."

The understanding in her tone threatened to undo him, and he turned away, swallowing hard against a tight throat. A moment later he felt the soft touch of her hand on his arm from behind.

"I know the pain of losing someone you love. You'll be in my prayers, Jason."

Prayers? The pain twisted deep inside. He and Beth used to pray together every night, their arms wrapped around each other as they thanked God for blessing them with so much love. He hadn't prayed since. He wasn't sure he knew how anymore.

Thank goodness Noah returned at that moment. He strode through the open doorway, his expression pensive. When he caught sight of Jason he gave a nod. "Still here, Gates?"

Evie answered in a bright voice. "I was just about to put him to work as a kitchen slave. Now that you've returned, he's escaped my whip."

Noah's face screwed up into a good-natured grimace. "I knew I should have accepted Louisa's offer of a cup of coffee."

Glad for an excuse to take his leave, Jason re-buttoned his coat. "I'll leave you to it, then. Thank you for the delicious meal. I haven't eaten food like that in a good long while."

"I look forward to serving you many more."

Her gracious smile didn't hold a trace of the sympathy he found so disturbing, though it lingered in her eyes. He dipped his head in farewell and made his escape.

FOUR

Tuesday, January 8, 1856

The sun had barely begun to rise when Jason joined a line of men making their way down the hill toward the mill. Yesterday's rain had stopped, at least for the moment, and the air held the chill of winter. Nothing like back East, but a frigid breeze stung his cheeks. He recognized several of the men from the restaurant the night before and dipped his head in a greeting here and there. As though in deference to the early hour and those still sleeping in the houses they passed, they spoke only in whispers and not to him at all, though he did overhear the occasional phrase that let him know he was a topic of several conversations.

". . . Evangeline's last night . . ."

". . . seems decent enough . . ."

Someone mentioned Michigan, and he hid a smile. He had not discussed his past last night, but the men obviously knew something about him. Probably from Yesler, which made sense. No doubt he'd been talking about the man he'd hired, describing his qualifications. Still, being the topic of discussion among strangers — even though they would soon be coworkers and hopefully friends — didn't sit well. He valued privacy above almost everything else. That was one reason he intended to keep to himself as much as possible here in Seattle, especially where gossipmongers like Madame Garritson were concerned.

He had dropped his guard a bit with Evie last night and let the information that he was a widower slip. No doubt that tidbit would spread like wind through a forest. But unlike Madame, Evie didn't seem the type to indulge in mean-spirited gossip.

The mill was situated at the bottom of Mill Street, directly on the shore end of the first of two piers. The *Fair Lady* lay in port at the second. In the dawning light, Jason took his bearings. A wide, muddy strip of bare land carved into the surrounding forest ran behind the buildings he had passed yesterday, and he recognized it immediately as the skids. Deep grooves bore evidence of the passage of many tons of logs, which could be sent sliding down the steep embankment to land directly into a cordoned-off area of the bay and floated into the mill. A tall smokestack belched great billowing clouds of white smoke that rose and dissipated into the rapidly lightening sky. The boiler was already going, then. He quickened his pace and passed by a handful of millworkers. He'd intended to arrive before the operation got started for the day.

He entered at the nearest end of the long mill shed and stopped to get his bearings. To his right lay the boiler, where a pair of workers were already feeding the fire with shovels full of wood chips and scrap lumber. Heat rolled toward him from that direction, a welcome relief from the cold outside. The welcome wouldn't last. Though the sides of this shed were open to the elements, the fires and the engine and the physical effort of the work would make the men warmer than was comfortable by the end of the first hour. The smell of sweating men and milled timber that lingered in the air would intensify, and by lunchtime he'd be praying for a wind off Elliott Bay to blow through the building and cool them off.

A man on the far side of the shed caught sight of him. He said something to the fellow he was talking to and then made his way down the length of the conveyer belt. His long-legged, confident strides and the erect set to his shoulders gave evidence of his self-assurance. Henry Yesler, if Jason were to hazard a guess. He wore his hair short, his mustache shaved, and his beard neatly combed. A liberal amount of gray colored the beard, but his dark hair had not yet surrendered to the silver touch of age.

He extended a hand when he neared and held Jason's gaze in a direct one of his own. "That you, Gates?"

"Yes, sir." His fingers were warm, his grip firm.

"Welcome. Sorry I didn't make it up the hill to meet you last night. We had some trouble with the engine, and repairs took longer than expected."

Jason tossed a glance over his shoulder toward the platform where the giant engine sat, its levers, pistons, and wheels dormant since it had not yet been started for the morning's shift. "I should have come down to help."

"Nah. Nothing you could have done." He dismissed Jason's chagrin with a grunt and then grinned. "Me either, for that matter, except hover over the mechanic and ask for an update every five minutes."

Jason returned the grin. "I'm sure that motivated him to hurry the job along."

"You don't know my mechanic." He rolled

his eyes. "He let me dither for an hour or so before he snapped. Almost took my head off. Told me to go shuffle papers or something and let him work. I backed off, and he had it fixed twenty minutes later."

His good-natured manner spoke of his confidence in the mechanic's abilities and a healthy realization of his own tendency to brood over the men's work. Jason made a mental note to stay out of the mechanic's way, or at least to hover from a distance.

Yesler turned and waved down the length of the shed. "This is our operation. You've worked mills before, so I expect you know your way around a saw."

Nodding, Jason inspected the equipment. The infeed deck, rollers, and head rig all looked standard from here. He'd put in his time operating every piece of equipment in the sawmill where he'd worked back in Michigan. The work of the sawyer suited him best, actually setting and operating the primary saw. Something about watching metal teeth rip into a rough log and turn it into clean, usable timber, about being the first to inhale the odors of nature that were released when a log was opened for the first time, gave him a sense of satisfaction like none other. His job here would be to manage the men who did the physical work.

Still, he intended to get his bearings by taking a hands-on approach. A man had to work with a piece of equipment before he really understood what it could do.

He nodded at Yesler. "Yes, sir, I know my way around a mill. You've got a nice outfit here."

"I bought the machinery down in San Francisco and shipped it up here. No proper wharf at the time. We had to throw it overboard and float it to shore, all except the engine. Loaded that on a raft." His head turned as he gazed around, an expression of proprietary satisfaction on his face. "Yep. It took us a while to smooth out the operation, but here we are four years later and doing great."

"I can't wait to get started."

"Good." Yesler slapped him on the back. " 'Course, you'll spend most of your time pushing a pencil, I'm afraid."

He arranged his features into an expansive grimace, and Jason laughed. "That's all right. Part of the job. Believe it or not, I enjoy the paperwork almost as much as the mill work."

"Now, that right there proves I made a good decision in hiring you." The man's smile became companionable, and the last vestiges of tension fled Jason's muscles.

They were going to get along just fine.

"Before you start going over the books, I'd like you to get your hands dirty. Work with the men, let them see you know what you're doing." He spied someone behind Jason. "In fact, here's somebody you need to meet first off."

Jason turned and saw a familiar face approaching. William Townsend, the man who'd arrived at the restaurant in David Denny's company and then left so abruptly.

"We met last night." He extended a hand. "Good to see you, Townsend."

The older man examined him with the same cautious gaze as the night before, and again Jason wondered about his position with Yesler. Why had he not been given the manager job?

After what seemed to be a longer-than-normal pause, the man's grip became firmer for a second before the release. "We don't stand on ceremony around here. Call me Will." He grinned. "It'll be nicer than some of the names the men have for me."

Feeling as though he had passed some sort of test, Jason grinned in reply. "Fair enough. I'm Jason."

Yesler jerked a nod and flashed a brief smile at each of them. "Right. Will, I'll leave Jason in your care. Walk him around, intro-

115

duce him to the men. I'll be in the office if you need me."

He started to turn away, but Will stopped him. "Don't know if you've heard, but David and Noah are planning to build a blockhouse up at the end of Cherry Street."

Yesler stopped, and his smile transformed into a grim line. "I heard. Are they going to start work this morning?"

Will nodded. "I told him this couldn't come at a worse time, what with that shipment due by the end of next week."

Uh-oh. Jason eyed his new boss. A tight timeline to meet a scheduled shipment meant double shifts in most mill houses. Would he forbid the men to work on the blockhouse?

He straightened and turned to face Yesler head-on. "I volunteered to help with the construction after hours. If that's a problem —"

The man cut him off with a swift gesture. "Not a bit. I've been telling David and Noah and anyone else who'll listen that my Indian friends are worried about these newcomers from the northern tribes. We've got to do something, and we can't afford to wait." He clapped Jason on the back a second time. "Glad you're throwing your support in that corner, Jason. I'll be putting

116

in my share of time up there too." He peered at them both from beneath thick eyebrows. " 'Course, we still have to meet that shipment. If it starts looking like we're going to come up short, you let me know. Sooner rather than later."

Will met his gaze without flinching. "We'll meet the shipment. Don't worry about that."

His certainty boosted Jason's confidence. If Will Townsend had anything to say about it, he believed they would.

"Good man."

Yesler gave a curt nod and then turned on his heel and headed for a door in the corner Jason hadn't noticed before. The wall beside it contained a large glass window, and he glimpsed a desk in a tiny dark room on the other side. The office, no doubt, with an opening so Yesler could keep an eye on the mill operations while he worked. Smart man.

When he disappeared through the door, he turned to find Will studying him through narrowed eyes. "He showed me your qualifications. You're young to have worked all the places you have."

It was a statement of fact, but was that a hint of doubt in his tone? Jason kept his expression impassive. The new man in an operation always had to prove himself. Didn't bother him.

"I started young. Worked alongside my father cutting white pine when I could barely hold my end of the crosscut. Then I got a job in the mill sweeping sawdust. Water powered. As soon as I operated my first mill saw, I was hooked." He allowed himself a smile at the memory.

The older man answered with a slow nod. "Yeah, me too. Sawing by hand's one thing, but then you get your first taste of power, and there's nothing else like it."

They exchanged a smile, an expression of connection that transcended age or geography and delved the depths of shared experience. Jason relaxed. He and Will were going to get along just fine.

"C'mon. There's Big Dog and Pelfrey. They're the off-bearers on this shift, and they've been here longest. I'll introduce you."

He took off down the length of the mill shed, heading toward the place where the giant Jason had met at the restaurant stood talking to another man.

As they walked, he eyed Will sideways. "Pardon my asking, but you seemed to be in a hurry to get out of there last night."

The man kept his gaze focused ahead, but

did his jaw tighten? "I remembered some- thing urgent I had to attend to at home."

Jason didn't believe him. If that were the truth, he would at least meet his gaze now. Will had left in a hurry the moment he'd been introduced to Kathryn. If he wasn't mistaken, and he didn't think he was, a look of recognition had flashed across the man's face in the instant before his hasty depar- ture.

"The lady who arrived on the ship with me. Have you met her before? Her name's Kathryn Bergert."

Had he not been watching closely for a reaction he might have missed the sudden bulge in Will's jaw, indicating clenched teeth.

"No." The word clipped short. "Never met a woman by that name."

He was lying. Jason was sure of it. But why?

It was none of his business, of course. As he himself had thought not half an hour past, a man's privacy should be considered his most prized possession. If Will wanted to conceal the reason for his abrupt depar- ture, that was his right. And if he chose to avoid the presence of an annoying, cloying woman, Jason completely understood and even applauded the desire.

But the secrecy was curious, nonetheless.

"I think I should tell you that I don't intend to stay in Seattle."

Kathryn didn't meet Madame's eye as she delivered the news. Instead, she focused on pouring tea into two matched cups, their finish crazed with fine, spidery cracks that crisscrossed over the entire surface. She set the pot down and covered it with a quilted cozy before sliding one filled teacup across the small table in Madame's sitting room. There were no saucers in evidence.

Madame had invited her to breakfast here, where it was her custom to cook a morning porridge over her small stove. Though she directed her guests to Evangeline's Café for their meals, she told Kathryn since she was to be the *assistant manager* — she spoke the title with a scorn that set Kathryn's teeth together — she could at least share her employer's breakfast.

"Running home to Daddy's house, are you?" The woman spoke in something akin to a jeer as she spooned a liberal amount of sugar from a crock, dumped it into her cup, and repeated the process twice. "I figured as much the moment I laid eyes on you. Flibbertigibbety gal like you doesn't have what it takes to last more than a week here."

Kathryn eyed her with distaste, both at the idea of drinking tea-flavored syrup and at the implication that she was somehow lacking the ability to succeed in an environment where Madame thrived.

She picked up her tea and aimed a cold eye over the rim. "What do you mean, flibbertigibbety? I am quite levelheaded, thank you."

Madame made a rude noise and added a glug of cream directly from the jug. "You're spoiled. Not your fault. Your parents encouraged it. When Philip saw you were too plain to attract a husband, he should have put you to work in his business instead of letting you spend your days playing with a paintbrush."

The teacup clattered to the table, and Kathryn stiffened her spine. What an ill-mannered thing to say, and directly to her face!

"I do not spend my days 'playing with a paintbrush.' Monsieur Rousseau at the San Francisco School of Fine Art says I have a fledgling talent unlike any he has seen before. Papa is discerning enough to want to encourage me in that pursuit."

At least, he had been at first. Their last unpleasant conversation threatened to replay itself in her mind — the one where

121

Papa insisted that she spent too much of her time in artistic pursuits and not enough in social activities that might one day lead to finding a suitable husband. He expressed the opinion that Monsieur Rousseau seemed far more interested in collecting his fees than in furthering his students' artistic ambitions. Kathryn had objected to his assessment, and had become rather more heated than she intended. The conversation had ended with his pronouncement that she was being sent to Seattle.

No reason to detail that conversation with Madame. She only hoped Papa had not shared his reasoning too freely in his letter to his cousin.

"And I am not plain," she added for good measure.

Madame cocked her head, eyes narrowed. "You may be right about that. You're no beauty, for sure, but you're not homely either. Good, high cheekbones. No pockmarks. Nose not too long, though it does turn up a mite. And at least you don't have a squint."

Uncomfortable at being the object of such scrutiny, Kathryn opened her mouth to object.

Madame continued before she could. "If you were to make a little effort, you might

122

even be pretty. You've got good hair, but pulling it back that way makes you look like a schoolmarm. And that blouse hangs on you like a sack. Why don't you put on a little rouge and a nice dress, pretty yourself up a bit?" She leaned over the table and fixed a gleaming eye on Kathryn. "Be friendly to the men, if you know what I mean."

The outrageous suggestion was accompanied by a waggling eyebrow that Kathryn found nearly as distasteful as Madame herself. Without a doubt, Papa had shared his intentions that his daughter would find a husband among the hundreds of unattached men living in Seattle. And apparently Madame was ready to accept the challenge.

Oh, Papa, of all the places in the world you could have sent me, why did it have to be here? And especially to this *woman?*

Her appetite was completely ruined. The mere idea of attempting to choke down porridge while seated at the same table with this odious woman threatened to send her stomach into revolt. Moving with extreme grace and composure, she rose and scooted her chair neatly beneath the table.

"I believe I'll begin work now. Thank you for the tea."

An amused grin twisted Madame's mouth

sideways. "As you wish. Before you start on the rooms, though, go next door and fetch a tray for Miss Everett. She's paid extra to have her meals delivered."

"Very well."

Kathryn kept her chin high and her eyes averted as she left the room. Perhaps her dwindling resources would allow for a decent breakfast at Evangeline's Café every now and then. Beginning her day in the company of the cheery Evie was certainly preferable to suffering Madame's advice on how to attract men.

A little later Kathryn climbed the stairs carrying a covered tray. Her mood was considerably improved after half an hour in Evie's company. The restaurant owner's chatter was pure delight after Madame's sarcastic barbs, and Kathryn had accepted her offer of tea while the tray was arranged. For the duration of her short stay, she would endeavor to spend as much time in the restaurant as she could, thereby escaping the Faulkner House.

Miss Everett had been installed in a second floor room at the opposite end of the hallway from Jason's. Since her hands were full, Kathryn used the toe of her boot to tap on the door.

A muffled answer came from within. "Yes?"

"It's me, Kathryn." Fresh from the cheerful atmosphere at Evangeline's, she adopted a lighthearted tone. "I've brought your breakfast tray."

There was a scuffling sound and then the door cracked open. A brown eye peered cautiously at her for a moment, and then the door swung open.

"It's flapjacks with butter and jam. And there are fresh eggs and bacon — fried crisp." She smiled into the solemn face. "It looks better than anything the ship's cook served us, I can tell you that."

A brief smile appeared on the woman's thin lips and then evaporated. During the voyage on the *Fair Lady,* Miss Everett had barely spoken five sentences. Kathryn's initial attempts to strike up a conversation met with no success, and she'd finally given up. The aura of sadness she'd sensed then was still apparent in the woman's rounded shoulders, her downcast expression, and the way her rare smiles affected only her lips but failed to dispel the heaviness in her eyes.

She reached for the tray, but Kathryn pulled it backward out of her reach. Last night she'd delivered supper into Miss Everett's hands and left her at the door. This morning she was determined to prove Madame wrong. She *could* succeed in Seattle, if she wanted, and that included succeeding at her job. The decision to leave wasn't a matter of being incapable. It was a matter of desire.

"I'll bring it in for you and keep you company for a minute if you like. While you eat I can tidy up your room."

Another shadowy smile acknowledged the offer. "Thank you, but as you can see I've already straightened up."

She stepped back to allow Kathryn an unobstructed view inside. Curious, Kathryn peered around her slight figure. The room would be considered small by most standards, but compared to the closet in which she slept, it was palatial. Though crowded. Two beds dominated the cramped space, the coverings of both neat and straight. An old, scratched trunk rested between them, and she spied the edge of Miss Everett's satchel peeking out from beneath the bed in the far corner. A book lay on the mattress, splayed open and facedown.

"I'll take that," the lady said softly, reaching again for her breakfast.

Since there would hardly be room for both of them to maneuver within the confines of the small space, Kathryn released the tray into her hands. She set it on the surface of the trunk, which she apparently intended to use as a makeshift table, and then turned to face Kathryn, her hands clasped tightly together in front of her.

"Madame Garritson promised to have someone remove the extra bed this morning, though she seemed unhappy about having two private rooms at one time." She cleared her throat, her eyes fixed on a place on the wall somewhere off to Kathryn's right. "I hated to mention it to her, but would it be possible to request a chair in its place?"

Yes, a chair would be a good addition. Situated there in the corner, she would have plenty of light to read by. That is, if the sun ever decided to put in an appearance in the dull, dreary, cloud-covered sky. She glanced around. A picture on the wall would work wonders in here, and some nicer curtains. Those dreary ones looked like they'd been made from worn-out burlap sacks.

"I'll pass along the request." She turned to go and then paused. "Tomorrow, leave the bed for me to make. I'm happy to do that for you." To her amazement, she meant it. She felt an urge to do something to bring a smile to this sad woman's face.

Miss Everett's solemn expression did not

change as she shook her head slowly. "I'm accustomed to looking after myself. It" — she bit down on her lower lip — "gives me something to do."

"Perhaps tonight you could join me for supper." She displayed an encouraging smile. "The proprietress of the café next door is a lovely woman, and she would enjoy meeting you."

Best not to mention the deluge of eager men who would also enjoy making her acquaintance. That would scare this shy violet off for sure.

A look of interest flashed across Miss Everett's features, and Kathryn thought she might accept. But in the next moment, the sad mask returned. She shook her head. "Thank you, but I think I'd prefer a tray here. At least for now."

Should she insist? Pull the woman out of her self-imposed isolation and into the only society Seattle had to offer, whether she liked it or not?

With a sigh, she nodded and turned to go. Miss Everett was a grown woman, older by several decades. Certainly old enough to make her own decisions. Whatever events had turned her into this sad, reclusive person were none of Kathryn's business.

Promising to return for the tray after she

finished her duties, she left.

Straightening the guest rooms proved not to be as onerous a task as she feared. True, the bed linens did not look as crisply immaculate as hers at home after Mrs. Porter was done with them, but they were at least neat. And though Madame spoke with grim satisfaction of chamber pots to be emptied, she did not find a single one. Apparently guests preferred the solitude of the privy out back. The occasional discarded article of clothing she merely folded with two careful fingers and laid neatly across the foot of whatever bunk was closest. Other than Miss Everett, the hotel was empty of guests, so the work went quickly without distractions. She finished all the rooms on the left-hand side of the hallway in less time than expected and started on the others with a much improved outlook. Running a hotel was not difficult in the least. She directed a smirk toward Madame's sitting room below.

She approached the room in the far corner, the one where Madame had installed Jason. After a perfunctory rap on the door with her knuckle, she pushed it open. Whereas most of the guests had left their bed linens in various states of disarray, Jason had taken care to smooth the coverings flat on the bunk in the corner. The second bunk had been stripped in preparation for removal. The linens lay neatly folded at the foot of the bare mattress. Well, he may be rude, but at least he was neat. In a rush of magnanimous charity, she decided to ask if Madame could spare a chair for this room as well.

Arranged on the smooth covering of the bed in the corner was an assortment of items — a tidy stack of clothing with a hat resting on top, a shaving kit, a —

She drew a sudden intake of breath. That was an artist's palette! The surface was a satisfying mishmash of hues and pigments, blended together in a rainbow-colored jumble. There were paintbrushes in varying sizes too, and made of expensive red sable. And those things there, what were they? She widened her eyes. Were they . . .

Her lungs emptied of air. She tiptoed into the room, gaze fixed on a half dozen narrow objects as long as her hand, some of them shriveled and malformed, the others rounded. Why, those were paints in tin tubes with screw-on lids. Monsieur Rousseau used these new paints in his own work, and touted them to all his students. The sealable tubes were so much more effective than pigskin bladders. And more expensive too. Though she had been trying to convince

Papa that the higher cost was worth the extra money because paint waste would be virtually eliminated, he refused to see reason.

So focused was she on admiring the tubes of paint that at first she did not see the canvas. When she did, a chill spread from the back of her neck down her spine and over her entire body, and for a moment she was paralyzed. It had been centered on the wall beside the door so that the person lying in bed could gaze on it with an unhindered view. And no wonder. It was stunning.

Tall birch trees lined a glassy stream and stretched limbs heavy with golden-green leaves across the water like slender, elegant ladies reaching for their lovers on the far shore. Sunlight streamed through the foliage, tinged with green as it poured onto the stream's shiny surface in bright, verdant pools. Leaves floated lazily on an invisible current in a carefree journey toward an aimless end. Tall grasses in hues ranging from bright gold to vibrant green to rich maroon clustered along the bank, soaking up stray rays of the sun that peeked between misty white clouds and flowed through the living canopy above.

Kathryn inched closer. With an effort, she

pulled herself from the grips of the painting to examine the details with an artist's eye. An exquisitely light touch had created the feather-soft look of the golden leaves, and an expert hand had blended gold to green. Bolder strokes gave the slender tree trunks the impression of strength, of permanence, though the details of peeling bark and a peek of living white wood beneath had been wrought with intricate care. And the light on the water! How had the painter managed to capture the exact hue, the feeling of movement, without physical evidence of a rippled surface? It was astounding. The work of a true artist. Why, even Monsieur's landscapes, while perhaps technically superior in the aspect of scope, did not portray the depth of feeling of this piece.

Something on the floor caught her eye. A piece of wood. With the toe of her boot she lifted the draped bed covering for a better look. It was the corner of a crate. A narrow, rectangular crate. She recognized it instantly as the one with which Jason had taken such care during the short journey from the ship. And no wonder, if it housed this masterpiece.

She stepped closer to the painting and searched for the artist's signature. There, in the bottom left corner. Peering closely at green letters that blended to near invisibility with the watery reflection of the leaves, she made out a set of initials. *JEG.*

Jason E. Gates.

Why, that rude man she had determined to avoid for the duration of her stay in Seattle was an accomplished artist!

Jason trudged up the hill in the company of a handful of millworkers. The muscles along the backs of his thighs, unaccustomed to such a steep grade, protested with burning twinges. His shoulders, too, were stiff and sore after a day of lifting heavy logs and stacking cut timber. It had been close to six weeks since he left the mill in Michigan, and his body would take a while to re-accustom itself to the work. He'd like nothing better than a hot supper and to stretch out in bed for a good night's sleep.

The second, at least, wouldn't happen for a while yet. He and the others planned to grab a bite to eat at Evangeline's and then head over to the blockhouse to work until the sun set.

Will, the daytime foreman, caught up to him. "Now that you've had a chance to see our outfit in action, what do you think?"

"You run a smooth mill operation. Everybody knows their job, and they work hard at it."

He'd done as much observing as working, and kept a careful eye out for areas where the process could benefit from improvement. To his surprise, he hadn't found any. In fact, he'd been impressed by the number of logs they managed to mill in the span of a single day. The crew worked together like they'd been doing it for years, and by talking to some of them throughout the day, he knew they had been.

Will snorted. "They were showing off for the new boss. We have a few who'll take advantage of a chance to slack off. But for the most part, we've got a good group of men."

At the top of the hill a few men bid farewell and veered off to the left where a row of small cabins and shacks lined the street. Most turned right in the direction of a handful of establishments along the left side of the wide avenue where the Faulkner House stood. A couple of the men ahead of Jason entered Coffinger's Dry Goods store, but the rest headed in the same direction as he was. The wide door of Evangeline's Café stood open, and a steady stream of customers turned at the colorful totem pole and entered.

Will showed no sign of stopping, but kept on in the direction of the larger, nicer homes that began just beyond the hotel. As they passed the pole, Jason craned his neck to look up at the top where the carved wings of an eagle were spread wide, as if to embrace the wharf and Elliott Bay at the bottom of the hill.

"What's the story behind this?" He slapped the pole as they walked by.

Will glanced up at it and shook his head. "It was here before me. Apparently it was a gift to Evie from the old Duwamish chief this town was named after. His way of saying welcome, not only to her but to all the settlers."

"Apparently not all of his people are as agreeable as him," Jason said drily.

"Definitely not."

They arrived at the Faulkner House, and Jason came to a halt. "You going down to the blockhouse?"

"For a bit. After I see to my grandson." His chest swelled with pride. "He's a rascal, and sometimes Louisa is waiting for me at the door, ready to hand him over. I need to make sure she's agreeable to watching him evenings too until the building is done."

Jason was curious to know how the man had come to have custody of his grandson,

135

but held his tongue. If Will wanted to tell him, he would choose his own time in which to do so.

"I'll see you down there."

He jerked a nod and turned toward the hotel. First, a quick visit to his room and the satchel where he stored his loose money, then he'd head next door for that supper. The door to the Faulkner House opened and a figure appeared. Kathryn. She stepped onto the porch, an expectant look on her face, her gaze fixed on him. Clearly, she was waiting for him.

Beside him, Will's eyes narrowed and his lips twisted into a scowl. He came to a halt.

"Hope you'll excuse me for saying so, but if I were you, I'd watch out for that woman."

Surprised, Jason looked at him. Why would he say that? "Do you know her?"

"Oh, I know her all right. You can find her kind everywhere." His gaze slid sideways and fixed on Jason. "If you take my advice, you'll keep your money close and your business even closer where that one's concerned." He jerked a farewell nod and continued up the street, his pace quick as though he could hardly wait to put some distance between himself and Kathryn.

Jason stared after his back for a second. What did he mean by *her kind*? He had not

136

exchanged a word with Kathryn last night. Maybe he assumed she was a man-hungry female and held strong opinions about women who traveled to Seattle alone in order to attract a husband. When he arrived with David last night she'd been recovering from her faint, drooping across the chair and surrounded by an audience of attentive men. Did he mean to beware women who feigned weakness in order to attract attention? No need to warn Jason off there. In fact, no need to warn him off *any* woman.

He kept a wary eye on Kathryn as he approached the hotel porch. Something had happened to excite her, and the smile she fixed on him was warmer than any he had seen from her.

She rushed forward to meet him as his foot touched the bottom porch step. "I've been waiting for you."

"Oh?" He eyed her with caution. "Why?"

"Because I've seen it."

"Seen what?"

"The painting." Enthusiasm bubbled in her voice. "It's beautiful! I've never seen color blended to such effect. I would have credited the use of the expensive paints, but when I looked closer I realized mere oil and pigment couldn't have achieved that level of beauty."

With her first words, his feet had halted as though the bottoms of his boots were stuck to the porch. A buzz started in his ears and intensified as her chatter continued.

He interrupted. "You entered my room?"

The gushing stream of words halted for a second. "Yes. To clean it, of course."

"My room did not need cleaning," he told her coldly.

She drew back, eyeing him with surprise. "I saw. Your bed was neat and orderly."

"And yet you entered anyway."

Blotches of color rose on her slender neck. "I saw your paints, and couldn't help —"

"Did you touch them?" The idea of this woman, or anyone for that matter, disturbing those art supplies sent a spear of anger straight through his skull.

Clearly offended now, she drew herself up. "Of course not. I only admired them. And then I saw your painting." Her throat moved with a swallow. "I was hoping to ask —"

He didn't wait to discover what she wanted to ask, but barged past her and into the hotel.

"Madame Garritson!"

Anger gave his voice an unexpected volume in the confines of the front room. A few seconds later the interior door opened and the rotund hotel manager appeared. At the same time, Kathryn followed him inside and came to a stop nearby.

"Perhaps I failed to make my wishes clear." With considerable effort, he wrestled his voice to a reasonable level. "When I arranged to pay for privacy, I expected that the belongings in my room would be safe from probing eyes. Yet I find that your *assistant* has entered my room and conducted a thorough investigation of the contents."

Kathryn sucked in an outraged gasp and planted her hands on her hips, eyes blazing. "I did no such thing! I only saw what was laid out in plain view."

"You had no business there to begin with," he snapped.

Madame's gaze slid between the two of them. To her credit, she maintained an unruffled manner. "Cleaning is a service we offer our guests, Mr. Gates. I'm sure my *assistant*" — her gaze skipped sideways to Kathryn and then back to his face — "meant no harm."

Her composure had a calming effect on him. No doubt she was right. He was tired from a full day's labor and overly sensitive when it came to those paints. And especially about that painting. Coming so close on the heels of Will's warning, Kathryn's unwitting intrusion had angered him unreasonably and prodded him into an embarrassing display of emotion.

He willed the angry buzzing in his ears to stop and rubbed his eyes with a finger and thumb before answering. "I'm accustomed to cleaning up after myself. I'd prefer to do so."

She shrugged her pudgy shoulders. "Less work for us." Then she turned and disappeared back into her lair.

Taking a deep breath, he turned to Kathryn. Outrage still simmered in her glare.

"I apologize for shouting at you." There. He'd done as courtesy demanded. Hopefully that would be enough.

Her anger dimmed into resentment and she gave a cautious nod. Jason turned on his heel and headed for the stairs.

Behind him, she cleared her throat. "Would it be possible for you to show me the technique for achieving that peculiar lighting effect?"

She had nerve, he had to give her that. A trait he found particularly annoying in a woman. He did not pause, but tossed his answer over his shoulder as he ascended the stairs.

"No. It would not."

FIVE

Few patrons sat at the tables in the restaurant when Kathryn arrived that evening. She entered and stopped in surprise, glancing around the room.

At her worktable in the corner, Evie caught sight of her and waved her across the room.

"I hoped you'd stop by tonight. It's pretty lonely here with all the men out working on the blockhouse. Sit here." She wiped her hands on her apron and pulled out the closest chair. "I'll get your supper and you can keep me company while I work."

Kathryn slid into her seat and Evie set a cup and saucer in front of her. Before long a pot of steaming tea joined them. Kathryn filled her cup. The pungent odor of the tea soothed the sour mood brought on by the encounter with Jason and his stubborn refusal to teach her. She inhaled deeply and heaved a sigh into her teacup.

Evie turned from her worktable. "Goodness, that was a heavy sigh. Is something wrong?"

She managed a weak smile. "I had a disagreeable encounter with Mr. Gates this evening."

"Oh?" Her smile became sympathetic, and she continued her efforts. "He is an interesting man. Many men are quiet, but him more than most, I think."

The echo of his shout for Madame still rang in her ears. "I wouldn't call him quiet."

"No?" She tilted her head. "Introspective, then."

That Kathryn could agree with. Most artists of her acquaintance were pensive, some preoccupied with their thoughts to the point of excluding the real world. Completely understandable, when their inner musings were filled with artistic contemplation that rendered external daily routines mundane. Though after this afternoon's display, Jason proved himself more temperamental than most.

Evie set a plate in front of her. "I hope you like venison."

"It's one of my favorites."

A thick slice of meat dominated the plate, alongside a mound of golden potatoes glistening with butter. The aroma, though tantalizing and rich with spices, failed to stir her feeble appetite. She took up the meat knife and cut a bite-sized piece. Evie watched for her reaction while she chewed.

"Very good. Some of the best venison I've ever had."

A relieved smile lit Evie's features and she returned to her work table.

The food was delicious, and normally Kathryn would have devoured every scrap and looked for more. She had no patience with women who denied their healthy appetites to pick at their food in order to impress men.

But today she found herself tempted to push the plate away and sit brooding over her teacup. Why would Jason react so angrily to a sincere appreciation of his work? And why the peremptory dismissal of her simple request? Perhaps he was one of those secretive artists who believed that sharing their technique somehow threatened their standing. The idea frustrated her in the extreme. Monsieur Rousseau freely shared his knowledge and skill, and felt that in doing so he furthered the cause of art. Maybe if she explained her teacher's stand on the matter Jason would see reason. After all, she only wanted a simple demonstration, not a commitment to teach her in the long term. Soon she would be gone and back in San Francisco. Why would it hurt to show her a few techniques in the next week?

Unless the next ship, too, had no room for her.

The thought brought with it a stark reminder of her precarious financial state. How long would her money last? And how much would the next ship charge for passage home? She cut another bite of the delicious venison. If she ate well at supper time she could save the expense of breakfast. Or if her situation became desperate, she could always force herself to suffer Madame's company over porridge and tea in the mornings.

In fact, she had no idea how much a meal was. Last night she had been so distracted by the ill tidings that she'd completely forgotten to pay for her supper. Evie must think her a freeloader. She jumped up so suddenly her chair fell backward.

Evie turned, eyes wide. "What's wrong? Is it the venison?"

"I didn't pay you last night. I am so sorry." She fumbled for her reticule, which had fallen from her lap to the floor when she rose. "Please forgive me. I'm accustomed to Papa taking care of these things."

Amused laughter filled the restaurant,

drawing the attention of the few customers seated around the room. "My dear, don't worry so. I didn't remember myself until you said so just now. People hereabouts are accustomed to paying when they can." Her laughter settled into a smile. "I trust you. Now sit down and finish your meal."

Relieved, Kathryn set her chair right and returned to her venison. She sliced into a perfectly roasted potato. No doubt there were some who took advantage of Evie's kindness, but she did not intend to be one of them. Papa modeled integrity in all his dealings, and she would do the same. But how much should she allot for food? She eyed the full plate before her. Best to figure out the costs before she ate her way through all her money.

She cleared her throat. "What is the cost of a meal?"

"Twenty-five cents for supper." With a long metal fork she opened the door of the big oven and delicious-smelling heat escaped into the room. "Ten for breakfast, unless you want eggs and then it's twelve." Her hands protected by a thick towel, she drew out a metal sheet covered with a row of potatoes and deposited it on the surface with a clang. "I serve a proper tea on Tuesdays and Fridays for ten cents. I make sweet bread and tea cakes special on those days."

A quick mental calculation made clear a sobering fact. Until she knew the exact price of her passage back to San Francisco, she had better make do with eating a substantial breakfast and forego supper. Perhaps that last-minute donation before she boarded the ship had been a bit hasty. But it had felt so good to be able to do something substantial for the cause of women's rights.

She looked up to find Evie studying her with a speculative stare and arranged a quick smile on her face. "Don't worry. I'll pay as I go along."

The woman's face cleared. "Oh, I'm not worried. In fact, I was wondering something." She averted her gaze, looking a touch uncomfortable. "But I don't want to offend you by asking."

Her manner piqued Kathryn's curiosity. "I'm not easily offended."

Evie's stare went on for a long moment, and then she seemed to reach a decision. "Okay, I'll just ask." She pulled out the chair directly opposite Kathryn's and dropped into it. "Noah told me this morning that his work at the blockhouse is going to take all his time, at least during daylight hours. Of course I told him I could manage here without him, but to be honest, it's harder than I thought. What with cooking and delivering the food to the tables and making sure everyone has clean plates and forks and plenty of coffee . . . well, I just can't manage on my own." She placed her forearms on the table and wilted over them. "Frankly, I ran myself to exhaustion this morning. And he was still here part of the time."

Her intent dawned on Kathryn. "Are you asking me to help?"

"Only if you want to," Evie hurried to say. "I'm afraid I can't pay you much, certainly not what Madame is paying you as her assistant. But of course your meals would be free. And it wouldn't have to interfere with your work at the Faulkner House, because the busy part of breakfast is usually over quickly and then the men go to work at the mill."

Pay? Kathryn's lip curled with scorn at the idea of Madame prying her hand open wide enough to pay her for cleaning guest rooms.

Evie leaned back in her chair. "I've offended you. I'm so sorry. You probably have maids and cooks and everything back home, and the idea of working in a restaurant is abhorrent to you." She started to rise.

147

"Please forget I said anything. I'm sure I can convince one or two of the Moreland girls to help."

"You misunderstand." Kathryn half-rose from her chair too and gestured Evie to stay. "I'm not offended in the slightest. I . . ."

What would her friends at the art studio say if they knew she had taken employment first as a hotel maid — no matter what lofty title she gave her duties — and then as a waitress in a restaurant? On the other hand, what did it matter? Her duties this morning had been accomplished in less than two hours and the rest of the day had been spent in dreamy contemplation of the techniques she would learn from Jason. Obviously that was not to be. Besides, it was only for a week or so, and the arrangement would solve the problem of paying for meals.

She smiled at Evie. "I don't know who the Moreland girls are, but please don't ask them. I can't think of a nicer place to spend my days than here in your company." That, at least, she meant wholeheartedly.

"Oh, thank goodness." Evie wiped her forehead with an exaggerated gesture. "The oldest Moreland girl chatters incessantly, and I'm not sure I can handle her first thing in the morning." She smiled into Kathryn's eyes. "Besides, I look forward to getting to know you better, even if it is for such a short time."

When Evie returned to the stove, Kathryn tackled her supper with renewed appetite. At least one element of her stay here in Seattle might prove to be enjoyable, even though it would be brief.

Dear Papa,
I pray this letter finds you and Mama well. If not, we have that in common since I am most assuredly *not* well, in the accepted definition of the word. Please tell Mama not to worry over my health. I do not refer to my physical well-being, but to my mental condition due to the circumstances in which I find myself.
Seattle is not at all as you were led to believe.

Kathryn lifted her quill and stared at the fire blazing in the Faulkner House's bare common room as she contemplated the last sentence. Madame's writing desk was small but well supplied, and at least the woman did not begrudge her the use of paper and ink. While Kathryn would have liked to take an accusatory tone in her letter, no doubt

Papa would react poorly to accusations of willful mistreatment. The better approach was to assume that he would be as shocked as she at the situation in which she found herself.

Cousin Mary Ann is a woman of . . .

She brushed the tip of the feather against her lips for a moment, considering words descriptive of Madame's character.

. . . harsh countenance, and acerbic of tongue. Not an hour past she dropped a crock of lye which shattered on impact, and she proceeded to blister my ears with words that were not even used by the sailors during the voyage here. I confess I was not familiar with most of them, but the vehemence with which she shouted spoke of their shocking and inappropriate intent. Furthermore, my position here is not what we were led to believe. Not five minutes after my arrival at the Faulkner House, Madame informed me of my duties, which include cleaning guest rooms. Imagine, Papa, your daughter — a hotel maid! You understand that I am not complaining about earning an honest wage, but I am not even to be paid. In exchange for my labors I am given lodging in a closet. Yes, Papa, a *closet*. Madame outfitted it with a cot, and beyond that not a single stick of furniture will fit in the cramped space. She expects me to purchase my own meals, and you know, Papa, the allowance you so generously provided will be used up quickly.

The words in that last sentence were carefully chosen, and she was satisfied with their veracity. No need to mention her arrangement with Evie.

To make matters worse, some of the guests are quite rude. In particular one gentleman raised his voice and shouted in a most disturbing display of temper. And speaking of gentlemen, there are few of those here. Men abound — that much of the reports we had of Seattle, at least, was true — but thus far I have not met a single man of business who is not married. The primary occupation here is lumber, either the cutting or milling of it. Said vocation requires no social graces. Nothing, in fact, beyond brute strength.

Wait. Papa might interpret that last bit as

151

arrogant. She chewed on a fingernail. If only there were a way to strike the words from the page without leaving a telltale smudge.

Not that there is anything wrong with physical labor, of course. I admire the tenacity of those who earn their living through sweat and muscle. But when I choose a husband, I have hopes he will display the manner, intelligence, and business acumen of my dear Papa, who is a model of these admirable qualities.

A smile settled over her lips as she wrote. Papa was not a gullible man and was never fooled by flattery. Yet he frequently adopted an indulgent smile and acquiesced to her requests when she plied him with the occasional compliment about his intellect. He did love her, and had been known even to dote upon her. He truly wanted her happiness and security, a fact upon which she depended as she prepared to conclude her missive.

Papa, I have saved the most disturbing news for last. Not four hours after our landing in Seattle, we received an alarming report. The Indians attacked a group of men nearby, and one poor soul was killed. The settlers here were most disturbed by this development, which apparently is the most recent of a string of similar assaults. It is said that a savage tribe is assembling in the surrounding forest to prepare for a major attack on the town. The men of Seattle have undertaken to build a fortress to shelter against the impending aggression. I was so distraught upon hearing the news that I fainted. Me! You know, Papa, that I have always enjoyed a sturdy constitution, and am not given to swooning, but the idea of ferocious savages swarming through the streets quite unnerved me.

If her previous pleas failed to move him, certainly the fear for her safety would convince him that this move was foolish and should be rectified with all haste.

That is why I have determined to leave Seattle as soon as I can arrange passage. Captain Baker did not have room for me on this voyage, but I am assured that another ship will arrive next week. I intend to be on that ship when it sets sail. My financial state being what it is, I may not have enough to cover the entire cost of the passage. I trust, dear Papa, that you will settle any debt I am forced to incur in this effort to ensure my safety. Again, please give my love to Mama and assure her that I am, at least for the moment, in good health.

Your loving daughter,
Kathryn

Six

Wednesday, January 9, 1856

Jason rose Wednesday morning well before the sun. His muscles protested the previous day's activity when he rolled off the mattress, and he sat for a moment in the straight chair that had replaced the spare bed sometime during his absence yesterday, massaging the stiffness from his shoulders. Thoughtful of Madame to supply the chair. He wouldn't have pegged her for the type to perform spontaneous kind gestures. At least, not without expecting some form of compensation in return.

A peaceful darkness occupied the room, and he dressed without lighting the lamp. The painting commanded his attention whenever there was light enough to admire it, and this morning he didn't have time to sit and brood over the memories it stirred. Work awaited, and he was eager to get his second day at the mill under way. This morning he would arrive in time to see the boiler lit for the day's labor.

He crept through the dark hotel corridor, stepping lightly so as not to make noise with his boots on the floor. Not that the sound of footsteps would disturb anyone who could sleep through the racket that filled the hotel during the night. A symphony of snores in varied tones and resonance echoed down the hallway and vibrated through the thin wooden doors. The loudest resembled the sound of a saw chewing its way through a log. Yet another reason he insisted on a private room.

Outside, he halted on the porch to draw fresh air into his lungs. The rich scent of the forest invaded his nostrils, combined with another, more domesticated aroma. Freshly baked biscuits. If he wasn't mistaken, the odor wafted from the direction of Evangeline's Café. It stirred up a rumble in his stomach. A biscuit or two with some of Evie's strawberry preserves and a mug of good, strong coffee would go down well.

When he entered the restaurant, he discovered that he was not the only early riser in Seattle. A handful of men were seated around the restaurant, platters of eggs, ham, and biscuits before them. A few were mill-workers, and he nodded a silent greeting to those he recognized. David and Noah were seated at the same table where he met them the night of his arrival, the plates before them empty but for a few crumbs. Noah waved him over.

"And I thought I would be the first customer of the day." He slid out a chair and dropped into it.

David, elbows planted on the tablecloth and an earthenware mug held before his lips, smiled over the rim. "We're really old farmers at heart, and used to getting started well before dawn."

"Farmers?" Jason shook his head. "I thought you were lumberjacks."

"Farmers. Jacks. Traders. Restaurant owners." Noah's frame shook with a laugh. "We're a little of everything, I guess. Have to be around here."

"Good morning, Jason." Standing before the stove and stirring something in a huge pot, Evie turned her head to greet him. "Coffee's coming right up."

He was about to reply when someone entered from the storage room in the corner. His mouth snapped shut. Were his eyes deceiving him?

"Good morning," Kathryn almost sang as she skirted the stove, snatching up a towel to shield her hand and grabbing the coffeepot in a single smooth movement. She bustled over to the table, taking a mug from a shelf on the way, and set it before him. "I trust you slept well."

"What are *you* doing here?" The question came out in a rude tone he didn't intend.

Hers were not the only eyebrows that arched. He shifted uncomfortably in his seat and avoided looking at either of the men at his table.

"I mean, I didn't expect to see you here."

"You'll be seeing a lot of me if you take your breakfasts and suppers here." She smiled sweetly, though he detected a hint of tartness in the sparkle in her eyes. "I've agreed to lend Evie a hand while Noah is occupied in building the blockhouse."

"You? A waitress?" The idea of an arrogant woman like her waiting tables almost made him laugh.

"I want to help, and I can't very well wield a hammer or ax, can I?"

She poured coffee into his mug with careful attention and then held up the pot with an inquiring gaze at Noah.

"I've had enough." He set his mug in the center of his empty plate and reached across the table for David's.

Kathryn leaned forward and snatched it first. "Cleaning up is my job. You two can get going."

They smiled their thanks and, with a farewell nod to Jason, left the table. Noah detoured to the stove to plant a goodbye kiss on Evie's cheek before following David out of the restaurant.

Kathryn stacked their plates and then hooked two fingers through the mugs' handles to carry them away. She awarded him another bright smile as she picked them up. He even heard her hum the snatch of a tune as she turned. He narrowed his eyes and watched her cross the room and deposit the mugs in a dish pail by the back door. The arrogance he'd seen her display seemed to have disappeared this morning, replaced by this cheery disposition. What happened to bring about this change in attitude? Especially since the last time he saw her he'd accused her of snooping through his things?

She returned by way of the stove, where she collected a plate from Evie to set before him. Two fluffy biscuits, each bigger than his fist, rested atop a thick slice of ham. A boiled egg, sliced in half and speckled with pepper, nestled up against a mound of potatoes that had been fried to golden perfection. Rounding the table, Kathryn reached for the butter plate at the far end

159

and scooted it toward him, then straightened.

"Now. What else can I bring you?"

He cocked his head and eyed her, not bothering to hide his suspicion. By all rights, she should be angry with him, or at least sullen. Why, then, this cheerful demeanor?

She returned his gaze with round eyes. "Is something wrong?"

"I'm wondering about the reason behind your pleasant disposition."

The smile wavered and annoyance flashed in her eyes. "I assure you, I am quite pleasant much of the time." With a visible effort, she conquered her annoyance. "I will concede that I haven't been in the best humor since our arrival, due to some unexpected developments in the arrangements. After all, we artists are known to have volatile tempers, aren't we?"

Her assumption that they shared a common talent or temperament irritated him. "Who says I have a volatile temper?"

Dainty muscles in her cheeks bulged as she clenched her teeth. Then she expelled a long breath. "I'm afraid we seem to have gotten off to a bad start. I'm . . . sorry for that."

The apology did not roll naturally off her

160

tongue. Jason saw the effort it cost her, and his conscience pricked. She was at least making an effort to be genial. Though he wanted nothing to do with her or any woman, except perhaps those safely attached to husbands, neither did he want to be at odds with anyone. It would be churlish of him to refuse the olive branch.

"I accept your apology. And I'm sorry I shouted at you."

With a quick glance around the room, she pulled out the chair across from him and slid into it. "You may have heard me say that I won't be staying long in Seattle. Be that as it may, it appears I will be here for another week or ten days. I hate to impose on your time, but . . ." A hopeful smile settled on her face. "Would you please consider giving me one or two lessons?"

His ire returned with double strength. The painting again. Unbelievable.

"No." The word blasted forth, clipped and harsh.

Kathryn reared back, eyes going wide. "I know you're busy. They wouldn't be long lessons, just a . . ."

"I said no." He punctuated his answer with a slap on the table, which drew the attention of everyone in the room. At the stove, Evie turned in surprise.

161

"You needn't shout." Petulant lines creased Kathryn's forehead. "I'd think you would be flattered that someone admires your talent enough to want to learn from you."

"Well, I'm not," he snapped.

Anger flashed in her eyes. "What was that about not having a volatile temper? I wouldn't ask at all, except your painting is so extraordinarily beautiful."

Yes, it was. Achingly so. Just looking at it brought back the happy days of its creation, the warmth of the sun, the trickle of the water, the breeze brushing his skin as delicately as the paintbrush caressed the canvas. Beth's laughter, the feel of her arms around his neck, pulling his lips down to hers.

He stood abruptly. From his pocket he pulled out a few coins, tossed them on the table, and then grabbed the biscuits off his plate. "I don't want to discuss that painting. Ever."

Without waiting for her answer he stomped out of the restaurant, aware that half a dozen astonished stares were fixed on his back.

"That is the rudest man I have ever met in all my days!"

Kathryn didn't bother to lower her voice or filter the anger from her tone. When the customers at the nearest table chuckled, she rounded on them, ready to pounce. The three men's faces cleared of mirth in an instant.

Evie spoke without leaving the stove. "Perhaps he isn't a morning person. Some people are positively cranky before they've had a cup or two of coffee."

"That's sure enough true for me," commented one of the customers as he lifted his mug and drained it.

"That was not simple crankiness." Kathryn snatched his plate off the table. "That was downright boorishness."

The man seated nearest the back door scraped his plate with a crust of biscuit. "He's a hard case for sure. Back in Michigan he had a reputation for keeping to himself."

The man seated next to him gave him a curious look. "You worked with him before?"

"Not directly. I was jacking and he was down at the mill. Only saw him once or twice when I was working the skids. Word was he knew his way around a sawmill, but kept quiet about his private life. When Yesler told us he'd hired a man named Gates I didn't put two and two together, not till I saw him yesterday."

Kathryn eyed him with interest. Someone who knew Jason from before would surely have heard of his talent. "Have you ever seen his paintings?"

The man looked at her with surprise. "Paintings? Nah. Like I said, he mostly kept to himself. Never heard tell of no paintings."

"Jason paints?" Evie looked after him at the empty door frame. "How interesting."

Kathryn followed her gaze. "He paints beautifully," she said with a touch of bitterness. "Only apparently he doesn't want to share his talent."

"Like I said." The man jerked a nod. "Private."

"He may have reasons for guarding his privacy that we know nothing about." The restaurant owner's voice took on a gentle tone. "We should respect that." With a bright smile that dismissed the subject she turned back to the stove. "I've almost got Miss Everett's tray ready. Kathryn, would you mind filling one of those small jam pots? There's one on the drying rack right outside the back door."

With one final grimace toward the empty chair where Jason had sat so briefly, Kathryn did as she was asked. Evie was a kind and gentle woman, quick to forgive and ready to think the best of everyone. Admirable qualities that Kathryn knew she should strive to exhibit. Why, look what she had accomplished here in the hinterlands of Washington Territory. Last night she'd shared a little of her history, how she had left her home in Tennessee and set her sights on starting her own business in the untamed wilds of a frontier settlement that at the time did not even have a name. And she had done so too. Hindered in her goal of hiring men to do the construction work for her, she and a handful of women friends had cleared this very plot of land with axes and saws and then worked alongside friendly natives to erect her restaurant. The first female business owner in Seattle. And this all occurred before she married Noah, proof that a single woman *could* succeed on her own in this progressive time. Evie's was a story to inspire the likes of Susan Anthony and Elizabeth Stanton, whose efforts to forward women's causes were gaining notoriety in the East. Evie's gentleness and kindness were inspirational and worth imitating.

Kathryn selected a jam pot from among the collection of dishes arranged on a drying rack beneath an awning that stretched the length of the restaurant, nearly as deep as the one that covered the Faulkner

House's front porch. As she turned, a splash of color caught her eye. A bushy patch of wild winter grasses had sprouted just beyond the railing and against the odds had produced a few yellow blooms. What a hopeful sight after the dreary rain that had saturated the town since their arrival!

On impulse, she skirted the railing and plucked a handful of the tiny blossoms. Just the thing to brighten Miss Everett's breakfast tray. Maybe it would bring a smile to her habitually sad countenance.

Rain had fallen in a steady drizzle all day, and heavy, gray clouds cast a gloomy pall over Kathryn's mood as well as the inside of the Faulkner House. All of the guests were out taking care of whatever business they had in the town and surrounding forest, rendering a tomb-like quality on the place. After a morning of mending, Madame settled in the single comfortable chair in her sitting room and immersed herself in a book. Kathryn sorted her paints and supplies and toyed with the idea of starting a new painting, but the walls of her tiny room flickering in the candlelight pressed in on her. Besides, the fumes from the oil of turpentine would become unbearable as soon as she unstoppered the jar. She made an attempt to join Madame for an afternoon of reading, but even her favorite book of poetry failed to hold her attention. Finally, she laid it aside and wandered over to the café.

The atmosphere inside the restaurant was drastically different from that of the hotel next door. As she stepped inside she was greeted with the happy laughter of children, a sound that coaxed a smile to her face.

"Miss Kathryn!" Inez slid out of her chair at the far end of the room and skipped down the center aisle to greet her. "Have you come to play dolls with us?"

"Why, perhaps I shall." Kathryn smiled down at the girl as she untied the laces of her bonnet. She didn't have much occasion to be around children beyond the ones she saw at the church meetings she attended with Mama and Papa. "My sister and I used to enjoy dolls when we were little."

"Oh, good." She clapped her hands, and then informed her in a disgusted tone, "John William refuses to do as I tell him."

Standing at the worktable beside Evie, Louisa half-turned and directed a laugh her way. "You've let yourself in for it now, Kathryn. She is a tyrant for sure, and will dominate your time if you let her."

"I have some to spare at the moment."

Kathryn followed the little girl back to her table, where another child sat playing quietly in a chair drawn closely up to the table. He was so short that at first the only part of him visible was the top of his head, bent over something in his lap. He looked up at her approach, and interest flashed in round eyes the deep green color of the sea on a sunny day. A dimple appeared in one round cheek.

"Are you a lady?" The words were precisely articulated in a high, childish voice.

Surprised at the unexpected question, she laughed. "Why, yes, I am."

"Miss Weesa is a lady. And Miss Evie." The news was delivered with a serious countenance. "Inez is a girl, and not a Miss."

From her position at the worktable, Louisa chuckled. "We're learning our manners." To the child she said, "Do you remember how to introduce yourself to a lady?"

Chubby hands deposited a collection of wooden toys on the table, and then he climbed out of his chair and stood formally before Kathryn on sturdy little legs. He stood a few inches shorter than Inez, with chubby cheeks and folds at his wrists that still resembled those of a roly-poly baby. With one arm across his stomach and the other held formally behind his back, he executed a perfect bow.

"I am John William Townsend." He straightened and added importantly, "I am a boy."

Charmed, Kathryn dropped into a deep, formal curtsy. "I am Miss Kathryn Bergert, and I am happy to make your acquaintance, Master Townsend."

Apparently that was the expected response, for a wide smile lit the child's face.

Inez's patience for manners had apparently worn thin. She inserted herself between them, took Kathryn's hand, and tugged her toward an empty chair. "You sit here. You may play with Rebecca, and I will have Rachel." She thrust a well-loved doll, the paint on its cloth face nearly worn off, toward Kathryn.

With a grin at Louisa and Evie, Kathryn did as instructed. John William returned to his chair but instead of sitting, stood on the seat on sturdy legs and began to arrange the wooden toys he had put down a moment before. Inez picked up a second doll, this one newer and wearing a blue dress that was a miniature replica of hers. She stood the doll's stuffed legs on the table.

"I'm glad you've come to visit, Rebecca. Won't you stay for tea?"

Holding her doll aloft, Kathryn responded with the expected answer. "Why, yes, Rachel. I would love some tea."

While Inez served her make-believe tea, John William piled his toys, a handful of wood chips sanded smooth and cut in various sizes, carefully on top of each other. Kathryn stirred invisible sugar into her pretend teacup, declined cream, and declared the apple cake "simply wonderful!" to Inez's delight.

The boy placed a block of wood on top of his pyramid and the pile toppled. Heaving a sigh, he began again. As he worked the tip of his tongue appeared between his sweet little lips in a gesture that reminded Kathryn of Papa when he was hard at work over his books. The thought made her smile.

"What are you building?"

"A blockhouse." His gaze flickered briefly to her face. "Just like my grandpa. It's gonna keep the town safe."

Evie approached and stood looking down at his handiwork. "Safe from what?"

The child thought a minute. "I don't know," he finally said, and shrugged in a gesture so adult that Kathryn couldn't hold back a chuckle.

"Speaking of tea," Evie said with a smile at Inez, "it's time for ours. Would you like milk with your apple cake?"

The little girl jumped out of her chair, curls bouncing. "Yes, please!"

"Me too!" shouted John William.

"All right. Put your toys away and I'll get it." She grinned at Kathryn. "Would you care to join us at the adult table?"

Against Inez's protests, Kathryn left the children to clean up their toys and switched tables. Louisa emerged from the storage room with a loaf of sweet bread. The three of them set the table with the lovely ivy cups and saucers and then settled themselves around the cheerfully steaming pot.

"You must be sure to join us tomorrow," Louisa said as she slid a slice of apple cake onto her plate. "There aren't many ladies in Seattle, but almost all of them come for tea on Thursdays. It's one of the highlights of the week."

"I hope the weather cooperates this week so the children can play outside." Evie glanced at the other table, where John William and Inez were applying themselves to cake and milk with enthusiasm. "They enjoy the time together almost as much as we do."

A tea would serve as a delightful diversion in an otherwise long and boring afternoon. And it would be nice to meet the other women of Seattle.

A thought occurred to her. "I wonder if I could persuade Miss Everett to come. It might cheer her up."

"Please do." Evie set her spoon down on her saucer and fixed an eager expression on Kathryn. "Tell us about Miss Everett. We're all wondering about her."

Louisa nodded. "Yes, do. Letitia was able to find out almost nothing, only that she wrote to Madame from her home in Nevada City several months ago to inquire about reserving a private room."

"And that she paid six months in advance," added Evie.

Kathryn regarded her with surprise. Paid in advance? She must have been absolutely certain that she would stay here. Why, then, would she hide out in her room and refuse to come out and meet the people of the town where she would spend the next six months?

"I don't know much about her. She seems sad, somehow." She thought about it a moment, and then shook her head. "She is shy, that much is certain. But when I deliver her supper tray I will try to convince her to come for tea."

"Speaking of supper, Noah suggested that we do something different tonight." Evie dribbled a thin stream of cream into her cup with one hand, stirring with the other. "We're putting together sandwiches and delivering them to the blockhouse."

"A sound idea. The men won't lose time coming here for their evening meal. They can make use of every minute of daylight." Louisa cut a bite of the moist sweet bread and speared it on the tines of her fork. "And you *do* know how to serve a good supper from the back of a wagon."

Evie nodded, and then explained to Kathryn, "When I first arrived in Seattle, every man in town was focused on cutting lumber for their first timber order. I worked at the cookhouse for a time, and toward the end when the timing got tight, Cookee used to deliver portable suppers to the cutting sites so the lumberjacks could keep working. That was before we built this place." A distant smile curved her lips as she swept the room with a fond gaze.

"I'll help however I can," Kathryn assured her. "But remember what I told you. I know nothing about cooking."

"Putting together a sandwich is not exactly cooking." Louisa sipped from her milky tea. "There's not a lot of skill involved in placing a slab of meat between two pieces of bread. Everything's already cooked."

Sandwiches were not served at the Berg-

173

ert household, since Papa considered them unsuitable for the dining room. Except the small fancy variety appropriate for tea. But she had eaten one on a picnic once. "I think I can handle that."

"And then I wondered if you would help me deliver them to the blockhouse." Evie's glance slid toward her friend. "Louisa has agreed to take the food to the men while I serve the guests here tonight. I thought maybe if you two do it together the first time, then you'd know the way. Tomorrow perhaps you'll feel comfortable enough to handle the delivery yourself."

The idea left her vaguely uneasy. Was it safe for a woman to wander around town alone? Was the blockhouse even in town, or would she be required to travel through the forest to get there? She would not agree to that.

Hesitation must have shown on her face, for Evie said, "Maybe you'd prefer to handle things here while I deliver supper to the men."

Actually, she would prefer to remain in the safety of the restaurant, but she didn't want to appear like a frightened child to these two fearless women who had conquered the wild frontier. No doubt they would laugh at her fears. Besides, she trusted that Evie would not send her into an unsafe situation.

She pasted on a brave smile. "No, I'd like to see the blockhouse. And some of the town as well. I've been here three days and seen nothing except the wharf and this street."

"Thank you." Evie's expression held a touch of relief. She relaxed against the back of her chair. "How I wish you were staying longer in Seattle. Already I feel like we've become friends."

Kathryn returned the warm smile. "I do too."

Beside her, Louisa shifted uncomfortably in her chair, one hand pushing against the side of her round belly. "This baby isn't fond of apple cake, apparently." Her fingers massaged the area for a minute, and then she settled back and picked up her cup. "Why are you leaving when you've only just arrived? Is Madame so very difficult to work for?"

Across the table, Evie chuckled. "I'm surprised you even have to ask that question. Would *you* want to work for her?"

"Not I." The answer came quickly, accompanied with a firm shake of her head.

Kathryn twisted her lips and answered with a wry tone. "Madame is actually quite

175

easy to work *with*." She emphasized the word, hoping to maintain a distinction. "Of course, it has only been two days, but I don't think she has bestirred herself to climb the stairs since I arrived. She stays in her sitting room mostly, or sometimes at the desk, answering correspondence or going over the finances. I'm fairly well on my own upstairs."

"I'm sure the upstairs are in capable hands, then, and I'm glad to hear she manages the business affairs." Evie set her fork down beside her plate. "I confess to feeling a bit sentimental about the Faulkner House, and would hate to see it fail due to mismanagement."

"Oh?"

Louisa aimed a smile at her friend. "Evie and Noah intended to build a boarding-house next door, but when Captain Faulkner approached them with the idea of a grand hotel, they sold the property to him."

Grand was not a word Kathryn would use to describe the Faulkner House. *Plain* was more like it. *Austere* came closer to the mark. "It could be grand," she said carefully, "with a few nice pieces of furniture, especially in the entry."

"Exactly," Evie agreed. "Walking into an empty room doesn't convey a sense of grandeur, or even of comfort. I've told Madame that many times, but of course she is limited in what she can do with Captain Faulkner gone so much of the time on business."

Judging from the jumbled appearance of Madame's personal rooms, Kathryn doubted she could achieve the desired effect even given the proper furnishings.

"So tell us. What makes you want to leave so quickly?" A grin teased the corners of Evie's mouth. "Don't you like our company?"

"Very much," Kathryn assured her. "It's only . . ." She lowered her gaze, her finger circling the rim of her saucer. If she complained about becoming a hotel maid, she would look like a pampered socialite to these hardworking women.

Louisa came to her rescue. "I think Kathryn is used to a bit more culture than our town has to offer." She raised her eyebrows as though questioning whether that was a correct assumption.

"That is most certainly true," Kathryn agreed. "I'm an artist, and enjoy discussions of technique and trends with other artists, of which San Francisco is in good supply. Here the only other artist I've met has scorned my every effort at conversation with bad-mannered determination to rebuff me."

"She means Jason," Evie told Louisa, then looked at Kathryn. "I've thought about his outburst this morning. I wonder if it has something to do with his wife."

Jason was married? The idea settled on her like a cloud. She'd never considered the possibility.

Louisa straightened, her expression perking with interest. "I didn't realize he was married. Why didn't he bring his wife with him?"

"She died." Evie's voice held an ocean of compassion. "He told me the other night, and I nearly cried at the sorrow in his eyes. He obviously still misses her very much."

"How did she die?" Kathryn asked.

Evie shook her head. "He didn't say, and I didn't have the heart to ask. Speaking of her seemed to cause him so much pain."

Kathryn sat back, her tea forgotten. No wonder he was so ill-tempered. No doubt his wife's death was somehow at the root of his reluctance to discuss his painting. Perhaps she had been his encourager. Certainly she would have to have been, married to a man with such talent. Perhaps he had even given up painting because of his grief. The very idea made her draw in a quick, horrified breath. To have been endowed with such ability and walk away from it, give it up to work in a lumber mill. The thought was inconceivable.

And yet, he had brought his art supplies to Seattle. The expensive tin paint tubes, his palette, his brushes. If he could not bring himself to leave them behind, then the longing to paint must still be there, buried beneath a mountain of grief.

She became aware that both ladies were watching her with curious expressions, and busied herself in picking up her teacup and draining the last of its contents.

"Perhaps that is the reason," she told Evie. "Grief can certainly affect a man's demeanor. Or a woman's. I will try to remember that the next time Mr. Gates attempts to take my head off with sharp words." Straightening her shoulders, she changed the subject. "If I'm to learn how to make sandwiches, perhaps we'd better start. If it involves kitchen implements, I'm bound to be a slow pupil."

For that confession she received an indulgent grin. "I think you'll master the skill quickly."

With an answering smile, Kathryn stood and began gathering the dishes. Her time in Seattle may be short, but at least she could put it to good use. Acquiring a few cooking skills would certainly pass the time, and she could enjoy the company of these two ladies. But now she had a more important goal. She must convince Jason to paint again. A gift like his must not be wasted.

SEVEN

The afternoon passed quickly, and Kathryn enjoyed working alongside Evie and Louisa immensely. Making sandwiches was so easy she felt embarrassed to have even joked about her lack of kitchen skills. The hardest part was cutting the ham. She produced many uneven slivers and jagged chunks before she finally got a feel for the knife. Even the children helped, standing side by side on chairs across the table from her. Inez directed John William's efforts and criticized his placement of meat on bread in an authoritative voice until her mother scolded her for being a tyrant. After that they fell into an easy partnership, with Inez laying out a row of bread, John William applying slices of meat with precise care, and Inez covering them with a second piece of bread.

When the light meal of sandwiches and molasses cakes was loaded in the back of a wagon along with the children, Kathryn and

Louisa waved goodbye to Evie and headed down the wide avenue. It was the first time Kathryn had ventured more than a few steps from the Faulkner House. She inspected the buildings they passed with a bit more interest than the evening of her arrival, when she had been overwhelmed by their primitive appearance. Knowing more of the town and its people, today they looked small, rugged, and entirely appropriate to such a young settlement. Most were small, square, and built of rough cut logs and had low roofs, but they passed a few larger homes, most even made of milled timber.

When their wagon started up an incline and approached a neat two-story building set in the center of a grassy piece of cleared land, she exclaimed to Louisa, "Why, that's an attractive home. With the window shutters and that beautiful porch railing, it's nicer than some I've seen in San Francisco."

A grin stole across the woman's face, and from the back of the wagon came Inez's piping voice. "That's *my* house. My papa made it."

Kathryn looked at Louisa in surprise. "David built that house?"

"He had help, of course. Most of the men in town showed up at one time or another to help with the building." Her gaze traveled to her home, but a faraway look came over her. "I love it, of course, but it was sad to be forced out of our little cabin in the swag. Nothing so grand as this, but I will always miss our first home, where we lived when we married. Especially since we left out of fear." They topped the hill, and she pulled the horse to a halt. "Take a look, Kathryn. This is the perfect place to see Seattle."

She was right. Had the thick layer of clouds not lain low in the sky, Kathryn could have seen for miles in all directions. Even with the low-lying clouds her view of the populated area was perfect. The town circled an inlet of the bay, which had been cordoned off by a series of corrals in the water at the closest end of the lumber mill. From here it looked like the buildings she had passed upon arrival were crowded together with hardly any space between them, but farther away from the wharf they spread out. Clusters of smaller buildings lay here and there with stretches of barren land between them. Crisscrossing paths connected them to each other, the dirt packed and grooved into avenues wide enough to accommodate all but the largest wagons. From this vantage point Kathryn could appreciate the scale of the town and the ambition of those who envisioned it.

Her friend watched her face, clearly expecting a reaction of some kind.

"It's bigger than I thought. How many people live here?"

"I'm not sure." Louisa cocked her head as she considered. "Around three hundred white settlers, I'd say, but we have a number of Duwamish friends who live in town as well."

"Apparently you expect the number to increase, judging by the amount of cleared land over there." Kathryn gestured toward the wide-open space to the right of the wharf.

"More men arrive with every ship that docks here. It's been rather astounding to watch Seattle expand. Four years ago there were only a handful of us." A look of sorrow passed over Louisa's face. "I mourn the loss of the forest. But I suppose that is the price of progress." She turned her head and looked to their right. "But we still have plenty left. I hope you can get out into the woods before you leave. You have no idea how beautiful it is when you're surrounded on all sides by trees taller than the tallest building, the leaves so thick you can barely see the sky between them. It's" — she inhaled a deep breath — "freeing, some-how."

Freeing? Given recent developments, wandering in the forest would soon find her free of her scalp. No, thank you. She intended to remain within the safety of the town for the remainder of her stay, however long that may be. But she smiled and replied with a noncommittal murmur.

"There's where we're going." Louisa pointed ahead.

The work area stood at the top of a knoll not far ahead of them. Looking at it, Kathryn immediately saw the wisdom in building the fort there. Its central location would allow access by most of the town, and the land around it had been cleared far enough that an approaching enemy would be spotted immediately. But the forest's edge did lie fairly close on two sides. Within gunshot range? A shiver rippled down her spine.

How far was the Faulkner House from here? She turned to look behind her. They had taken one turn and the hotel lay hidden behind a rise in the land, but they had not traveled very far. Perhaps half a mile. Certainly near enough to reach safety within a reasonable amount of time. Provided, of course, the streets weren't swarming with savage enemies.

"They see us." Louisa lifted an arm above her head and waved.

At the building site, one of the men waved back. David Denny, Kathryn identified. Beside him another man straightened from his work, and her pulse skipped when she identified his broad shoulders and dark, curling hair. Jason. Somehow she must find the proper way to approach him about continuing his painting.

"They've seen us." Louisa flipped the reins and the wagon began to roll forward.

The work stopped at their approach, and in no time the wagon was surrounded by eager, smiling men. And not only eager for sandwiches, either. Kathryn found herself inundated with offers of assistance to climb down. Jason, of course, was not among those who crowded her side of the wagon. She took one of the dozens of hands lifted toward her and stepped from the sideboard to the ground.

Smiling her thanks, she made her way around the wagon to the back. The children waited at the edge of the bed beside the crates containing the results of their afternoon's labor. A quick count of heads showed her that they had made plenty of sandwiches for the work crew to eat three or four each. Evie had been afraid they would run out.

Noah stepped up beside her and took charge. "Let's get going so we can get as much done as possible before the light fails completely. Form a line here."

He gestured with both hands and the men moved to obey. Louisa and Kathryn stood at the back of the wagon, distributing sandwiches and sweet cakes. To a man, the millworkers voiced polite thanks as they received the meal from her hands, and Kathryn made certain to smile into each face.

"I want down," demanded a small voice behind her.

Kathryn looked up to find John William standing over her. He extended his chubby arms toward her, and she reached for the child. Before she could grasp him, someone pushed by her, jostling her away.

"Come here, boy," said a rough voice.

Surprised, she turned to see who had spoken so harshly and found herself looking into the stern countenance of the boy's grandfather. The glare the narrowed eyes fixed on her was so full of menace she took an involuntary step backward.

He lifted John William to the ground and immediately snatched up his hand. "We're going home now."

"But I don't want to go home," the child

whined. "I want to see the fort."

"There's nothing to see yet." The words were clipped and full of impatience. "We have things to do at home."

Before she could even bid the child good-bye, he was pulled away from her and disappeared behind the line of men waiting for their supper. Why, if she didn't know better, she would think the man was trying to get the child away from her. She turned to Louisa, astonished by such a rude display from a grown man. Her friend was staring after the pair with a surprised expression.

"Have I done something to offend him?" Kathryn asked.

Louisa shook her head. "It certainly looks that way."

"But how? I've never spoken a word to him."

"He *is* very protective of his grandson," Louisa said slowly. "Perhaps he's cautious of strangers."

Kathryn stiffened. Did he think she would harm a child? The very idea was offensive.

"I'll ask him tomorrow morning when he brings John William for the day." Louisa dismissed the incident with a quick smile, though she did glance once more in the direction in which the rude man had disappeared.

■ ■ ■ ■

Will Townsend stomped away from the building site, dragging his grandson beside him. Fury still buzzed in his brain. Fury — and fear. The sight of John William's arms outstretched to that woman had sent a spear of alarm straight through his heart.

Who did she think she was to show up here and casually insert herself into the daily lives of his friends and grandson? And on a flimsy claim of kinship with Madame Garritson, no less. He wouldn't believe it for a minute except Madame herself had verified the distant relationship when he stopped by the Faulkner House to inquire the other night.

"Ow, Grandpa. Let go my hand."

The child's plaintive whimper drew his attention from his brooding, and he realized he was practically dragging the boy down the street by the arm. Immediately contrite, he relaxed his grip.

"I'm sorry. I didn't mean to hold you so tightly."

John William rubbed his wrist with the fingers of his other hand and turned a reproachful look up at him. "I wanted to pass out sandwiches. I made them, but I

189

didn't get to pass them out."

Those green eyes never failed to move Will. A hundred memories blew through his mind like a warm breeze. *Oh, John. If only you could see how much like you your son is. More every day.* His throat tightened, and for a moment he could not speak. When he did, he forced a light, conversational tone.

"You made sandwiches today?"

The child gave an eager nod, reproach forgotten. "Me and Inez did." His little chest puffed importantly. "I put the meat on after Miss Kathryn cut it."

A chill invaded his blood. With an effort, he kept his boots moving up the street. "Miss Kathryn was at the restaurant, you say?"

"Uh huh. With Miss Weesa and Miss Inez. She played dolls with Inez and blocks with me. She's a good builder."

"Is she, now?"

The idea of that woman sitting beside John William, touching his toys, touching *him* . . . Will set his teeth. What game was she playing, really? Whatever it was, he would not let his grandson be caught in the cross fire. If Louisa insisted on spending time in Kathryn's presence he would make other arrangements for John William's daily care, and he would do it immediately.

190

With an abrupt move, he turned on his heel. "Let's go this way."

The child complied. "Are we going back to the blockhouse so I can eat a sandwich?"

"No. I've just remembered an errand I need to run down by the wharf." He swept the child up and settled him on one arm.

"I can walk," John William complained. "I'm not a baby."

"I know, but I can walk faster because my legs are longer."

"Can we go see Captain Baker's ship?"

The child's love for all things nautical normally brought a smile to his grandfather's face, but not tonight. "Another time. I want to be safely home before it gets too late."

John William studied him with a serious expression. "Are you afraid of the mean Indians, Grandpa?"

Will returned his gaze calmly. No sense in upsetting the child. "No, I'm not afraid."

Not, at least, of the Indians.

When the sandwiches had been distributed and the men had taken seats on piles of logs or in dirt to eat them, Kathryn was able to inspect the building. A trench had been dug, and the beginnings of the walls lay deep inside. She walked to the edge and peered down, judging the thickness of the wall with satisfaction. The blockhouse would be sturdy with its foundation buried in earth this way. Louisa and David came up beside her.

"Goodness, I can't believe how much progress you've made," Louisa exclaimed, one hand resting on her husband's arm and the other pressing into the small of her back.

"The work is going quickly." He gave a satisfied nod. "I think we'll be finished within a couple of weeks."

"The sooner the better." They wandered away, David pointing out something in the length of timber down in the trench.

Kathryn glanced around the area. Everywhere she looked men tried to catch her eye with broad smiles and nods. She answered absently in kind. Then she caught sight of the object of her search. There. Jason had selected a stump a little apart from the others and sat with his back to them, staring across the bay. Gathering her courage, she made her way around the building site in that direction.

He turned at her approach, and she ignored the way his body stiffened when he caught sight of her.

"How is the sandwich?" Surely he could not take offense at a benign question like that one.

His answer was given without taking his eyes from the vista in front of him. "Fine. Good. Thank you for bringing it."

Encouraged by his polite tone, she ventured an observation. "The view is beautiful from here, don't you think?"

For a moment he did not answer. When he did, his voice was guarded. "Not particularly."

"You don't find it beautiful? The way the wind whips the water into froth and the heavy clouds turning it dark and almost forbidding?"

"I wasn't looking there. I was looking at the mill."

She directed her gaze to the mill, where black smoke belched from the smokestack and an untidy mass of logs cluttered the corralled waters of the inlet. "It does give the area a rather dismal appearance," she admitted.

Though he did not look at her, she watched his profile and saw his lips tighten into an impatient line. "If you had any concept of the ingenuity that has gone into building and equipping that mill you wouldn't call it dismal. I find it inspiring."

She leaped on the word. "Do you plan to paint it? The view from here would make for an interesting scene." Ugly, in her opinion, and not even close to the beauty of the landscape in his room, but she did not voice that opinion. If he was inspired by ugly buildings, then he should paint ugly buildings.

Now he did look at her, and uttered a disgusted grunt. "Did I not clearly forbid you to talk to me of painting?"

Irritation crackled along her nerves. Why, he spoke to her as if she were no more than a child, and an aggravating one at that. She snapped a reply. "I do not respond well to rudely shouted commands." With an effort, she calmed herself. "Besides, you *requested* that I not speak of *the* painting, not of painting in general."

"Then please let me make that *request* officially now." He spoke through clenched teeth. "Do not speak to me of paint in any form. Nor of canvas, brushes, pigment, oils, lighting, or any other aspect of art." With a jerk, he turned his head away from her, a clear dismissal.

"But why?" Frustration overcame her, and she resorted to pleading. "With a talent like yours —"

He stopped her by raising a finger and fixing a stern look on her face. "Not. Another. Word."

Anger erupted in her stomach. Surely he was the most infuriating artist in the world. Rudeness of this magnitude could not be excused under the guise of creative temperament. With a jerk that set her skirts whirling about her ankles she left him alone on his stump. If he insisted on ignoring his talent, what was it to her? Let him rot away in anonymity here in this backwoods, primitive territory.

EIGHT

Thursday, January 10, 1856

Kathryn rose before the sun, dressed quickly, and tiptoed through the hotel so as not to disturb Madame or any of the guests. Serving the café's breakfast diners platters of steaming hot food that Evie produced in extraordinary volume was one of the highlights of her day. She was becoming familiar with the men, and prided herself on the ability to bid "good morning" to Big Dog, Red, Murphy, Lowry, Samuels, and the others by name.

Two things made her sad. First, the announcement toward the end of the meal that the *Fair Lady* had set sail with the tide. By all rights, she should be on that ship. At least Captain Baker had promised to have her letter delivered to Papa the moment they moored on San Francisco's pier.

The second thing that made her sad — and a little angry — was Jason's absence.

Apparently he would rather skip breakfast completely than risk seeing her. The idea sat bitterly in her stomach. Perhaps she should tell him that she would abide by his wishes. She would not, under any circumstances, discuss art with him again. In fact, she would not discuss *anything* with him. Let him scowl and glower and squander his talent. It mattered to her not in the least.

The sun was well along its ascent when she carried a laden tray up the hotel's stairs and rapped her toe on Miss Everett's door.

"Time for breakfast," she called in a cheery voice.

The handle turned, a crack appeared, and the lady peered out. With a quick smile, she opened the door wide. Kathryn entered and deposited the tray on the small table she had procured from Madame. The surface of the table was no wider than the tray, the perfect size for this small room. She straightened and looked around. The addition of a few personal items, like a cozy afghan on the bed and a basin and pitcher in the far corner, gave the room a crowded but cheery look. She noted the wilted blossoms in a cup beside a Bible on the nightstand. This afternoon she would look outside for fresh ones.

Miss Everett's gaze flickered across her

face and then she cast her eyes downward. "Thank you."

"You're most welcome."

Sunlight streamed through the east-facing window and cast a bright glow into the little room. "Why, look," Kathryn exclaimed. "The sun does shine here after all. I'd begun to think I wouldn't see it again until I returned to California."

"It promises to be a beautiful day," Miss Everett agreed. "Just before you came I was admiring Mount Rainier. I have a perfect view from my chair."

Kathryn looked out the north window where she gestured. When she caught sight of the mountain, her breath snagged in her chest. A huge, majestic pyramid towered above the forest that butted up nearly to the back of the hotel, its steeply sloping sides covered in snow. Jagged rocky precipices around the top third stood bare and exposed in the sunlight, lending a sense of wildness that a completely snow-covered peak would not imply.

"It's stunning." Her voice came out in an awed whisper. "I can't believe I haven't noticed it before."

"Perhaps you've been too busy." Miss Everett gave her a kind smile. "Whereas I have done nothing for days but sit here and stare out the window."

Kathryn drank in the vista before her. Tall, slender trunks of the cedar trees, the deep green of the fir boughs, the shining white of the snow-capped mountain, and the azure blue of a cloudless sky. Could such a dazzling contrast of colors be captured in oils on canvas? Oh, if only her skills approached the level of Jason's. But even if she failed, how could a student of art like herself gaze on such beauty and not at least try? Excitement flickered deep inside her at the prospect. As soon as she finished her hotel chores, she would go outside with her easel, palette, and one of the canvases she'd packed and start a new painting. With luck the weather would hold for as long as it took to absorb the view and get the basic lines down. She had a few hours before the afternoon tea.

The tea. She cast a quick glance at Miss Everett. How to approach the subject of the afternoon tea without being dismissed out of hand? She had given the matter considerable thought, and come to the conclusion that Miss Everett's reticence was due to a case of shyness the likes of which Kathryn had never seen. Left to her own devices, she might spend the entire six months within the confines of this room, stepping foot outside only for an occasional visit to the necessary. In cases like this, what was needed was a friendly push.

She cleared her throat. "Mrs. Hughes asked me to convey an invitation. It seems most of the women in Seattle gather at the café on Thursday afternoons for tea, and they would like to meet you."

The shadowy smile vanished and lady's brow creased. She averted her eyes. "I'm not ready —"

"Of course you are. You've been here three days already and haven't met a soul outside of Madame and myself." With a quick glance over her shoulder to ensure she was not overheard, she went on in a low voice. "Let me assure you, Madame is not typical of the manners and character of the ladies in Seattle."

That elicited a faint upward turn of the lips.

Encouraged, Kathryn continued. "I'm told there are no more than twenty ladies and twice that many children."

"Twenty?" Her already pale face went white, and she shrank back toward the corner. "Please convey my appreciation for the invitation, but I don't think —"

"Nonsense." Kathryn strode forward and grabbed her cold hand. "I'll stay by your side the entire time, and I promise to defend you from any hostile approach they may attempt."

She assumed a wide grin, and was rewarded with a hesitant smile.

"I'm sure you think me foolish for taking sanctuary here." Miss Everett's glance circled the room. "Back in Nevada City my mother often chided me for being too timid. She wanted me to be more adventurous. That's why I paid for six months' lodging in advance. I knew if I didn't, it would be far too easy to flee back home, where things are familiar. I've never been comfortable talking with strangers."

"You talk to me," Kathryn pointed out. "Until ten days ago I was a stranger."

Her smile came to the fore. "I doubt you're ever considered a stranger for long. You're so outspoken."

Was that a good thing? Papa would have said no, that ladies should be soft-spoken and demure. But many of the women Kathryn admired back home were considered outspoken to the extreme. Papa would have called them pushy. She decided to accept the statement as a compliment. "Thank you. I will call for you a few minutes before four and we will go together."

She fled quickly, closing the door behind

201

her before Miss Everett could refuse.

Jason hurried up the streets, his stride as long as he could stretch his legs. Over a mug of coffee as strong as wagon grease during the men's lunch break, Henry had revealed his plans for an expansion of the mill. The concept had merit, and Jason's enthusiasm ignited as he listened to the ideas. After two and a half days of studying Henry Yesler, Jason's respect for the man had grown tremendously. A visionary with lofty goals for both the mill and the town, Henry was a man to be admired and followed.

His skills in execution fell slightly short of the mark, though. His visions were exemplary, but rather lofty. He needed men around him who could translate those visions into work that could actually be accomplished. Jason was just such a man.

In the case of the proposed mill expansion, Hudson Lumber Mill back in Michigan had undertaken a similar project when Jason worked there. When he told Henry he had brought some sketches with him, the man's excitement had made him bubble like a boiling soup pot. He'd sent Jason to retrieve the sketches with all speed.

His boots pounded on the Faulkner House's porch and echoed off the hotel walls as he bounded up the stairs. In his room, he threw open the lid of his steamer trunk and began rummaging inside. Where had he put that satchel? Ah. There it was.

The smell struck him at the same time his fingers closed around the leather. He jerked upright. No need to wonder at the odor; he knew it as well as he knew the scent of the rose water Beth used to dab on every morning when she dressed. Invisible fingers squeezed his heart, and he shut his eyes against the tide of memories that pounded like fists against his brain. Oil of turpentine. But where was it coming from? He glanced at the paint supplies he'd arranged in the corner when the spare bed had been removed, intending at some point to wrap them up and store them out of sight where they could no longer taunt him. No, he hadn't brought oil of turpentine for fear the container would leak and saturate the other items in the trunk. Where then?

He spied the window, which he had cracked open before leaving. Was the odor seeping in from outside? Moving like a fearful child, he edged close to the window and peered through it. The sun rode high in a clear blue sky, illuminating the landscape behind the hotel in a bright light he had never seen. The mountain, which he had

admired often since his arrival, stood senti-
nel over a forest so deep the inside looked
black as night. These things he noted in
passing, for he located the source of the
odor immediately.

In a wide stretch of grassy clearing behind
the hotel sat Kathryn. In fact, she had
positioned herself directly beneath his
north-facing window. Before her stood an
easel, a flimsy portable one no taller than a
child. To accommodate the lack of height,
she had laid a blanket on the grass and arranged herself on it facing a small canvas.
She wore a knit shawl around her shoulders
against the chill. Her skirts spread out
around her in an unconsciously graceful
fan, and she had removed her bonnet to
reveal a tail of dark hair curling down her
back. She was absorbed in her work, bending forward and applying her brush with
light, sweeping strokes. From here he could
easily see her progress. She had completed
a rough sketch of the landscape, her focus,
of course, being the mountain. Now she was
blocking the forest with the primary green.

His throat constricted to the point that
breathing was impossible, but Jason was unable to tear his eyes away. He watched in a
sort of self-inflicted torture. When she
leaned back and swished her brush in

turpentine, he was jerked out of the nightmarish trance. With more force than necessary, he slammed the window shut, not only against the agonizing smell but from the far more disturbing sight of a painter before an easel.

Below, Kathryn started and turned, scanning the building. Their eyes met through the glass, but only for a second. Then Jason snatched the curtain closed over the window. He grabbed the satchel containing his sketches and strode from the room, his boots vibrating the hotel floor with every step.

A loud bang jerked Kathryn out of her intense concentration on the painting. Alarm zipped through her. A gunshot? An instant later she recognized the sound and willed her pulse to slow. Not a gunshot, but a window. Turning, she scanned the hotel until her gaze snagged on a figure watching her from the second floor.

Jason.

Hope sprang up in her like a blossom to full bloom in an instant. Surely a true master like him could not look upon a piece of art unfolding without wanting to see it become the best it could possibly be. Maybe he would come down and offer a suggestion or two.

But no. Her hopes wilted when she caught sight of his expression. Even from this distance and through the glass, anger blazed in his eyes. Then he yanked the curtain closed.

Seething, she set her teeth. What right had he to glare at her like that? She'd done nothing wrong . . . this time. Was she not free to pursue her own activities without drawing his wrathful disapproval? How could she ever have thought him nice, his manners courtly, even for a minute?

Well, she'd show him. She would finish this painting before she left Seattle, and use every skill she possessed to make it her best so far. And then she would give it to Evie as a gift to be hung on the wall at the café where he would see it during every meal.

With that goal in mind, she picked up her paintbrush.

Kathryn rapped on Miss Everett's door, fully expecting the reticent lady not to answer. Or, if she did, to have a list of excuses why she could not make the journey next door for tea. Armed with ready answers and a determination to pull her from the room by force if necessary, Kathryn stiffened her spine and lifted her hand to knock a second time.

To her surprise, the door opened and Miss Everett stood before her already dressed in her coat and bonnet.

She dropped her hand. "I'm a few minutes early, but I see you're ready. Good."

"I'd rather meet people one at a time as they arrive than walk into a crowded room." Deep creases in the woman's high, pale brow bore witness to the extent of her anxiety. With jerky, nervous gestures she fetched a small reticule from the chair. "Shall we leave?"

They might have been going to a funeral, judging by her wary tone. Smiling encouragement, Kathryn led her out of the room, down the stairs, and out into the sunshine. She paused a moment on the porch to breathe in the fresh air, scented not with rain for once but with pine and cedar.

"If this weather is any indication of the springtime and summer, I can see why the townspeople choose to stay here." With a nod she invited Miss Everett to walk at her side as they left the porch and headed next door. "I could find sufficient inspiration in Mount Rainier alone to keep me here for a few years."

"I saw you painting this afternoon." Miss

Everett took small, dragging steps that made Kathryn want to grab her arm and pull her along.

"Oh?" Some artists guarded their unfinished projects jealously in order to make a grand presentation of the finished piece. She cared not one whit if someone watched her art unfold, and in fact found encouragement along the way motivating. "And what did you think?"

"Me?" After a quick smile, she averted her eyes. "I couldn't see very clearly from my window. And besides, I know nothing about painting."

Kathryn would have pressed for an opinion had they not at that moment arrived at the restaurant. The door stood open, and they entered to find a handful of ladies already seated around the room. One table was in use as a buffet, the surface covered with platters of tea cakes, pies, small sandwiches on thinly sliced bread, and an assortment of pastries. Since she knew Evie had not made pastries, they must have been the work of one of the other ladies.

Louisa caught sight of them and interrupted her conversation with a large woman seated next to her. She stood and hurried across the room with the waddling gait employed by expecting women the world over.

"Kathryn, you brought her!" She pulled Kathryn into a quick hug, and then startled Miss Everett by doing the same to her. "We are so glad to finally meet you. I am Louisa Denny. Welcome to Seattle."

"I . . ." Miss Everett cast an anxious glance at Kathryn, swallowed, and then managed to whisper an introduction. "My name is Helen Everett."

Helen? In the ten days of their acquaintance Kathryn had never heard her Christian name. And, she was chagrined to realize, she had not thought to ask.

Louisa tucked Helen's hand in the crook of her arm and pulled her forward. "Come and meet the others." She stopped and, turning to Kathryn, extended her other hand. "You too. We've become friends so quickly I almost forgot you're new too."

Some people were gifted with the ability to put people immediately at ease, and Louisa had that gift in abundance. Within minutes she had drawn Helen out from behind her wall of reserve and had her sharing details that Kathryn had never heard.

"I decided to leave Nevada City when my mother died two months ago," Helen explained in her hushed voice.

Kathryn felt a rush of sympathy for her reticent friend.

"Oh, my dear, I'm so sorry." Beside her, the gray-haired woman who had been introduced as Mrs. Moreland laid a comforting hand on Helen's arm. "I lost my own mother a year ago."

"She had been ill for a long time." Helen sat quietly with her hands folded in her lap. "All my life, really. I've cared for her ever since I was a child."

The tall woman, who Kathryn recognized as Letitia Coffinger, owner of the dry goods store next door, spoke in a voice as big as her large-boned frame. "So now that you're free from nursing duties, you've decided to come to Seattle and find a husband."

Helen's normally pale face burned bright red, and her head drooped forward.

"Letitia," scolded Evie, "there are any number of reasons to move to Seattle."

The big woman waved that off with a flick of her fingers in the air. "This town has two things in abundance. Men and trees. I assume Helen is not here to try her hand at lumberjacking, so that leaves men."

Helen made no reply, either because of her bashful nature or because Letitia's assumption was correct. Looking at the color riding high on her cheeks, Kathryn thought

210

the reason might be a blend of the two. Certainly there was opportunity, if a husband was what she was after. But somehow Kathryn had a hard time picturing shy Helen in the company of rowdy men like Big Dog or Red. She needed someone more mature, more stable.

Then Letitia turned in her seat and fixed a sharp gaze on Kathryn. "And what about you? Are you here to find a husband as well?"

"Certainly not." Kathryn emphasized her answer with a swift shake of her head. "I came to assist Madame in the management of the Faulkner House."

"She told me she hired you to be a maid," said Letitia. Kathryn was about to protest, but the shrewd eyes narrowed. "But you could do that in San Francisco, where there are a far greater number of hotels. So my question stands. Why did you choose Seattle?"

Really, the woman was quite pushy! But there was no malice in her questions, only a sincere desire to know the answers. So nosy, but in an almost engaging sort of way.

Unable to hold that piercing gaze, Kathryn averted her eyes. "Actually, the journey was my father's idea. I didn't want to leave California, but he insisted. He wanted me to . . ." She toyed with the handle of her teacup. There was no reason to lie. She lifted her chin and glanced around the table. "To find a husband," she admitted.

The ladies laughed, Letitia loudest of all. Even Helen joined in, and Kathryn found herself relaxing. The ladies of Seattle might not be as progressive in their views as some she knew in San Francisco, but their company was enjoyable.

The restaurant filled almost at once when a large group arrived. Chatting women entered, many of them carrying a platter of sweet cakes or a loaf of nut bread, and soon the first buffet table overflowed to a second. Children darted in to snatch a treat and then raced through the open back door to rejoin their friends. A handful of girls commandeered their own table and sat with their heads close, whispering and giggling. Talking of boys, no doubt. Kathryn remembered herself at that age, when she and Susan would draw frowns from Papa for whispering in church and stealing glances at Bobby Frye.

Inez ran in, caught sight of Kathryn, and charged across the room to throw her arms around her for a quick hug. She was gone as quickly as she appeared, leaving Kathryn to smile after her.

She spoke to Louisa. "I expected to see John William racing behind her. I suppose he's outside playing with the other children."

Louisa shook her head. "Will didn't bring him to the house today. I saw him carrying John William down the street toward the mill early this morning, but he was already too far away to hear me call. I can't imagine Henry Yesler encouraging him to bring a three-year-old to the mill, but . . ." She shrugged. "I'll ask David when he gets home from the blockhouse tonight."

"Oh, that blockhouse." Mrs. Butler, seated at the next table, turned around in her chair to insert herself into the conversation. "My Hillory speaks of nothing else when visitors come calling. Says it's a foolish undertaking and a complete waste of effort and good lumber."

Because Kathryn was seated across from Louisa, she could watch her expression change. Her lips pursed into a knot and fire flashed in her eyes. Setting her teacup down with extreme care, she turned to face Mrs. Butler.

"He says so, does he?"

A lady at yet another table emitted a high-pitched laugh. "My husband says the same. Those men are working themselves to exhaustion, and for what reason?" She asked the question of the women at her table.

"Exactly," agreed Mrs. Butler. "They're building a fortress that will never see a day's use. Why, it's ridiculous, that's what it is."

The cords in Louisa's neck stood out and her fingers pressed so tightly Kathryn feared for the fragility of her delicate teacup. "They scoffed at Noah for building the ark too," she snapped.

All around the room, silent ladies stared awkwardly into their cups or busied themselves cutting bites of cake or pie. The girls at the far table stopped giggling to watch with wide eyes and dangling jaws. Mrs. Butler opened her mouth to reply, but the woman next to her placed a restraining hand on her arm.

When the tension stretched to a nearly unbearable level, Evie stood and spoke in a bright voice. "I believe I'll have another slice of bread with some of that delicious blackberry jam. Who made that?"

"I did," answered Letitia, hefting herself out of her chair and snatching up her plate. "And I believe I'll join you."

Mrs. Butler and Louisa both turned back around and Kathryn released a pent-up breath. She exchanged a glance with Helen, who had watched the near-argument with

214

wide-eyed alarm.

Louisa lifted her teacup and spoke in a low voice to Kathryn over the rim. "I truly hope they're right."

Kathryn leaned over her plate and whispered an answer. "And if they aren't, I hope they live long enough for you to point out their mistake."

At that Louisa giggled, and the last of the tension fled.

NINE

Tuesday, January 15, 1856

"Kathryn! A moment before you leave."

Kathryn stopped in the center of the hotel's empty front room and waited for Madame to appear through the doorway to her private area.

Madame waddled in carrying a bundle. "I need you to take this laundry down to Princess Angeline."

"Princess?" Astonished, Kathryn could only stare at the woman. "Seattle has a princess?"

In the week since her arrival, no one had mentioned the presence of royalty. Surely someone would have. And would the lady not have come to tea last Thursday night?

Madame emitted the raucous cackle that had ceased to grate on Kathryn's nerves and now caused only mild annoyance. "In a way. She's the old Indian chief's daughter. Earns money as a laundress." She thrust the

216

bundle, which Kathryn saw was a bedsheet gathered around a mound of clothing, into her arms. "Tell her to have someone bring it up tomorrow when it's finished."

Kathryn tried to push it back. "But I'm due next door to deliver sandwiches to the men working on the blockhouse."

Madame whisked her hands behind her back. "I know that. Princess Angeline's house is not far from there, down on the waterfront. It won't take you a minute to drop by after you're finished serving."

"I don't know the way." A whine crept into her voice, though she deplored the sound of it. "And Louisa isn't going with me this evening. I'll be alone."

"So ask someone. Everyone knows Princess Angeline." The woman turned her physically around and gave her a shove toward the door.

"But . . ."

Further protests would be a waste of breath. Madame had made good her retreat and closed the door to her sitting room behind her. Settling the laundry into a sturdier bundle, Kathryn headed next door. Perhaps in Evie she would find a sympathetic ear, and possibly a companion to show her the way.

She was mistaken.

"Oh, Princess Angeline's cabin is easy to find." The cheerful restaurant owner didn't pause in her task of loading a crate of sandwiches onto the back of the wagon, which was hitched and ready. "Just go down the hill and when you get to the pier, turn right. Hers is the first house on the left past the dock."

"Is it . . . safe?"

Evie gave her a quizzical look, which cleared after a moment. "Perfectly safe. You won't go anywhere near the forest." A smile settled on her face, no doubt intended to be reassuring. "Only you may want to leave the wagon by the pier and walk. The ground down by the water tends to be too muddy for a heavy wagon during the rainy season." Then she bustled back inside the restaurant for another load of sandwiches.

Still uneasy, Kathryn stowed Madame's laundry on the front bench. If only Louisa had not felt so tired after the tea. And if only Kathryn had not felt so confident in her ability to deliver the sandwiches on her own that she urged her to go home to put her swollen feet up.

Thanks to the assistance of many of the ladies who stayed after the tea to help assemble sandwiches, she got an early start. With a jaunty wave that projected more confidence than she felt, she climbed up onto the wagon and picked up the reins. Though a handful of men, like David and Noah, had been working at the blockhouse all day, the bulk of the evening workers would not yet have left the lumber mill, which meant she had some extra time. Might as well get the unpleasant task out of the way first. She directed the horse toward the main road leading to the wharf and flicked the reins.

The sun had been out all day, and though lower, still dominated the western sky. As she headed down the hill, she scanned the town below her. The avenue down which she traveled was the same one Carter had taken when he delivered her, Helen, and Jason to the Faulkner House. Had that really only been a week ago? She shook her head, chuckling to herself. Seemed like months.

She followed the length of the road with her eyes to the place where it ended at the wharf. Another road, narrower than this one, ran along the front of the dock to Yesler's Mill on the left, and to the right . . .

Ah, there. She sat straighter on the bench and stretched her sight in that direction. The wooden platform of the dock ended, and then there was a long empty stretch and, beyond that, a line of small, square, steep-roofed houses perched on the water-front. Shacks, really. That first one must be Princess Angeline's.

Imagine, a princess living in a shack and working as a laundress. Actually, now that she gave it some thought, Kathryn found the idea admirable. Presumably the daughter of a chief would enjoy some measure of status had she moved to the reservation with her father's people. Instead she chose to live here among white settlers and earn her own living. A woman like that was to be commended for her independence, something Kathryn had found more of in Seattle than she anticipated.

Movement around the house in question drew her attention. She squinted to focus across the distance. Children, if she weren't mistaken, running after one another around the building. A cheerful stream of white smoke rose from the chimney, creating a homey appearance. A few knots in her stomach unraveled, and Kathryn flicked the reins to prod the horse forward.

When she rolled through town, she again drew attention from those inside the buildings lining the wide street. Though the men stared with that same hungry intensity they displayed upon her arrival, she must be growing accustomed to it. She even recognized several of them from the restaurant, and nodded a greeting here and there.

At the end of the street she turned and traveled for a distance with the wharf on her left. No ship sat at the pier, but the *Decatur* was still anchored nearby in the bay. Whistles and a few shouts reached her, and she saw that the ship's deck was lined with Marines in military uniforms, all of them staring at her. Feeling a bit less confident where sailors were concerned, she lifted a hand and gave them a hesitant wave, and then schooled her eyes forward.

When the wooden dock ended abruptly, she drew the horse to a halt. The first of the little huts lay about seventy-five yards in front of her, the road a barren path stretching between them. The idea of leaving the wagon and covering the distance on foot was not appealing. The ground, though moist enough to muddy her boots, seemed solid. It had not rained all day, and the sun had probably hardened the ground enough to handle the weight of the wagon. She flicked the reins and urged the horse forward.

When she drew near, she saw that she had been correct in thinking of Angeline's home as a shack. This dwelling could be called a cabin only by the loosest definition of the word. Constructed of split cedar with the cracks filled by what appeared to be crumbling mud, it leaned noticeably to one side. There was no porch and a rough block of wood had been set before the open door in place of a proper stair. On the right a collection of barrels and old lumber, apparently left over from the construction, had been tossed into a haphazard pile. A pungent odor dominated the air, an unlikely blend of rotting fish and lye that set Kathryn to coughing.

She halted her wagon and sat staring at the open doorway. Someone was sitting inside. Surely decorum dictated that the woman come outside to greet her visitor, but she made no move. After a moment's hesitation, Kathryn climbed down from the bench and then gathered Madame's bundle. Though she had not heard a sound, when she turned around an Indian woman stood behind her, arms folded and hands hidden beneath a multicolored shawl that appeared to have been made for someone twice her size.

"Oh!" Kathryn jumped back and bumped against the sideboard. She emitted a nervous laugh. "You startled me."

The face before her did not change in the slightest. Eyes as dark as midnight fixed on her calmly. A wide nose spread across above thin lips with a distinct downward turn at the edges, giving her a grim countenance. Her dark skin had a weathered look that defied age, and her brow held traces of what promised to become heavy creases later in life. Her hair was black without a hint of silver, and she wore it parted in the center and pulled partially back in an untidy arrangement that left the ends to straggle across her shoulders.

Kathryn swallowed. "P— Princess Angeline?"

Though the woman before her looked nothing like anyone's idea of royalty, she held herself with an easy regal bearing that gave Kathryn the urge to drop into a formal curtsy. She controlled the impulse, but when the Indian lady dipped her head, she managed a composed nod in return.

"My name is Kathryn Bergert. I recently arrived from San Francisco."

"I know who you are." The voice, unexpectedly low, was heavily accented but each word was precisely articulated.

"You do?"

Again the regal dip of her head. "Not so big a place, this town."

"Well, yes." Kathryn glanced over her shoulder in the direction of the town. "I suppose news of newcomers spreads rather quickly."

"Especially white lady newcomers." For the first time, the hint of a smile tugged at the corners of those thin, solemn lips. One hand emerged from within the folds of the shawl and gestured toward the bundle in Kathryn's hands. "For me?"

"Oh." She had momentarily forgotten her errand. "Yes, of course. Madame Garritson instructed me to bring her laundry, and asked if you could have someone deliver it tomorrow to the Faulkner House."

Again the stately incline of her head, and she waved toward the shack. Kathryn assumed she was being instructed to put the laundry inside. Moving with quick, awkward steps, she did so, though she did not enter the dwelling but merely extended her hand inside to deposit the bundle near the door. The quick glimpse she took of the interior showed a single room, sparsely furnished but tidy and clean.

She turned to find the woman watching her with that same unreadable, impassive expression. Was she expected to deliver the laundry and leave, or would that be considered impolite? This was, after all, the daughter of a chief.

"Angeline," she said after casting around

for something to say. "It's a beautiful name."

"*Princess* Angeline," the woman corrected.

"Of course." Kathryn cleared her throat. Should she call her by a title? Were Indian princesses addressed as *Your Highness,* as English ones were? "I'm sorry, um . . . Princess."

A twinkle appeared in the black eyes. "That is my white man's name given by my friend Letitia."

"Letitia Coffinger?" Kathryn asked, surprised when the woman nodded. "Then what is your, ur, your Indian name?"

"*Duwamish* name," she corrected gently. "To my people I am known as Kikisoblu, daughter of Sealth. Letitia Coffinger did not think it a name that suited me."

Actually, she looked far more like a Kikisoblu than an Angeline, but Kathryn kept the opinion to herself. Something about this lady's tranquil manner and barely revealed humor put her at ease, and she risked a hesitant smile into the broad face. "Both names are lovely."

A string of children, their laughter filling the air, came charging around the house. Catching sight of her, they screeched to a halt a few feet away and fell silent. Perhaps a dozen children stared at her with open

225

curiosity. Kathryn gave them a hesitant smile, and then a smaller one pushed through from behind. She saw a flash of white skin and blond hair, and in the next instant the child dashed forward and threw himself around her skirt, hugging her knees with enthusiasm.

"Miss Kathryn! Did you come to play with me?"

"Why, hello there." Surprised, she bent down to return John William's embrace. "I didn't know you were here or I would have made a special point to come and play with you. I'm afraid I don't have time right now."

So this was where Will Townsend had been taking his grandson. She glanced up to give Princess Angeline an inquisitive look, but found no answers in her face.

John William heaved a dramatic sigh. "It's okay. I left my blocks at Miss Weesa's house. I miss Miss Weesa." His smile returned, and he gestured to his companions. "But I have lots of kids to play with today. C'mon!"

The last was shouted toward the other children, and then they were gone, running off toward the next little shack down the road.

Straightening, she turned to face Princess Angeline. "I wondered who'd been minding him. I know Louisa has missed him since his grandfather decided to take him somewhere else. She's had the care of him since they first arrived. No matter how tired she is, she insists he has never been a burden."

She mentioned the reason almost as a question. Will's excuse to Louisa had not rung true from the beginning. No matter how far along with child Louisa was, she rarely suffered from lack of energy. But Kathryn kept her doubts to herself.

For a moment she thought Princess Angeline would not answer. When she did, it was in the same toneless voice that Kathryn found impossible to interpret.

"He feels safer knowing the boy is with an Indian woman than a white woman."

Interesting. Why did he give a different reason to Princess Angeline than to Louisa?

The woman paused, as though considering whether or not to continue. When she did, it was in a voice so low Kathryn had to lean close to hear. "Though red skin will be no safer than white in the days to come."

Fear blew its icy breath against the nape of Kathryn's neck, and questions about Will Townsend evaporated. "You mean there really will be an Indian attack?"

Black eyes held hers while the woman gave a shallow nod. "Klickitats, Nisquallies, Muckleshoots. They are not happy with the white men, or with the redskins who befriend them."

Kathryn cast an apprehensive glance behind her toward the knoll where the blockhouse was being built. "How soon?"

The shawl-covered shoulders lifted in a shrug. "Soon. Already our houses overflow with those who fear living in the woods where they have spent their whole lives."

Kathryn looked in the direction the young ones had run. "You mean those little ones are refugees?"

"I do not know the word. They came with their parents, who hope the white men and their guns will save their children from slaughter."

Mouth dry, Kathryn looked again toward the knoll. "I hope that blockhouse is big enough for everyone. Looks like it's going to be awfully crowded inside."

It was a halfhearted attempt at humor but Princess Angeline nodded, her expression serious.

With a renewed sense of urgency, Kathryn bid her farewell and climbed onto the wagon. She forced herself to restraint and did not push the horse into a run, but her fingers ached from her tight grip on the reins. A strong urge to glance continually over her shoulder at the dark places between the trees possessed her. Were hostile eyes fixed on her from those shadowy places?

So preoccupied was she that a sudden pitch of the wagon took her by surprise. The horse came to a halt.

"What's the matter?" Fright made her voice high, her words pinched. She flicked the reins with impatience. "Come on. Move."

The animal made an attempt to obey, but the wagon moved forward only a few inches before stopping and rolling slowly backward. Leaning over the edge, she saw why. The wheels were mired in mud. Apparently she had failed to notice a soggy place in the road.

"No, no, no!"

Now she did look back, prepared to shout to Princess Angeline for help. Not a soul in sight. Apparently the lady had gone inside, and the children with her. Besides, she had covered more than half the distance to the wharf. Twisting back around toward the front, she scanned the area before her. A small boat, loaded with sailors, was just approaching the dock from the direction of the *Decatur*. Relief washed over her.

"Hello!" She cupped her hands around her mouth. "Over here." Waving wildly, she drew their attention and several waved back.

"I'm stuck," she shouted. "Will you help me?"

"Hang tight, girlie," came the answer, along with a few whoops and a loud whistle that made her more than a little uneasy. Still, what choice did she have? She glanced at the ground below her. Perhaps the sacrifice of her shoes wasn't a bad choice after all. But no, she couldn't abandon the horse, wagon, and four crates of sandwiches in the mud.

The rowboat pulled alongside the dock and a group of sailors climbed out. They hurried along the wharf, eager faces fixed on her, and jumped from the platform to the road. Mud splattered when their boots hit the ground. A new kind of fear kindled to life in her at the sight of the intent, almost wolfish gazes some of them fixed on her as they neared.

At their approach the group parted, encircling the wagon. She was surrounded by what seemed an entire battalion.

"Over here, girlie." A pair of hands at her right lifted toward her. "I'll help you down."

Another time she might have informed the man that she hadn't been called *girlie* since she was a child in pinafores, but at that moment she found it hard to speak around the frightened lump that had arisen in her throat.

A lean, wiry sailor beside him scowled. "Shove off, Terry. Ye'll drop her like you dropped that crate of apples last summer." He thrust his hands toward Kathryn as well. "Come to me, gal. Old Barney'll take care of you."

"I'd like to take care of her myself," said someone on the other side, and the sly tone in his voice gave the words a meaning that sent heat into Kathryn's face. A chorus of snickers answered him.

"I won't either drop her." The first man, Terry, placed a hand on Barney's chest and shoved. "C'mere, girl."

She had better move quickly or a fight might erupt. Forcing a shaky smile, she reached down to take the proffered arm. Instead he grasped her hand and in the next instant she found herself pulled roughly off the wagon and swung up into a pair of surprisingly strong arms.

The man hefted her as though testing her weight, a most unpleasant sensation that caused her to issue a tiny, surprised exclamation.

"She ain't no heavier than a young'un."

"I ain't never seen no young'un with a body like that," said someone, and this time the comment was met with a chorus of raucous guffaws.

Kathryn mastered her frozen tongue. "Please, put me down."

"You'll sink in mud up to your pretty little knees," said Terry with a low, disturbing rumble in his voice.

Horrified at the mention of her knees in the company of these woman-hungry seamen, Kathryn pushed at his shoulder with a balled fist. "I can manage."

He ignored her and started toward the dock. Before he had gone three steps, another man jumped in front of him. "Let me have a go with her."

Without warning she was wrenched bodily from Terry's arms. Startled, she gave a little scream. The others seemed to find that funny, and her face burned anew at the sound of their rough laughter.

"My turn."

Barney tried to jerk her away, an act that so infuriated Terry that he gave a bellow that left her ears ringing. His arms tightened like steel cables and she was crushed against a stone-like chest. Someone grabbed her coat at the back of her neck and pulled, and the buttoned collar pressed against her throat. Choking, she began to kick her feet.

"Put me down this instant!"

Her command went unheard, muffled by a muscled chest and drowned out by the men's rowdy laughter. Fear gave way to fury. She balled her fists and began beating her captor's face. Startled, his grip loosened. That was the moment Barney had been waiting for, and she was jerked roughly away. Drawing a deep breath, she let out a scream, the volume fed by anger.

"Hey! What's going on here?"

The shout rode over the top of the sailors' ruckus. They fell silent and moved quickly to form a wall in front of her.

"Nothing that concerns you," answered Terry, the man whose face she had hit. "You boys go on about your business."

But Kathryn recognized the voice. She twisted around, still held tight in the seaman's grip, and spied Big Dog towering head and shoulders above a handful of millworkers. Apparently their shift at the mill had ended at exactly the right time.

Red spoke in a voice that held all the menace of a growling wolf. "I don't know who you are, boy, but you'd better put that lady down real gentle-like."

Feeling a bit braver with the arrival of her friends, Kathryn reached up and grabbed Barney's ear between her thumb and finger. When she gave a vicious twist, he shouted,

"Ow!" and dropped her. She stumbled for a step, but landed with her feet moving and pushed her way between two sailors. Never had she been so happy to see anyone as these men who one week ago had been complete strangers.

"We didn't hurt her none," said one of the sailors. "She asked us for help, that's all."

"For *help*." Now that she stood in the protective presence of her friends, she gave her anger full head. "I didn't ask to be insulted and manhandled."

Big Dog stepped in front of her and drew himself up to his full threatening height. "Here in Seattle we don't take kindly to people insulting ladies."

"Yeah." Murphy moved beside him while rolling his sleeve up above a flexing muscle. "Especially not by a pack of bilge rats."

To a man, the sailors' expressions hardened, and she saw several hands clench into fists. This could get out of hand quickly.

"It's okay. I'm not hurt." She forced a smile and flashed it equally between both groups. "No harm done."

She might as well have not spoken for all the attention paid to her. Narrow-eyed glares were exchanged as the men on both sides moved to stand shoulder to shoulder in two lines facing each other.

The spokesman for the sailors, Terry, turned his head and spat without interrupting his glare at Big Dog. "Who you callin' *bilge rat,* dirtbag?"

Swallowing, Kathryn lifted her chin and spoke loudly. "Really. I'm fine. And I did ask for their help."

"I think he was talking to you, bilge rat." Big Dog took another step forward, and as one the line of millworkers moved with him. "Only maybe he should have said *squid.*"

In the face of a glare from a mountainous man like Big Dog, Kathryn would have melted into her boots. The seaman did no such thing. Incredulous, she watched as his chest inflated and a furious grimace settled over his mouth.

"I'm gonna swab the deck with your ugly carcass."

As the last word left his lips, the man pulled back a balled fist and, quicker than she could blink, landed a shot on Big Dog's jaw. The crack seemed to resonate in a pregnant silence that lasted a fraction of a second. That was how long it took the huge man to land his own punch and send the seaman sprawling in the mud.

That blow ignited a wildfire. The two lines flew at each other and her ears filled with growls, shouts, and the sickening thud of fists on flesh. Someone was thrown backward, and she was almost knocked off her feet when he glanced off her shoulder on the way to the ground.

"Get outta here, Miss Kathryn," shouted Murphy as he picked himself up and dove back into the fray.

She did. With a speed that would have made the cavalry proud, she lifted her skirts and dashed across the short distance to the dock, where she turned to watch in dismay as her friends defended her honor.

"G'night, Don," Jason called with a wave for the evening shift foreman. "If you need anything, send a message up the hill."

The man acknowledged Jason from his position near the head rig before returning to his work. Jason nodded his farewells at the workers he passed on his way to the shack's exit, where Will waited. As soon as the blockhouse was finished, he intended to spend his evenings here, working alongside Don so he could get to know him as he had Will. Henry had given him a frank rundown on the strengths and weaknesses of both men yesterday.

"Donald's a good operator." Seated behind his desk in the crowded office, he'd leaned over the surface toward Jason and kept his voice low. "The men respect him. But he doesn't read, and when he adds two and two he comes up with twenty-two. That's why I couldn't give him your job."

One question answered, at least. Jason had leaned on his hands, which were planted on the edge of the desk, and asked in an equally low tone, "And what about Will? Seems to me like he would make a fine mill manager."

"Trying to give away your job already?" Henry had grinned up at him, and then waved off his protests. "Truth be told, I offered him the job. He turned it down on account of his grandson. Said he couldn't expect Louisa Denny to keep the boy day *and* night."

As he passed by the engine, which chugged along with a satisfactory rumble, Jason watched Will talking with one of the men who was making an adjustment to the rollers. It couldn't be easy raising a boy alone. The fact that the man took the task so seriously spoke well of him. If he'd had a son when Beth died . . .

He shied away from the thought and the accompanying stab of grief. Lengthening his stride, he approached the pair.

"Everything all right here?" He inspected

the roller where it connected to the infeed deck.

"Fine." Will slapped the man on the back. "Coleman knows what he's doing. Been here since Henry built the place."

Coleman's chest swelled at the praise, and Jason nodded his approval. Then he and Will left, walking side by side down the narrow street that skirted the inlet. A load of logs was floating there, waiting to be milled. Jason and Will shared the companionable silence of men who worked together, respected one another, and were quickly becoming friends.

When they reached the intersection where Jason turned to go up First Street toward the blockhouse, Will stopped.

"I'll join you shortly. Want to go check on John William first."

Why, then, wasn't he heading up to the Denny home? Jason started to ask, but at that moment the sound of men's shouts reached him.

"What in the world?"

He whirled and looked in the direction the noise had come. There, a few yards past the wharf, a brawl was taking place. It didn't take more than a glance to recognize Big Dog, and the flash of red hair beside him had to be Red. Half the brawlers wore flannel, the other uniforms, all of them covered in mud. And no wonder. As he watched, Big Dog grabbed a sailor in his powerful hands, lifted him bodily, and tossed him to the ground. The man landed with a splat that sent mud showering the area. He rolled over and leaped to his feet, then charged back into the fray.

Jason's gaze was drawn to a lone woman standing at the edge of the wooden dock. Even from this distance he recognized Kathryn's profile. What in the world was she doing down here? Her posture stiff, she stood watching the fight with both hands clasped over her mouth.

He and Will exchanged a quick glance and took off at a run. Plowing into the battle, Jason headed toward Big Dog, who seemed to be at the center of the melee.

"Hold off!" When the huge man drew back a fist in preparation for landing another punch on the sailor in front of him, Jason hooked an elbow around his arm and held tight. "Stop this right now!"

Big Dog tried to shake him off, lifting Jason completely off his feet, but then caught sight of his face. He hesitated, and for a second Jason thought he'd been successful in stopping the fight. In the next instant, pain exploded in his face and he found himself on his backside, rubbing his jaw.

"Hey!" bellowed the big man. "That's my boss, you stinking squid." He charged forward to retaliate.

The blast of a gun from somewhere behind him stopped the fight. Jason turned to see a horse galloping toward them, Noah Hughes in the saddle with a rifle aimed straight into the air. The men grew still.

"What is going on here?" His shout held almost as much force as the gunshot. "I looked down here from up on the knoll to see a bunch of men rolling around in the mud, beating each other bloody."

"They insulted a lady." Red stood straight, his nose held high with self-righteous indignity. "No man among us is gonna let 'em get away with that."

"We were *helping* her." A sailor nearby shot a poisonous glare toward Red. "She *asked* us to help."

Big Dog folded his arms across his powerful chest. "Didn't look like help to me. You were tossing her back and forth like a rag doll."

Heads turned toward the dock, where Kathryn stood as though frozen in place. Her eyes were wide as dinner plates. She lowered her hands from her mouth, and cleared her throat. "M–my wagon got stuck

240

in the mud." Tears trembled in her voice, and Jason almost felt sorry for her. "I didn't mean to cause" — she swept a hand toward the men, who were a sorry sight indeed, covered in blood and mud — "this."

Noah cleared his throat. "Sounds to me like a misunderstanding."

"It weren't neither!" shouted someone Jason couldn't see.

"Yeah, and we ain't about to let no dirty —"

"Hold it right there." Jason cut the man off before another insult could reignite the brawl. He picked himself up off the ground and cast a stern glance around the group. "Let's all go about our business. I know my crew has somewhere to be. And if you sailors don't, maybe we ought to send someone over to the ship to see what Captain Gansevoort has to say about the matter."

The suggestion brought the desired effect. The sailors began snatching up their hats and making a hasty retreat.

When they were gone, Noah nudged his horse toward the dock. "Are you all right?" he asked Kathryn.

She gave a shaky nod.

He addressed the men. "Why don't some of you get that wagon out of the mud so

Miss Bergert can be on her way?"

Jason stood off to one side while they hurried to obey. When the wagon stood on more or less solid ground, they helped her onto the bench. In a trembling voice, Kathryn thanked them over and over for coming to her aid. When Noah suggested that some of the men see her safely back to the Faulkner House, she protested that she had to deliver the sandwiches to the blockhouse. They headed in that direction, Noah walking his horse beside the wagon and her rescuers surrounding her on all sides.

Jason stood watching their departure, running a tentative finger over what was rapidly becoming a swollen jaw. An experimental wiggle told him it wasn't broken, thank the Lord.

Will came up beside him. "What did I tell you about that woman? She's trouble."

Surprised at the vehemence in his voice, Jason looked at the man. "I'm not sure this was her fault."

"Of course it was," he snapped. "What did she expect, hanging around the docks by herself? What was she doing down here anyway?"

He cast a quick glance over his shoulder at a row of shacks lining the waterfront. "Maybe she had an errand." Jason kept his tone carefully even. What had Kathryn done to provoke Will's anger? Obviously something more than a visit to the wharf.

Unpleasant laughter erupted. "An errand involving a boatful of sailors?"

The crude insinuation shocked Jason, especially coming from a man who was normally calm and even soft-spoken. "I don't think that's called for," he said by way of mild reproof.

Will's lips tightened. "You don't know her kind. I do."

Jason shook his head. Arrogant, irritating, occasionally flirtatious, and obstinate in the extreme. There was plenty to criticize about Kathryn. But whatever else she might be, she was a lady. Of that Jason was certain.

"Don't you think you're being a little hard on her?" He studied the man. "What has she done to make you dislike her so much?"

For a moment, he thought Will might answer. Then the man jerked his head sideways. "Take my advice and cut a wide path around her."

He walked off. Not toward town, but toward the shacks lining the waterfront. Jason stared after him for a minute and then shook his head. Somewhere in Will's past he had been dealt a harsh blow by an untrustworthy woman. Unfortunately for

Kathryn, she obviously reminded him of that woman.

Brushing the worst of the mud off the seat of his trousers, Jason took off for the blockhouse.

Will left Jason behind, barely mindful of the mud that sucked at his boots. A sick knot wrenched tight in the pit of his stomach. That woman hadn't been here but a few days and already she'd caused a riot. Somehow she managed to slither her way into the affections of the men.

Well, he knew how. Hadn't he seen her in action before? He kicked a chunk of wood out of his way with enough force to send it flying several yards. She was well aware of the effect her femininity would have on a bunch of woman-hungry men, and she didn't hesitate to use it to her advantage.

Now it looked like even Jason was in danger of falling for her charms. That she had set her sights on the handsome mill manager Will didn't doubt. He'd seen the way she looked at him when that sailor punched him, the way her gaze kept returning to him. Will shook his head. How could a sharp man like Jason not see through her schemes? Sure, she appeared innocent and frail, standing there on the pier watching the chaos she had caused. She even managed to look like she was close to tears. For all he knew, that might not have been faked. No doubt she'd bitten off more than she could chew when she played her flirtatious game with a boatload of sailors. She set out to enjoy a little sport with them, intent on spending an evening watching them vie for her attention. But then things had gotten out of hand.

What was she doing down here anyway? He lifted his head, searching the area ahead of him. An Indian woman picked her way across the muddy street, her feet bare and a wide, shallow basket propped on her hip. From one of the distant huts came the wail of a baby. High-pitched laughter drew his attention to the place where a group of children played at some game not far from where the familiar figure of Princess Angeline stood over a fire pit stirring a huge pot with a board. John William's blond hair stood out starkly against the black hair of the Indian children.

An invisible hand snaked into his gut and squeezed. Had Kathryn come down here to see his grandson?

"John William!"

The children all looked up at his shout. John William's face lit with a smile that would normally have warmed his grandfather's heart. Today nothing could penetrate the chill that invaded his chest.

"Time to go."

The child came obediently to his side. With a nod of thanks to Princess Angeline, Will turned and headed toward town with his grandson at his side.

"Are we going to the blockhouse?" the child asked.

"Not tonight."

"But you said you'd show me —"

At a sharp glance, the boy fell silent. Will automatically shortened his stride so John William didn't have to run to keep up, thoughts whirling in his mind. He couldn't stand by and watch Jason get his heart handed to him by a trollop. Nor would he let her near John William. Somehow he would have to find a way to reveal the kind of woman she really was beneath that innocent mask she wore.

TEN

"I don't understand why he would tell me one thing and Princess Angeline another."

Louisa's brow knit together as she stacked sweet cakes on a platter for transport to the blockhouse late the next afternoon. For once little Inez was not underfoot, begging Kathryn to play dolls with her. She'd been invited to spend the day with the Morelands learning to sew.

"Maybe he didn't want to worry you." Evie handed a square of linen across the table for Louisa to cover the cakes. "After all, you are expecting a baby."

"So?" A cross look stole over Louisa's face. "I'm not an invalid to be fussed over. And I'm not a leper to be avoided, either."

"Of course you aren't." Kathryn carried an empty crate from the storage room and set it on a chair to be loaded with sandwiches. "I'm sure he's only avoiding you

247

because he doesn't want to upset you."

"I don't mean Will," she said. "I'm talking about Jason Gates."

Kathryn halted her work to peer at Louisa. "Jason avoids you?"

"Yes, he does. Whenever I enter the room, he makes an excuse to leave." A petulant frown settled on her face. "It's as though I've done something to offend him *and* Will, though I can't imagine what."

And Kathryn thought she was the only one he disliked. Although lately Jason didn't seem to be as quick to avoid her as he once had. Probably because she had ceased speaking to him — about painting, or about anything else. Still, he had returned to the restaurant for breakfast, and even awarded her the occasional quick smile when she loaded his plate with an extra portion of the fried potatoes and onions for which he'd expressed a preference.

"Have you mentioned it to David?" Evie asked.

"Oh, him." Louisa dismissed her husband with a wave. "He's so obsessed with finishing the blockhouse he doesn't think about anything else. When I mentioned it, he got that annoying solicitous look on his face and patted my hand and told me I'm imagining things. As though being in the family way has addled my brains."

Evie picked up the tray of sweet cakes and grinned at her friend. "I can't imagine David ever doubting your intelligence, dear."

"Wait and see," snapped Louisa. "When it's your turn Noah will treat you like you've lost every bit of good sense the Lord gave you."

Evie went still. Kathryn glanced at her, noting the sudden whiteness of her face.

Louisa's eyes widened as she realized what she'd said. She grabbed Evie's hand. "I'm sorry. That was thoughtless of me. Forgive me."

"It's okay." A brave smile flashed across her lips. "Really. Being a mother would be one of the greatest blessings of my life, but since I can't have babies of my own, I'll enjoy yours."

She whirled and hurried into the storage room, but not before Kathryn spied the glisten of moisture in her eyes.

Louisa slapped a hand across her mouth. "David's right," she whispered. "My brains *are* addled."

Kathryn gave her a sympathetic grimace when a distant voice drifted through the open window. "Ship in the bay!"

Louisa perked upright. "That must be the *Leonesa.*" She projected her voice toward the storage room. "Evie, did you hear that?"

"I did." Evie returned to the room, her arms full of cooled bread loaves. She smiled with forced brightness. "I have an idea. As soon as we get these crates filled let's go down to meet the ship. I haven't seen Captain Johnson in months."

Good. After yesterday's disastrous errand, Kathryn had vowed never to venture anywhere near the waterfront alone. But in the company of her well-respected friends, she would be safe from further incidents. And she did so want to speak with the captain of the *Leonesa*. Maybe he carried Papa's answer to her letter, hopefully in the form of additional funds and notice of his arrangements for her return to San Francisco.

She reached for a loaf and began to slice.

"I'm sorry, ma'am." Captain Johnson smoothed his hair and replaced his hat, which he had removed when introduced to Kathryn. "If there's a letter it'll be in the mailbag, but no one contacted me about booking passage."

They stood on the dock at the end of the pier where the *Leonesa,* sails lowered, had been moored. The crew worked to secure the ropes while the captain came ashore to greet the harbormaster, a man named James

Garvey, whom she had not seen since he met the *Fair Lady* the evening she arrived.

Kathryn bit down on her lip and tried to keep her disappointment from showing. Perhaps it was not reasonable to expect an answer so soon. Captain Baker probably only had a few days to deliver her letter to Papa before the *Leonesa* set sail. Still, he had promised to see to it immediately.

Evie placed a sympathetic hand on her arm. "Miles Coffinger is the postmaster, but since he's back East checking into a business venture, Letitia's handling his duties. She's very fast in sorting the mail. We'll drop by on the way home and ask her to bring over the letter as soon as she can."

If the mailbag included a letter at all, which Kathryn doubted. Surely Papa would have hand-delivered a notice to the *Leonesa* when he read of her precarious situation here. She smiled her thanks, and then directed a question at Captain Johnson.

"Do you have room for me on the return voyage?"

Without hesitation he nodded. "Though you might have to share the cabin with a few barrels of pickled salmon if we run out of storage room."

"At least they won't wake me with snoring," she joked, and then cleared her throat.

"How much is the passage?"

"Forty dollars."

With an effort, she kept her expression impassive. The price was nearly twice what Papa had paid for her ticket on the *Fair Lady*. Of course she had shared that cabin with Helen, but a forty-dollar passage would take every remaining cent she had in her possession.

"Fine," she managed in an even tone.

"We'll hoist anchor with the tide Friday morning." The man turned toward the harbormaster and the two wandered away, talking of barrels and cargo and the like.

"Must you leave so soon?" Louisa placed an arm around her shoulders and hugged. "We enjoy your company so much."

"Yes, we do." Evie nodded agreement. "I don't know how I'll manage after you're gone."

Moved by their unstinting expressions of friendship, she smiled at both ladies. "The blockhouse is almost finished, and then you'll have your husbands back. You won't even notice I'm gone."

"Not true. We'll miss you terribly." Evie tilted her head to the side, her expression kind. "We do understand. The threat of an attack is hard on everyone, but Seattle is our home. If I hadn't made a commitment

252

to this town and the people here, I'd book my passage along with you."

"Me too." Louisa squeezed her shoulders once more before releasing her. "Oh, look. There are Reverend Blaine and Roberta, back from California. Yoo-hoo, Roberta!"

A couple stood amid a group of passengers on board the *Leonesa,* waiting for the captain to approve the lowering of the gangway so they could disembark. They waved back.

"Oh, I wish you were staying until Sunday," Evie told Kathryn. "Church meetings are as much fun as our Thursday afternoon teas."

"Well, almost." Louisa grinned, and then with a final wave toward the minister and his wife, turned away. "I'd better get up the hill. It's nearly time for the Morelands to bring Inez home."

Kathryn fell into step between her friends. She would miss these ladies, and though she was astonished to realize it, she would miss Seattle too. The people here had worked hard to carve their lives out of the forest, and she had grown to respect their determination to persevere. An image of Jason arose in her mind's eye, and she was more than a little astonished to realize she would miss him too.

■ ■ ■ ■

Letitia entered the café the next morning while calling out in a singsong voice. "Kathryn, there's something in the post for you."

Kathryn straightened from her task of scraping the last of the gravy from a stack of dirty plates into the bucket of pig slops. Her mood, which had taken a disturbing downward spiral as breakfast drew to an end with no sign of Jason, brightened at the news. Papa *had* written after all.

She exchanged a smile with Helen, who was seated nearby sipping her tea and waiting to accompany her back to the Faulkner House. Letitia wove between the tables, waving an envelope above her head.

"And guess what arrived on board the *Leonesa*?" She made her announcement to the room, clearly delighted to have news to bestow. "A piano."

Creases appeared on Evie's forehead. "Who on earth bought a piano?"

"Madame Garritson. Apparently she's finally going to do something with that empty front room." She delivered the letter into Kathryn's hands as though bestowing a jewel.

Though interesting, the arrival of a piano

254

for the Faulkner House paled as she inspected the envelope. Her name stretched luxuriously across the front in Papa's familiar script above the address of *Faulkner House, Seattle in Washington Territory.* The back side bore his trademark maroon wax seal with an ornate *B* indentation. She took it from the woman's hands and suffered a momentary pang of disappointment. The envelope was light, and very thin. Too thin to contain anything more than a sheet of paper. No money, then. A letter of credit, perhaps?

Three sets of eyes watched while she sank into the nearest chair and broke the seal. Inside was a single sheet of Papa's expensive stationery with a monogrammed *B* that matched the one in the wax seal.

Dear Daughter,

The omission of her name warned of the tone of the letter. Papa addressed her as *daughter* when he sought to remind her of her subordinate position in his household, usually prefacing a reprimand. Apprehension stabbed at her. Had he somehow discovered her shameful secret?

Your mother and I are delighted to hear

of your safe arrival and good health. I have long known that exposure to sea air promotes a strong constitution.

I imagine the revelation of the nature of your duties came as a surprise. Let me assure you, Cousin Mary Ann did not misrepresent the position in her correspondence to me. I held back certain details because I knew you would balk at performing tasks that you consider beneath you. Let me remind you that my first position —

Kathryn set her jaw, irritation tightening her muscles to steel. Remind her? What need, when all her life he took every opportunity to describe his lowly beginnings and the grueling efforts that led to his eventual success in California's financial industry? She should have known better than to complain about her duties at the Faulkner House. At least he made no mention of the shameful incident she hoped he would never find out about.

She briefly scanned the next few chiding sentences. What had he to say about the Indians?

With regard to the rest of your letter, I made some inquiries into the Indian situation and was assured by my friend Senator Weller that the matter has been thoroughly investigated. Governor Stevens himself reports that San Francisco and New York are in greater danger of an Indian attack than Seattle. The senator was aware that some of the townspeople lean toward an alarmist viewpoint. My advice is to align yourself with those of a more levelheaded nature. Your mother sends her love.

Warmly,
Your Father

Aware of the watching gazes fixed on her, Kathryn folded the letter and reinserted it into the envelope calmly. Not only had Papa refused to acknowledge the danger, he had ignored her hints that she would soon run out of money. Perhaps her request had been too subtle? No. He'd understood her perfectly. His denial had been tacit but clear. She was to stay here and stop worrying about a looming attack that he refused to consider a real threat.

Should she leave anyway? She did have the money for passage on the *Leonesa*, though barely. Papa would be furious when she arrived. What would he do? Surely he wouldn't deny her room and board. Mama wouldn't hear of it. But he certainly would not bother to hide his displeasure.

She tried to picture herself standing before him, head bowed, enduring what was sure to be a highly unpleasant lecture. What choice would she have but to endure the chastisement? After all, she had no means of supporting herself.

The thought stabbed at her, leaving a distinctly unpleasant taste in her mouth. Here she was, a perfectly capable woman, begging her father for money. What would Mrs. Stanton and Miss Anthony think? Why, they would advise her to stiffen her backbone, to find a job, and make her own way rather than continuing to rely on her father as though she were an invalid. And she *could* support herself. Had she not proven that since arriving in Seattle? Surely she could manage quite nicely in San Francisco, where opportunity abounded.

Still, the chiding tone of Papa's message stung.

Pocketing the letter, she cleared her throat and made an announcement to the trio watching her. "It appears I shall not be leaving immediately after all."

And if she died in an Indian attack that Papa refused to believe was inevitable, it would serve him right if Mama never spoke to him again.

"Okay, hold it there. That's perfect."

Jason placed the nail and pounded it in place. Three blows and it sank through the plank, securely embedded in wood all the way up to the head. He gave the board a strong tug, pleased when it did not move. To be safe he would have liked to place a second steel wire beside the first, but nails were in short supply in Seattle. They'd used every spare one on this blockhouse. Forty feet square and as sturdy as any fortress back East, it would stand firm against everything an attacker could throw at it except maybe a howitzer. And the Indians definitely didn't have access to one of those.

"I'm good," he called over to Big Dog, who had just secured the other end of the plank at the blockhouse's corner.

"That'll do it for this one," the huge man answered, and then called down to Red on the ground, "We're ready. Send up the next board."

But Red shook his head. "Time for a break. Supper's here."

Jason straightened and looked toward the main road. Sure enough, a wagon had just pulled up to a halt at the bottom of the knoll. A trio of men dropped their tools and took off at a run to help Kathryn climb down from the bench. The sight of her profile, that old-fashioned bonnet concealing her face and her black cloak enshrouding every womanly curve, lifted his spirits. He would never have thought it possible, but living in this male-dominated town was starting to get to him. Until he moved here he didn't realize how much the mere presence of a woman changed a man's attitude. It had nothing to do with attraction, either. Men acted differently when a woman was around. Manners came out. Courtesy became an unspoken code. In many ways, the world was a better place with a woman in the vicinity.

While Big Dog made haste shinnying down one of the poles they used as a makeshift ladder, Jason took his time. He always hung back and watched the men fawn over Kathryn while she distributed the light supper she delivered every evening. No sense joining the throng and having her mistake him for one of her drooling admirers. They were fools anyway. Why fawn over what they couldn't have? She'd made no secret of the fact that she was returning to San Francisco at the first opportunity. The arrival of the *Leonesa* yesterday no doubt heralded her departure.

When the last of the men had received his supper from Kathryn's hands, he sauntered over to the back of the wagon. "Got anything left, or did that swarm of locusts eat it all?"

A smile touched her lips, and she pulled out a bundle from behind a crate in the back of the wagon. "I saved something for you."

Now, there was no reason for the sudden thud inside his rib cage. He drew his brows down and almost snatched the bundle from her, mumbling a quick "Thanks."

The hurt look that erased her smile caused him a guilty pang. No sense being rude, especially when she wanted so badly to please him. He stopped in the act of turning away.

"Thank you," he repeated, this time more deliberately. "I appreciate it."

When he unwrapped the cloth, he found two sandwiches, a half-dozen molasses cakes, and a thick wedge of raisin pie.

"I feel I must warn you." A wry smile turned her lips into a crooked line. "I made the pie. It's not very good."

The effort it cost her pride to say that was obvious. A laugh rose in his throat, but he bit it back. "I'm sure it's fine."

"No, really." She fixed a wide, earnest look

on him. "Evie stood at my elbow every minute, but it came out all wrong anyway. I . . ." She bit her lip. "I've never baked a pie before today."

A touch of color appeared high on her cheeks. Twin locks of hair had escaped the severe knot she habitually wore at the nape of her neck. When she stood there like that, looking humble and a little embarrassed, she looked . . . quite attractive.

The thought struck him like a bad smell.

He jerked the cloth back in place over the plate and then lifted the whole as if in tribute. "Thank you again. I wish you safe journey tomorrow."

When he turned to go, she stopped him. "Jason?"

He didn't answer, but did pause and wait for her to continue.

"I'm not leaving tomorrow. My plans have changed." Her shoulders heaved in a laugh. "I hope this fort is as sturdy as it looks, because as it turns out, I'm staying. At least for a while."

If Big Dog had hit the back of his head with a piece of milled lumber, Jason couldn't have been more stunned. Or more displeased. She was staying? As in, not leaving?

"Why?" The question snapped off his tongue before he could temper his tone.

"You said you were leaving at the first opportunity."

Kathryn drew back, offended. Her eyes narrowed. "Maybe I changed my mind. I wasn't aware that I needed to obtain your approval first."

What was that thought a moment ago about her being attractive? He'd most definitely been mistaken. Why, look at that jutting jaw, that obstinate glint in her eyes. Never had he seen a woman who possessed stubbornness in greater quantity than Kathryn.

A suitable answer failed to present itself amid the roiling thoughts that whipped through his mind. Instead he slammed the plate containing his supper down on the bed of the wagon with a crack.

As he left, he heard Red venture a tentative inquiry. "If he's not gonna eat that pie, can I have it?"

Thursday, January 17, 1856
Jason left the Faulkner House long before sunup. He passed between the totem pole and the café, glancing hopefully at the cracks between the shutters closed over the windows. No sign of light. Every so often when he went to work early Evie was already up, making coffee and getting a head start

263

on breakfast. Not this morning, though. With a sigh he took a half-loaf of bread he'd begged from her the night before from his satchel and bit into the slightly stale crust. A fresh biscuit and a thick, juicy ham steak would have gone down well this morning. Not to mention a cup of Evie's coffee, which was far superior to the stuff the men down at the mill kept going all day. He could wait a few minutes . . .

No. The risk that he'd run into Kathryn was too great. She'd taken to rising almost as early as Evie.

Irritated, he cast a backward glance at the Faulkner House, half afraid that he would see the door open and her figure emerging onto the porch. He lengthened his stride and hurried down the dark street. Was it not enough that he had lost much of the night's sleep because of her? Her revelation that she was not returning to San Francisco had played over and over in his thoughts as he lay in the dark room. What had happened to change her mind? From the very first day she arrived in Seattle she'd made no secret of the fact that she would put the town behind her at the first opportunity. Why, then, when the chance presented itself, was she staying?

When he rounded a corner that put the

Faulkner House and Evangeline's Café out of sight, he settled into an easier gait. When there was no danger of running into her, he could relax. But when the possibility of seeing her arose, tension spread from his gut outward.

Angry with himself, he kicked at a clump of dirt that he could barely see on the dark road. Over the past several days, he had found her less irritating than before. He'd spent hours last night considering the reason. She had lost the edge of arrogance that had sharpened her personality when they first arrived in Seattle. In recent days she'd become almost pleasant to be around. She smiled more often, and her features seemed . . . softer, or something. What was the reason behind the change? Perhaps working in a servant's role had tempered her pride, or perhaps it was the gentler influence of Louisa and Evie.

Or maybe it was his attitude that had changed when she finally stopped plaguing him about art. He'd been on the verge of telling her the truth about the painting that hung in his room simply to shut her up. But then she'd changed her attitude on her own, thank the Lord. The less he had to talk about that painting, the better he felt.

The painting. The scene rose in his mind

with such force that he could feel the sunlight on his arms even here, in Seattle's chilly predawn darkness. Could feel Beth's feather-soft kiss brush against his lips. Pain squeezed his heart, but not the old pain to which he'd grown accustomed in the years since Beth's death. In the long, sleepless hours on his bunk last night he'd realized there was a new element to the grief that clutched at his throat and caused his breath to labor in his chest. A traitorous idea had snaked its way into his thoughts.

Maybe he *could,* one day . . . love someone else.

The disloyal thought punched at his heart with a guilty fist. A prayer, the first since his wife's death, formed in his mind.

No, Lord. I love Beth. I'll always love Beth. You gave her to me, and I promised to love her forever.

Then why did Kathryn's image swim before him in the darkness of the night? Why did the memory of her standing on the dock, hands clasped over her mouth in horror as she watched two dozen men beat each other to a pulp over her — why did he wake to that image in his mind before he even opened his eyes?

The Almighty remained silent, leaving Jason to grasp for reasons on his own.

It's because I'm in a place where women are so scarce. The few who are here command the attention of every man, not only me. Does she have any idea how often her name comes up at the mill or at the blockhouse? No wonder I can't get her off my mind.

For that reason alone it was better for her to leave Seattle. Let her go back to San Francisco, where she belonged. But now it looked like that wasn't going to happen.

A movement in the darkness ahead drew Jason out of his thoughts. He stopped on the street and glanced around. So distracting had his thoughts been that he walked right past his turn down First Street. Left to themselves his feet had followed a familiar course and carried him toward the blockhouse instead of the mill. Now he'd have to double back. A good thing he was early this morning.

But what had moved? Hard to tell in the dark, but he'd swear he saw a black shape run down the knoll and disappear into the forest. He stood stock-still, eyes scanning, ears on high alert.

What was that scurrying noise, that rustling in the trees to his right? He narrowed his lids and squinted in that direction, but the forest was pitch-black, impossible to see inside. Probably a deer. He dismissed that thought. Deer were known to bed down at night. The shape he'd glimpsed was too big to be a raccoon or a possum. A cougar maybe? His mouth went dry at the thought. David and Noah had described some of the giant cats that inhabited these woods. There had been a handful of attacks on livestock and even children of families that lived in the forest, but the cougars tended to avoid the cleared areas of town.

Besides, the shape he'd seen — or *might* have seen — had been upright. Like a person.

He started up the knoll, senses on high alert. David's advice returned to him with force: *Maybe we should all start carrying our long rifles with us. I'm gonna keep mine handy.* Reports kept coming in that hostile tribes were amassing in the woods, the attack force growing bigger every day. David and Noah and the others had discussed posting a guard on the blockhouse at night to guard against possible sabotage, but hadn't done it yet. Maybe they should.

Jason approached the knoll from the bay side, opposite the closest point of the forest. He circled upward, his head moving constantly to scan the area around him. Nothing moved. The half-finished walls rose high above him, sturdy but still roofless. Everything looked exactly as it had when he and the others left at sundown last night.

Crouching, ready to run if the need arose, he crept toward the open place in the wall that would soon become the door. Inside, the second floor platform they had begun a few days before created even darker shadows toward the back. His muscles twitching with nerves, he peered into the darkness and inched forward.

The smell hit him just inside. He jerked upright, nose twitching to identify the location. Somewhere off to the right. Turning in that direction, the odor grew stronger with every inch. He had not taken two steps when he found the source. There, by his foot, was an empty bottle. Running a pair of fingers down the wooden boards, they came away wet with a faintly oily residue. He crouched down to inspect the bottle and spied a few items littering the dirt. Picking one up, he verified what he had suspected when he first identified the smell. An unlit match.

Holding his fingers before his nose, he sniffed the familiar odor, mind racing. Oil of turpentine. No doubt at all. And he knew only one person in all of Seattle in possession of oil of turpentine.

ELEVEN

"It's ridiculous!" The force with which Evie applied her rolling pin to the lump of dough kept Jason on the other side of the café's dining room, well out of swinging distance. "Kathryn would no more sabotage the blockhouse than I would."

The evidence — the empty bottle and eight unburned matches — lay on the table beside Jason.

"How can you be sure?" Noah adopted an even, almost placating tone to address his wife. "You've only known her a little over a week. We all have."

The glare she turned on him held almost as much force as her rolling pin, and Jason marveled at Noah's ability to return it without flinching.

"Where is Kathryn?" Jason asked, hoping to diffuse a marital battle before it began. "Isn't she usually here by now?"

Evie turned that fiery glare his way. "Just

because she's a little later than usual proves nothing. A woman should be able to sleep late every now and then without making everyone suspicious."

He was about to agree when a new voice entered the conversation.

"Suspicious of what?"

Jason jerked around to see Kathryn enter through the open doorway, her fingers fumbling with the button at the neck of her cloak.

At the sight of her, Evie burst into tears. She abandoned the biscuit dough and charged across the room to throw her arms around her friend. "Oh, Kathryn! I believe in you. Don't think for a minute I don't."

Noah's mouth dangled open, consternation etched on his face as he stared at his wife. His gaze flickered to Jason and he shook his head, clearly baffled.

Kathryn seemed equally perplexed at the normally composed restaurant owner's behavior. "Well . . . thank you." She patted Evie's back, casting a questioning glance first at Noah and then Jason. "I appreciate your confidence in me. But would you tell me why?"

Evie straightened and took a step backward, blotting her eyes with her apron. "I'm sorry. I shouldn't have cried all over you

271

like that. It's just that —" Her mouth snapped shut and she turned a narrow-lidded glare toward Jason. "You tell her."

He swallowed convulsively, unaccustomed to being on the receiving end of feminine ire. Beth never lost her temper like this.

He arrested the thought. Now was not the time to dwell on the past, not with Kathryn's expectant gaze fixed on him.

Clearing his throat, he adopted an even tone. "There's been an attempt to sabotage the blockhouse."

As he described his discovery, he watched a series of emotions flicker across her features. Shock, concern, dismay, and finally, a dawning disbelief.

"But surely you don't suspect *me.*" Her hand flew to her chest and her glance flickered from Evie to Noah and finally came to rest once again on Jason. "I most certainly did not do anything so vile. And I'll prove it."

She whirled and ran from the restaurant. The sound of her running footsteps faded, and an awkward silence fell on the room. Jason stared at a knot in one of the logs on the wall, listening to Evie's sniffle.

A minute later the back door opened and Kathryn stepped inside. Her eyes looked larger than normal in her pale face. "It's gone. My oil of turpentine is gone. I'd left it by the back door because of the smell. My room is small, and . . ." She lifted a fearful gaze toward Jason. "I didn't do it. What possible reason would I have to do such a terrible thing?"

"Exactly." Evie had gained control over her tears, and now she looped an arm through Kathryn's and stood by her side, spine stiff. "It makes no sense. We don't believe it for an instant. Do we?" The glare that slid between Noah and Jason became intense as both women waited for their answer.

Actually, Jason did not believe Kathryn would attempt such a violent act. For one thing, she had made no secret of her fear of the looming Indian attack. Destroying the place where she and the others would take refuge made no sense. Besides, he could not envision Kathryn creeping through the forest in the dark all the way to the blockhouse, and he had definitely seen the saboteur scurry into the forest. And finally, he could not forget her expression as she watched the riot she had caused the other day. She had been appalled by the violence. Under no circumstances would he describe her as gentle, but neither would he believe her capable of vandalism on a scale such as this.

"No." He voiced his answer with the confidence he felt. "I don't believe you did this."

Grateful tears sparkled in her eyes, and the sight of them caused a sympathetic pang in his chest.

"Neither do I." Noah stepped toward his wife, who slipped her arms around his waist and buried her face in his sleeve. "But someone obviously wanted us to suspect you."

Jason agreed. "That's true. The oil of turpentine is clear evidence that points to you."

"Not necessarily." Evie raised her head. "If the bottle was sitting outside in plain sight, anyone could have picked it up. It might have been a scout from one of the hostile tribes." She looked up at her husband. "Our Indian friends have told us they're keeping watch over the town."

"It's possible one of them snatched it and decided to do mischief." He remembered the night a week ago when they'd first agreed to build the blockhouse. An argument had nearly broken out between those who saw the necessity for action and those who accused them of being alarmists and spreading panic without cause. "Or it need not have been an Indian scout. There are plenty of people right here in Seattle who don't support the blockhouse."

Noah nodded, his expression sober. He and David had been the target for a lot of verbal jabs and taunts.

"Thank goodness you arrived in time." Kathryn folded her arms and hugged her middle in a gesture that reminded him of a frightened child. "When I think of what might have happened if you'd been a few minutes later . . ."

Noah rubbed a hand across his mouth, shaking his head. "I'm not sure the vandal actually intended to set a fire. If it wasn't one of the hostiles, that is."

Jason narrowed his eyes, trying to guess where the man's thoughts had taken him. "What about the matches?"

"They could have been placed there on purpose. Think about it. If someone really wanted to set a fire that would do some damage, wouldn't they use a lot more fuel than what was in that little bottle?" He gestured toward the empty bottle. "Why not lamp oil? Comes in bigger containers and is far more accessible."

"Do Indians use lamp oil?" asked Kathryn.

"They use dogfish oil." Evie wrinkled her nose. "It stinks even worse than turpentine."

Jason considered Noah's point. "You're right."

"So we've got two possible culprits." Noah raised a finger. "Indian scouts intent on destroying our efforts to protect ourselves, and who happened across your oil of turpentine." He lifted a second finger. "Or one of our own who found the bottle and decided to cause a bit of mischief."

"There's a third possibility, and I'm afraid it's the most logical." Jason turned an apologetic look on her. "Someone in town dislikes you enough to want to cast suspicion on you."

Her mouth dropped open, shock registering on her face.

"That's absurd." Evie drew herself up in staunch defense of her friend. "Kathryn's only been here ten days and already everyone loves her."

Not everyone. Jason held his tongue, but Will's warnings resounded in his mind. The man made no effort to hide his intense dislike for her, at least not to Jason. One way or another, he intended to discover why.

Who hates me enough to try to turn everyone against me?

The question gnawed at Kathryn after Jason left. Her hands busied themselves in

276

preparing for the breakfast crowd that would arrive shortly while she tried to assemble a list. Could it be one of the sailors from the other day? At supper last night Red told her word leaked out that Captain Gansevoort had been furious when he learned about the brawl. Those involved had been denied liberty for an indefinite period of time. Maybe one of them was bitter enough to sneak ashore for a bit of mischief.

She went into the storage room after another stack of plates. That could be the case, but she doubted it. For one thing, how many of those sailors knew about her painting? None that she was aware of. The townspeople, on the other hand, did. She talked openly of the inspiring view from the hotel's back porch and her struggles to capture the majesty of Mount Rainier on her canvas. Plenty of the diners at the café spoke disdainfully of the construction project. Even so, she could not think of a single one who would have any cause to cast aspersions on her. She had done nothing to cause anyone to dislike her.

And yet, there was one who disliked her without cause.

With a handful of forks from the bin resting on the topmost plate, she hefted the stack. Will Townsend had disliked her from her first night in Seattle. Why? She couldn't imagine. A few discreet questions to Evie and Louisa had produced the fact that he was well respected and highly regarded by everyone in town. He was a good provider for John William, who clearly adored him. He'd answered Louisa's questions regarding the change in the little boy's daily care with the assurance that this was a temporary change only, to give her a much-needed break from the active child so she could save her strength for the birth. Louisa protested the need, but had been satisfied that there was no hidden reason behind the change.

Kathryn wasn't so sure. Was she somehow at fault?

She carried the plates into the dining room and skirted past Evie, who stood in front of her huge frying pan, turning a thick slab of sizzling bacon. The more Kathryn thought about it, the more certain she became. Will Townsend had stolen her oil of turpentine in order to cast suspicion on her. He wanted to make her look bad in front of her friends. No, in front of the entire town.

Well, she wasn't going to let him get away with it.

She set the plates down on the table with force. Evie turned to give her a surprised look.

"I've got to check on something," she mumbled as she snatched her cloak and bonnet off the peg.

"Now?"

"I won't be long."

"But what about —"

She didn't wait to hear the rest of the question, but hurried through the door. A colorful dawn was still several minutes from breaking, and the eastern sky behind the restaurant showed hints of pink and red streaks. A string of early risers were heading for the café, and she greeted them with a distracted smile as she hurried past. Louisa had pointed out the Townsend home the day she gave Evie a wagon tour of Seattle. It wasn't far. Hopefully she could catch him before he left for the mill.

She gathered her skirts and increased her pace to as close to a run as decorum allowed.

The glow of lamplight shone in the window. Relieved, she approached the door and then paused to gather her composure. What would she say? Accuse the man of trying to defame her?

No, she would not resort to accusations. Instead she would demand to know the reason behind his instant and intense hatred of her. Forcing her breath to return to normal, she squared her shoulders and knocked on the door.

A scurrying sounded inside and she heard the latch lift. The door cracked open and was then thrown wide.

"Miss Kathryn!" John William, still dressed in a long nightshirt, leaped forward to wrap his arms around her skirt in an enthusiastic hug. "Grandpa, look who came calling." He lifted his head to beam up at her. "Am I staying with you today while my grandpa is at work?"

Words evaporated from her mind. How could she have forgotten about the child? She couldn't very well shout at his grandfather in front of him. Maybe this impromptu visit wasn't such a good idea.

She knelt and returned the child's embrace. "Not today, sweetheart. I have to work at the hotel. I came to talk to —"

"John William!"

The coldness in Will's voice startled both of them. He had appeared from a back room and stood glaring in their direction, his face full of fury. The boy turned a wide-eyed question on his grandfather while Kathryn's pulse kicked into a gallop.

The man made a visible effort to control himself as he addressed the boy. "Go get dressed."

"But Miss Kathryn is here to visit."

"I said *go!*"

Though he did not shout, his tone held an undeniable command. John William gave her a confused look and then obeyed.

Kathryn straightened and waited for the child to leave the room. She glanced once into Will's face, but quickly looked away from the fierce anger she saw there. Blood sped through her veins, propelled by a racing heart that pounded like a drum in her ears. When the boy disappeared into the bedroom, Will stomped toward her and she beat a quick retreat to small patch of grass in front of the house. He stopped on the square platform that served as a porch, pulling the door closed behind him.

"What are you doing here?" he spat.

Words momentarily failed her. "I — I wanted to —" A spasm took her throat. "To talk to you about something that happened last night. Or —" She shook her head. "This morning, rather."

"No." He chopped off the word. "I mean what are you doing *here*? Why are you in Seattle?"

Taken aback, she stared at him. "I came to help Madame at the Faulkner House."

"Don't bother repeating that tale to me. We both know better."

Was the man mad? She tried again. "My father sent me to work with Madame Garritson, who is a distant cousin."

A smirk appeared, though anger still snapped in his eyes. "Does your father know what you really are, or have you fooled him along with everyone else?"

An initial flash of guilt stabbed at her. No, he couldn't possibly be aware of that shameful incident in San Francisco. He'd been here, in Seattle, at the time. He had obviously confused her with someone else, that was all. She drew herself up. "You've made a mistake. My father is —"

"Philip Bergert. I know who he is, *Kathryn*." He spoke her name with a sneer. "You might fool him and everyone else into thinking you're a mannered lady, but you and I both know better."

He stepped forward and came right up to her. Though she tried to hold her ground, she took an involuntary backward step. She was face-to-face with a lunatic. Would he strike her?

Instead, he searched her face as though trying to see her thoughts. Whatever he found there dampened the fire in his eyes. His shoulders slumped, and when he spoke, his whisper held a hint of agony. "I don't know what game you're playing but I will not let you ruin everything. We're happy here. Do you understand that? Leave Seattle. Just leave."

Before she could gather her thoughts to answer, he turned and stomped back into the house. The door closed with a solid thud, leaving her standing outside.

Was the man insane? A moment before she would have said yes, but that last plea gave her pause. Was she imagining things, or had she detected a touch of fear in his tone? He seemed truly afraid that she would — how had he put it? — *ruin everything,* simply by her presence.

A slow realization stole over her. There was only one explanation for his behavior.

He knew.

Somehow, he knew her secret. And he was threatening to ruin her reputation by exposing her.

This is ridiculous. It's not like I'm a criminal.

But Papa would certainly think so, if he knew what had happened. And what about her new friends? Evie, and Louisa, and — she swallowed — Jason? She could not bear it if he knew of that shameful night. He would certainly not believe her innocent of vandalism against the blockhouse then. No one would.

Perhaps she should leave, really leave.

Start a new life back East among ladies like Mrs. Stanton and Miss Anthony. Surely she would find acceptance among them. But since she could barely afford a ticket to San Francisco, certainly she could not pay for passage to New York. She sniffled. Besides, she'd found friends here in Seattle. And what of . . . of Jason? A painful prickle of tears assaulted her eyes, and she blinked furiously against them as she thrust the traitorous thought to the back of her mind. One more thing *not* to think about.

With a sickening sense of shame, she turned toward the café. It had been a mistake to come to Will's house. And she had not even confronted him about the oil of turpentine, either. Nor would she. Without a doubt, he had perpetrated the vandalism to implicate her in order to scare her away from Seattle. It wouldn't work, because even if she wanted to leave, she could not. No, her best course now would be to avoid him as much as possible and hope he held his tongue.

TWELVE

How to approach Will without accusing him outright? Jason struggled with the question throughout the day. Word of the near-disaster had spread like a cold wave at high tide, and the men talked of nothing else as they worked. The general consensus was that the vandal had been a sailor from the *Decatur,* trying to avenge his buddies who'd been denied liberty because of Kathryn. If that were the case, Jason hoped the man was never found out. Judging by the vehemence with which the millworkers vowed to defend her honor, he might not survive the encounter.

Paperwork consumed the morning. After the first week of Jason working alongside the men, Henry had opened his files and turned over the office. Jason's time was more and more devoted to the design of an improved water system for the town, an idea that everyone in Seattle heartily applauded.

Jason was nearing his second week of immersing himself in the mill's accounts. It was long, tedious work that sent cramps through his fingers by the end of the day, but he found the labor consuming and exhausting in a different way from the physical effort of milling timber.

Until today.

He tossed the pencil on an open account book and massaged the stiffness from his fingers while he stared through the office window. Will and another man were fiddling with a roller that kept jamming. They'd been at it off and on for the past hour. Excuse enough to interrupt his paperwork to check on their progress.

Jason left the office, nodding at the working men as he made his way to the end of the infeed deck. Will looked up at his approach.

"How's the repair coming?" He pitched his voice loud to be heard over the noise of the engine and the buzz of the main saw as it chewed through lumber.

"It's not," Will shouted in answer. "The roller was shot, so we're replacing it. Don't have a spare, so we had to take one off the front end." He pointed toward the outside edge of the roller belt, where Big Dog and a trio of others were about ready to heft a dripping log.

"Can we rig a replacement?"

Will jerked a thumb over his shoulder to where Murphy bent over a worktable intent on a task. "Already working on it."

"Good man."

He almost raised an arm to slap Will on the shoulder, but the gesture seemed awkward, almost condescending, for someone with far more experience leading this crew than he. Another reason he struggled with how to approach his question. He couldn't afford to alienate Will with a false accusation. If it *was* false.

"Have you got a minute?" Jason jerked a thumb toward a deserted place outside the shed. "Want to ask you something."

When they stepped out from beneath the roof's wide overhang, the noise dimmed considerably. The sun shone today for the third day in a row, and the temperature was warm enough that he didn't need his heavy coat. Both were unusual for January, according to the men. Some had espoused the opinion that the break in the weather was a sign from the Good Lord that He wanted the blockhouse finished sooner rather than later and was holding off the rain until the last shingle was in place.

Jason and Will stood side by side watching

the loading of the log on the roller belt. "What's your take on the incident at the blockhouse this morning?"

There. No beating around the bush, and no accusation. Just a simple question.

Will didn't look at him. "The men seem partial to the sailor theory."

"I didn't ask what the men think."

A cautious nod. "I think if we let them keep talking like that, we'll have another fight on our hands. They're whipping themselves up."

Jason turned his head and studied the man. "You're avoiding my question."

Will pursed his lips for a second. "You know my opinion of the *lady* in question." He spoke the word as though he doubted the veracity of it. Jason drew breath to contradict him, but he went on. "Everyone seems so certain of her innocence. I pity the man who dares to disagree."

"So you think Kathryn crept through the forest and spread oil of turpentine on the building, and then . . . what? Lost her nerve and ran off without striking a match?" The idea, spelled out like that, sounded ludicrous.

Will didn't seem to think so. "She needn't have crept through the forest. A black-cloaked figure in the dark could walk fairly

288

openly through that part of town. There are no houses close enough to see, and there were no moon or stars last night." He turned then and faced Jason head-on. "Or so I'm told. I wouldn't know, since I was at home with my grandson, sleeping soundly."

Ah. The man knew where Jason's questions were leading, and provided his alibi before the accusation could be voiced.

All right, so maybe he didn't do it. But that doesn't mean Kathryn did.

Jason planted a boot heel in the dirt. "I don't believe her capable of such a desperate act. She has no reason to want the fortress destroyed. Besides, she's a frail woman. I can't imagine her wandering through town alone in the dark."

Of course, she *did* venture down to the waterfront alone just two days past. The reminder gave Jason pause. But that had been in full daylight.

Will's mouth twitched, and Jason thought he might mention the incident, but he did not. "It could have been hostile Indians," he conceded.

Despite his words, he believed her guilty. Jason saw it in the set of his jaw, in the way he wouldn't look Jason in the eye. But he had determined to keep his opinion to himself.

Fine. That was probably the safest course of action, given the men's fervent defense of Kathryn.

"Yes. It certainly could."

And maybe that was the answer after all. Unless the culprit confessed, they would never know.

All through the afternoon the numbers in the ledger on Jason's desk kept blurring, replaced by the image of dark, tear-filled eyes. What could it hurt to check on the girl, just to make sure she was all right? Using the excuse of an errand at Coffinger's, he left the mill a few minutes early.

He strode into the café expecting to find Kathryn working at Evie's side. But the restaurant owner was alone.

"Jason. I didn't expect to see you here." She fixed an inquisitive look on him. "Can I get you an early supper?"

"No, thank you. I thought Kathryn would be here." He glanced toward the storeroom doorway, half expecting her to appear at the mention of her name. "Have you seen her?"

Evie's smile might have widened a fraction, or it might not have. Either way, he chose to ignore the added brightness in her tone when she answered.

"She's usually here by now, but I think

she lost track of time. I stepped outside a while ago and saw her next door, hard at work on her painting. She was so engrossed she didn't even notice me."

Her painting. The idea of seeing her paint left a sour taste in his mouth. "Well, I'd hate to interrupt her." He turned to go.

"No, wait!" Evie leaped up from her chair and hurried over to stop him. "I'm sure she wouldn't mind. In fact, I was just about to peek my head outside and call to her." A guileless smile spread across her lips. "I need her help. If you don't mind telling her so, you'll be saving me the effort."

He found himself practically shoved across the room and through the back door. Playing matchmaker, was she? Well, her efforts were wasted here. She'd have a far greater chance of success with Murphy, or Lowry, or one of the others. But while he was here, he might as well check on Kathryn. With a scowl for Evie's lack of subtlety, he straightened his coat with a tug and headed next door.

Kathryn had once again spread her blanket on the grass, and she sat at a graceful angle, leaning forward toward her short easel. She held her brush in an easy three-fingered grip and applied paint in minute brushstrokes. The familiar posture squeezed

291

his heart in his chest, and he almost turned back. He must have made an unconscious sound, for she looked up.

"Jason." The pensive lines in her forehead cleared, and a delighted smile pressed dimples in the smooth skin of her cheeks. "What are you doing here? You're usually at the mill at this time of day."

The clasp holding her hair in place had come loose and dangled in a mass of dark curls down her back. With an unconscious gesture she pushed back a lock, tucking it behind her ear, while she waited for his answer. The less severe arrangement made her appear . . . softer. Or something.

He stopped at the edge of the blanket and shoved his hands into his coat pockets. "I'm on my way to the blockhouse, and thought I'd check to see if you're feeling okay."

The sun was behind him, and she shaded her eyes to look up into his face. Her bonnet lay discarded on the grass, and the skin across her nose had turned pink from prolonged exposure. A healthy glow seemed to radiate from her smile.

"Do you mean have I recovered from the shock of someone making me out to be a traitor and a vandal?" Her lips twisted into a sardonic line, and then she heaved a sigh. "I suppose so. There was a steady stream of ladies to and from the hotel this morning to assure me of their belief in my innocence."

"That's good. I'm glad." Now that he'd reassured himself on that matter, he edged backward toward a hasty escape.

"Wait." She leaped to her feet and hurried forward with an outstretched hand. Just before she touched his arm she stopped and clasped her hands in front of her waist. "Now that you're here . . . I know I promised not to mention painting again, but . . ." Her gaze slid toward her canvas.

She was nothing if not persistent. Served him right. He should have known better than to approach an artist at work. Instead of the irritation that had overtaken him every other time she begged for his advice, he experienced a sense of surrender. Maybe if he told her the truth, painful though the words were to speak, she would stop plaguing him once and for all.

"I can't advise you on technique, Kathryn." When she would have protested, he held up a finger. "I don't know anything about painting because I am not an artist."

That took her aback. "Many artists doubt their ability. You should not. The beautiful landscape in your room is proof of your talent. And I saw your palette, the brushes, the tubes of oils."

"They belonged to my wife. To Beth." There. He'd said her name aloud, and though he felt as if someone had wrapped steel bands around his chest, it wasn't as painful as he'd feared. "She was the artist."

Kathryn's brows drew together as she digested the news. "The initials on the painting are JEG. Not Jason E. Gates?"

"My middle name is Leonard. JEG stands for Julia Elizabeth Gates. She went by Beth, because she insisted *Julia* sounded like an old dowager aunt." The hint of a laugh escaped on a breath at the bittersweet memory of Beth planting her hands on her hips and insisting on the nickname.

"Oh."

He went on in a softer voice, fighting a flood of emotions. Best get it all out at once, so they could put the topic behind them. "That painting is of a place that was special to us. The place where I proposed, in fact. She —" He swallowed. "She painted it as a wedding gift for me."

Compassionate tears flooded her face. "I'm sorry, Jason."

Tears prickled behind his eyes in answer. He tore his gaze away, shifting his weight from one foot to another as he looked out over the treetops at the majestic mountain peak looming in the distance.

"No harm done. You couldn't have known." He forced a bright tone, ready to end this painful conversation. "So you see, it's no use asking for my help on matters of art."

Thankfully, she matched his forced smile and adopted a casual tone that mirrored his. "Ah, well. Advice on lighting would be of no use to me at this point anyway." She folded her arms and aimed a jaundiced eye toward her canvas. "The scale is all wrong, and I'm at a loss on how to fix it."

An automatic reply rose to his lips, an encouraging vote of confidence that she would figure it out in time, but the words died unspoken when his gaze fell on her painting. He looked at it.

Blinked.

Looked at it again.

Squinted his eyes to refocus.

"Well." When he realized she was watching him for a reaction, he quickly cleared his expression. "It's quite . . ." He grasped for a description that would not offend her, but came up blank. "Quite colorful," he finally blurted.

The truth was, the painting was terrible. Probably the ugliest and most amateurish attempt he'd ever seen.

Hurt appeared in her eyes. "You don't like it."

"I didn't say that," he responded hastily. He'd learned from living with Beth that an artist could be extremely passionate about her work, and usually took criticism personally. "The trees are very . . . tall. And green." She watched him closely, obviously expecting more. Folding an arm across his middle, he planted an elbow on it and tapped a finger on his mouth as he made a show of studying the canvas, casting about for something encouraging to point out. "The scale of the mountain isn't exactly right, as you say, but the composition is, um, artistic. I like the way you have the rising sun peeking over that rocky ledge."

"That is not the sun rising," she informed him in a flat tone. "It's supposed to be mid-afternoon, and that yellow spot is a reflection of the light on the snow."

"Ah. Well." He flashed an apologetic smile. "As I said, I'm not an artist. Nor am I an art critic."

"You hate it."

Did that tremble in her voice hint of an impending onslaught of tears? Nothing in the world made him more uncomfortable than a woman's tears. All Beth had to do was sniffle and he would fall all over himself to placate her. Either that, or beat a hasty retreat before the storm broke.

Which seemed like the best course of action in the current situation.

"I don't hate it. Not at all." He took a backward step. "And you know what they say. Beauty is in the skin of the — No, I mean in the *eye* of the beholder." An awkward laugh escaped as he backed up even further. "I almost said *skin deep,* but of course that's mixing metaphors. Or something."

Egad, he'd begun to *babble.*

"I have to go. Don't want to be late for the blockhouse." He whirled, and had almost reached the corner of the hotel when he remembered his errand. "Oh, and Evie asked me to tell you she needs your help."

He shouted the last over his shoulder without turning. The gentlemanly thing would be to stay and help her clean up her painting supplies. In this instance, he felt justified in *not* doing as good manners dictated.

A gloomy fog settled over Kathryn when Jason disappeared between the buildings. The haste with which he took his departure told her everything she wanted to know about her painting. No matter what he said, he *did*

297

hate it. And no wonder. She studied it with new eyes, trying to see it as he would. Was it really as terrible as all that?

Someone approached from the café and she glanced up to find Evie striding across the grass, wiping her hands on her apron.

"I saw Jason leave, so I knew your work had already been interrupted. The first of the ladies have begun to arrive for tea."

Was it really that late? "I'm sorry. I lost track of time." She bent and began gathering her supplies from the blanket.

"Don't worry about it. I've almost got everything — oh."

Kathryn looked up to find Evie staring at her painting with the same horrified fascination she might display upon finding a rat's nest in her storeroom. She straightened and came to stand beside her friend to inspect her work.

"It's not very good, is it? Tell the truth." She couldn't stop a hopeful tone from creeping in at the end. Maybe it wasn't as bad as all that.

Evie's expression became apologetic and she shook her head. "No, I'm afraid it isn't."

At least she expressed her honest opinion. The sign of a true friend.

Kathryn's shoulders slumped. "I've studied and practiced as hard as I can, but no matter what I do, my paintings never turn out the way I envision."

"You've mentioned your art teacher in San Francisco. What does he say about your work?"

"That I have a natural talent, and that I'm improving at a remarkable rate."

Lines appeared between Evie's brows and she looked again at the painting. "Really?"

"Papa says Monsieur Rousseau's encouragement has nothing to do with my talent, and everything to do with the high price he charges for my lessons." A sigh gathered deep in Kathryn's lungs and she blew it out. "He's right, isn't he?"

A compassionate smile crept over her friend's face. "Perhaps there *is* some truth to your papa's opinion."

Curiously, the realization was not as devastating as it might have been. When she'd taken her first lesson three years ago, she'd been hopeful that she had finally found her life's ambition. She dreamed that her paintings would be admired by renowned critics and sought after by collectors. Galleries would display her work, and students would try to copy her techniques. But if she was honest, she had begun long ago to suspect that she wasn't nearly as talented as Monsieur insisted. Her determination to paint had found more and more strength in proving Papa wrong than in striving to improve.

Not that she would *ever* admit that to him.

She turned a resigned smile on Evie. "I don't suppose you want to hang this in the restaurant. It has the distinction of being the last painting ever created by Kathryn Bergert, an artist who achieved notoriety for her lamentable lack of talent."

Evie laughed and slipped an arm around her. "I would be honored to hang it in a very special place." She squeezed Kathryn's waist. "In my storeroom."

She helped Kathryn gather the supplies and fold the blanket. When Evie headed for the café, Kathryn took her paints, brushes, palette, and other articles, bundled them in a square of linen, and placed them in the bottom of her trunk. Kneeling on the floor, she covered them with a stack of books. There. Her artistic dreams buried beneath the eloquence of Jane Austen and Alfred Tennyson. Maybe one day she would discover her true talent and dream a new dream.

She sat back on her heels. At least she finally uncovered the reason behind Jason's coolness toward her. How painful it must have been for him to hear her blathering on about art every time she saw him. He could never fall in love with another painter. The reminder would be too —

She stilled, her hands frozen in the act of shutting the trunk lid. Love? Who said anything about love?

The second ladies' tea since Kathryn's arrival was even better attended than the first. With the arrival of Roberta Blaine, the minister's wife, conversation focused on the news she brought from their visit with her sister in El Dorado. Kathryn listened with half an ear, nodding at the appropriate time and mechanically washing down a slice of nut bread with tea.

When had she fallen in love with Jason Gates? The idea was so astonishing, so surprising, so . . . well, so entirely unwelcome. Perhaps she wasn't really in love with him. The soft, fluttery sensation in her stomach whenever her mind conjured his image hadn't been there yesterday, had it? No, it had begun this morning, when he looked her in the eye and declared his belief in her innocence. This was gratitude, not love.

But deep inside she knew that was not true. With dawning dismay, she admitted the truth.

I'm in love with Jason Gates.

"What do you think, Kathryn?" Louisa's voice broke through her musing.

Kathryn jerked upright, tea sloshing into her saucer over the rim of her cup. "What?" The faces of the ladies seated around her snapped into focus, all of them pointed her way. She cast about in her mind for a shred of the conversation that had been going on around her and came up empty.

"Someone's head is in the clouds today," Letitia teased in her singsong voice

With a bashful nod, she admitted, "I was thinking about something else. I'm sorry." She looked at Louisa. "What did you say?"

The answer never came, because at that moment a pair of men appeared in the restaurant's doorway. The ladies looked up to find two sailors in crisp uniforms staring into the room. Kathryn stiffened in her chair. The two were familiar. They were Barney and another man whose name she did not know. Both had been among the group who'd treated her so roughly two days past. In fact, Barney bore evidence of the fight in the form of an ugly purple bruise beneath his left eye.

They snatched their sailor caps off their heads and twisted them in their hands.

"We're looking for Miss Kathryn Bergert."

Every eye turned her way, and at that moment Barney saw her. He nudged his partner with an elbow and nodded toward her.

"Miss Bergert, could we speak to you outside, ma'am?"

"Certainly not." Evie rose and took up a protective stance beside her.

"We don't mean no harm," the other man hurried to say. His gaze fixed on Kathryn's face. "There's some of us out here who want to apologize for what happened the other day."

Though cautious to place herself in their proximity, she hesitated to dismiss them outright. Their manner was far more humble than it had been on Tuesday, almost servile. Rumors that the *Decatur*'s captain had berated them harshly might be true. Perhaps an apology was part of their punishment.

With a quick nod at Evie, she rose and crossed to the door. The sailors backed up and she stopped just inside. No sense putting herself in danger of being manhandled again.

Outside a group of six men congregated around the totem pole. Several sported bruises and one man had a bandage wrapped around his forehead. She hid a smile. This lot had certainly gotten as good

303

as they gave in their skirmish with her mill-worker friends.

At her appearance, with a group of curious women crowding the doorway behind her to watch, the sailors snapped to attention. Barney seemed to have been given the role of official spokesperson.

"Miss Bergert, we apologize for our behavior. It was not befitting of Navy men. You was asking for our help, and we shoulda treated you like a lady, which you are." His speech, obviously rehearsed, evoked nods from those standing around him. "Furthermore, we pledge that if you need our help in the future, we will come to your aid."

One of his buddies added, "That goes for all you ladies, and the whole town too. That's why we're here. If there's an attack, you can count on the *Decatur*'s crew."

"Well." Letitia stepped up beside Kathryn. "That's quite reassuring."

"Yes, it is," Kathryn agreed. "And I accept your apology."

At that moment, a wagon came into view from the direction of the wharf. Carter, the wiry delivery man, walked at the front, guiding his mule. A huge crate dominated the wagon bed. He caught sight of the group by the totem pole and picked up his pace.

"Am I glad to see you boys!" he called

out. "I could use some help unloading this here heavy box."

Letitia aimed a smile down her long nose at the sailors. "You did pledge to answer a call for help."

With a shrug, the sailors slapped their hats on their heads and fell in beside Carter as he passed the restaurant, headed next door.

Louisa peeked through the doorway. "What in the world does he have in there?"

"Were I to venture a guess," said Letitia, "I'd say it's Madame's piano."

"A piano?" Helen pushed her way past the ladies to stand in the doorway beside Kathryn. "Madame has a piano?"

"It just arrived on the *Leonesa.* She's finally going to put some furnishings in that empty front room, though she told me herself she doesn't play." Letitia rolled her eyes as she turned away.

The rest of the ladies returned to their teacups, leaving Helen and Kathryn in the doorway.

"I play," Helen said quietly. "Hymns, mostly, and a few romantic pieces. Mother enjoyed listening to music after dinner."

Kathryn watched as a pair of sailors hopped up in the back of Carter's wagon and the rest formed two lines at the rear, ready to catch the heavy crate when it slid out. An idea took root. Perhaps she had no talent for art, but what about music? She'd always admired musicians, but never had an opportunity to try it herself.

"Would you teach me?" she asked Helen. When the woman replied with a thoughtful nod, she smiled. Perhaps one day she could even hold a recital for her friends in the Faulkner House's front room. She would save a special seat in the front row for Jason.

THIRTEEN

Monday, January 21, 1856

Jason knelt on the pitched roof and positioned a split cedar shake. David placed the nail carefully, lifted his hammer, and after a dramatic pause, pounded it in place.

"There. That's the last one." He sat back on his heels and pitched his voice to be heard by everyone in the vicinity. "Gentlemen, we have finished our blockhouse."

Around the roof and on the ground, the men cheered. Jason scanned the even rows of shakes that covered the roof and satisfaction settled over him like a warm blanket. Look at all they'd accomplished. And not only the fortress construction. On the ground he watched as the men shook hands, congratulating themselves on completing the job. Noah clapped Will on the back and Big Dog lifted a giant fist above his head in communal victory. These men had been strangers two weeks ago. Now he counted them as friends.

"We've still got work to do inside." David stood, feet spaced shoulder-width apart on the steep roof, and looked down over the celebration. "I'd like to shore up that front wall some more, and I'm not sure the platform is secure enough. I wouldn't want it to collapse while we're trying to fire our rifles."

Jason had climbed up on the inside deck earlier today to check the height of the firing holes on the upper level. He'd mimicked resting a rifle in the opening to aim and determined that the position was perfect for most men — with the possible exception of Big Dog, who would have to stoop no matter what.

"It's secure enough," he told David. "You've done a good job."

"*We've* done a good job." David let a satisfied smile roam over the men. "I'd venture to say half the town has hammered a nail or two in the past three weeks." Then he shook his head and fixed a sardonic eye on Jason. "The other half prefers taunts to hammers."

"They'll come around." Jason set his jaw with grim certainty. "When the fighting starts they'll be falling all over themselves with gratitude."

They shinnied down a pole to join the others. Noah approached and shook their hands in turn. "Some of us were talking just now. We're going to need to stockpile supplies in here. Food, water, gunpowder."

David agreed with a nod. "I've thought the same. Been meaning to take a wagon out to the cabin for a week now. I've got some watertight barrels, camp bedding, and the like stored out there. Louisa has a bee in her bonnet over fetching them back here. We might need them before this is over."

"Why don't I go after them now? There are still a couple of hours of daylight left." Noah glanced around the area. "You stay here and see to cleaning up, then go on home. Surprise your wife by showing up early for once."

"I'm not going to let you go alone," David protested. "That's asking for trouble."

Jason eyed the sun. In another hour or so they'd have this place cleaned up. Plenty of time to head back to the restaurant for the first decent meal since construction on the blockhouse began. Noah had informed his wife that there would be no need to deliver sandwiches tonight, and she'd announced her intention to cook up an extra special supper to celebrate the end of the long days. An uncomfortable twitch began in his gut.

Kathryn would be there, helping Evie dish up generous portions and talking with the customers. Talking with him. Would she mention that terrible painting? Should he mention it? And if not, then what else did they have to talk about? For the first time in a long time he felt tongue-tied around a woman. And the realization made him want to escape.

"I'll go," he volunteered with a quick smile at Noah. "I've been in Seattle three weeks and the only thing I've seen is the mill, the hotel, and this blockhouse. Been itching to get out into the forest and take a look around."

David cocked his head. "It would be good to get home early for once."

"It's settled then," said Noah. "Let's get the extra timber out of that cart and get going."

They recruited some men to unload the wagon they'd used to haul wood from the mill and then hitched up David's horse. Jason found himself looking forward to getting out into the trees. He'd been raised in the Michigan forests, hanging around his dad and other lumberjacks from the time he was ten years old. There was a peace to be found in the woods that he'd never felt anywhere else. And *this* forest was like nothing he'd ever seen back East. The giant cedars and fir trees surrounding Seattle had been calling to him since he first saw them from the deck of the *Fair Lady.*

A thought occurred to him as they started walking down the sloping side of the knoll. "I guess we're safe enough?"

"Oh, yeah." Carrying the horse's lead rope loosely, Noah nodded. "The cabin's not more than a couple of miles from here and the road's well-traveled. We'd have heard if there'd been any hostiles sighted in this area."

"That's good enough for me."

"You ever hear about how we came to pick this place?"

Jason shook his head. "No, but it sounds like a good walking story."

The two men set an easy pace, and soon the last of the town's buildings fell behind them and they passed into the forest.

Men crowded into the restaurant as expected, their moods high while they congratulated each other over heaping plates of venison, stewed tomatoes, corn cakes, and potatoes drenched in butter. The arrival of fresh supplies on the *Leonesa* had filled the café's storage room to capacity, and Evie dipped into her supplies generously.

Kathryn bustled from table to table, refilling coffee mugs and empty platters and serving up unstinting gratitude along with huge slices of raisin pie and sweet cream. The news of Jason's and Noah's errand came as a relief. After her startling realization this afternoon she was not looking forward to seeing him. What would she say? How would she act? Would he detect her feelings when he looked at her? She devoutly hoped not, and whispered a prayer to that effect.

The pies were quickly becoming a memory when a messenger arrived. An Indian woman ran into the dining room and immediately doubled over, panting.

One look at the fear in her wide eyes and everyone fell silent.

"Kikisoblu sends word," she stammered. "White woman come. She hurt, bleeding. Say husband dead, house burned. She run away with girl, come here."

While Kathryn tried to make sense of the broken English, Red jumped out of his chair. "Who did it?"

"Nisquallies." The woman choked out the word. "They coming! They coming!"

"Now?" Kathryn's voice rose on a panicked note.

But the woman shook her head, dark hair

waving around her head. "Soon. Very soon. Kikisoblu says three days, maybe two."

Evie went to the woman's side with a mug of water and waited while she drained it. "Are the injured lady and her daughter going to be okay?"

"Girl scared, but okay." She shook her head again. "Kikisoblu take lady to white doctor man and send me here."

"She'll be at Doc Maynard's then," said someone.

"Who is it?" asked Evie. "Did Princess Angeline tell you her name?"

"Yes. She named . . ." The Indian woman screwed up her face, and pounded on her head with a fist. Then her expression cleared. "Cox."

Evie's hand flew to cover her mouth. "Not Rebecca Cox?"

The woman nodded. "Rebecca Cox. And a girl with her."

"That's William Cox's wife." Red spoke in a grim voice. "That means William is dead."

Evie wavered on her feet, and for a moment Kathryn thought she might faint. Her face turned deathly pale and she spoke in a horrified whisper. "Indians have burned the Cox cabin. Dear Lord, no."

Silence reigned for a few seconds, and then the dining room erupted in activity.

Men leaped out of their chairs and headed for the door.

"Don't you worry, Miss Evie," said Big Dog as he snatched his coat off the peg. "We'll get them."

Kathryn stood to one side, watching the restaurant empty. When every man had gone, leaving her alone with the Indian messenger and Evie, she shook her head. "Surely they don't intend to launch an attack against the Nisquallies."

"That's not where they're going." Evie's voice choked on a sob. "The Cox house is less than a mile from David and Louisa's cabin." She pressed a fist against her mouth and drew a shuddering breath. "Jason and Noah are walking right into their path."

"And that's how I ended up with the prettiest wife in all of Seattle." Noah finished with a grin.

Jason shook his head, laughing. "I can't believe she and a handful of women cleared that patch of land with a handsaw and axes."

Noah raised a hand in a vow. "It's the honest truth. You should have seen her expression when I told her it was *my* land. Why, we were at Arthur's place, not too far from here over that way."

He pointed westward, and Jason automatically followed the direction of his finger. His gaze was drawn upward, above the canopy of trees, where a thick cloud of black smoke billowed into the sky. The odor struck him then, and he realized he'd been smelling smoke for the past few minutes.

"Something's on fire."

Noah looked, and his laughter dissolved. "That's too big to be a cook fire."

They both came to a halt. A bad feeling settled in the pit of Jason's stomach. "You say Arthur Denny's place is empty these days?"

"Yeah, but it's a mile or two beyond that. I think that's close to where William Cox's place is. I hope everything's okay."

A heavy suspicion stole over Jason that everything was *not* okay at the Cox place. "We'd better go see if he needs help."

Noah was already leading the horse to the side of the path, where he looped the lead around a low-hanging branch. The wagon, piled high with collapsible cots, a couple of barrels, and two crates full of odds and ends left over from Seattle's early lumberjack days, was far too wide to navigate the dense forest. Jason grabbed the rifle he'd borrowed from David and tossed Noah's to him, and then they took off through the trees.

315

Having been raised in the woods, Jason prided himself on his ability to tread silently, a skill necessary for hunting deer and other wild game to add to the camp's supper pot. He was glad to see Noah possessed the skill as well, and fell in behind him as they slipped from the cover of one thick tree trunk to the next. After every step or so, they paused to listen. The only sound besides the call of birds and the occasional scurry of an unseen animal was a distant drone that grew louder as they neared the source of the pillar of black smoke. A chill rose up his spine when he identified the sound as burning wood. A loud crack echoed toward them, as though of thick logs giving way.

The space between the trees in front of them grew lighter, and Noah slowed. The smell of smoke was stronger here, and now Jason glimpsed the glow of flames just ahead. Bending almost double, they crept forward, heads in constant movement as they scanned the area for signs of life. Nothing moved.

They came to a halt inside the tree line. In front of Jason was a wide clearing. On the far side stood the burning remains of a cabin, one wall still standing but the rest reduced to a pile of blazing rubble. A long rectangle at the other end of the clearing had been plowed for a garden, empty at this time of year. Between the two the ground was littered with what proved to be, on closer inspection, broken dishes and smashed furniture.

Noah let out an exclamation and dashed from the cover of the trees. At first Jason started to call after him to come back, but then he spied the reason. On the other side of the clearing lay a man's inert form. With a cautious glance around the area, he ran after Noah.

He came to a halt beside his friend, who stood looking down at the body.

"It's William."

Noah turned away, eyes closed, and after a glance Jason did too. Blood stained the man's clothing from at least half a dozen wounds, and three arrows were still embedded in his flesh. But the sight that Jason knew would haunt his dreams for years to come was far more gruesome. William Cox had been scalped.

"I don't see anyone else." Clearly shaken, Noah's head moved as he scanned the clearing. "I guess we'd better search the area. He has a wife and daughter."

Jason closed his eyes, trying not to imagine their fate.

Suddenly Noah dropped into a near-crouch. "Did you hear that?"

"What?"

"Someone's coming."

They both dashed for the cover of the trees. Once out of sight, they halted. Jason strained to hear the direction whoever-it-was approached from, praying it was from behind them and not ahead. He clutched his rifle in both hands, his finger hovering near the trigger. When the intruders burst into the clearing, it took a moment for their identities to register. At least twenty men swarmed through the trees and came to a halt as a group.

He recognized Big Dog towering over the others at the same moment Noah shouted, "David!"

Such a strong wave of relief hit Jason that he almost didn't trust his knees to hold him. They ran out to meet their friends who, to a man, wore grim expressions as they took in the grisly sight of the ruined cabin and its former occupant.

David Denny grabbed Noah and pulled him into a rough embrace, while Jason was subjected to a dozen handshakes and relieved exclamations. Before anyone could speak, a distant explosion blasted the air, rolling toward them over the tops of the trees. Jason instinctively ducked.

Noah's eyes bugged. "What was that?"

"A howitzer. We sent a messenger to Captain Gansevoort before we came after you." David glanced at the body and then cast a narrow-eyed look toward the woods. "We asked him to let everyone within earshot know the *Decatur* wasn't going to stand by and watch while people are killed."

Jason followed David's gaze. The skin on the back of his neck crawled with the weight of imagined watchers from inside the swiftly darkening shadows. "Think it'll make a difference?"

Noah shook his head slowly. "I don't know, but it sure makes me feel better."

Jason had to agree. If it came down to a fight — and judging by the destruction around him, it very well could — it was good to know they had a military warship on their side. Maybe that would provide a strong enough deterrent and no more lives would be lost.

A phrase from the past filtered through the fear that crowded his thoughts. *Some trust in chariots, and some in horses: but we will remember the name of the LORD our God.* The scripture rang in his mind, spoken from the pulpit by the minister of the church he and Beth had attended years ago.

Maybe now would be a good time to take up praying again in earnest.

FOURTEEN

Tension crackled inside the restaurant, so thick Kathryn could not force herself to sit still. Neither could Evie, who, between pacing between the front and back windows, scrubbed at the tabletops with such vengeance Kathryn wouldn't be surprised if she sanded right through. Louisa sat in a chair in the corner, rocking a fretful Inez and biting her lip until a drop of blood appeared.

"They'll be fine," Letitia Coffinger announced for the fifth time. Seated near Louisa, her hands busily worked a string of spun wool with two knitting needles. From the calm set of her shoulders and the domestic activity of her hands, she appeared completely unconcerned. But when Kathryn came near to refill her teacup, she saw the way the woman's foot tapped a nervous cadence on the floor.

"If my Miles were here, he would set these Nisqually people right in no time, and the

Mucklemoots and Cookiecutters too."

Louisa managed to flash a quick smile. "They're Muckleshoots and Klickitats."

The woman interrupted her knitting long enough to dismiss the correction with a brusque wave. "Miles has always maintained good relations with the natives, no matter what they call themselves."

Evie did not look up from her furious scrubbing. "Thank the Lord he's safe back in Tennessee, Letitia. If Chief Seattle couldn't talk sense to the chiefs of these northern tribes, Miles wouldn't stand a chance." With a suddenness that spoke to how close to tears she was, Evie halted her work and collapsed over the table, her head dropping onto her arms as she surrendered to sobs. "Oh, *where* are they?"

Kathryn rushed to her side. Her stomach was a mass of knots and tears lodged in her own throat. Her feelings for Jason were so new, so fresh and strong, they threatened to choke her. How horribly unfair to lose her love only hours after she had found him!

Lord, keep them safe! Please, please, please let the men find them in time.

She fought down a wave of rising panic and wrapped Evie's shuddering form in a comforting hug. "They'll be fine. I'm certain of it."

A lie, but a necessary one to calm her friend. Evie's sobs were nearing hysteria. Kathryn exchanged concerned glances with Louisa and Letitia, who had left their chairs to form a comforting circle around their friend.

After a moment, Evie made an effort to regain her composure. She straightened and used the corner of her apron to dab at streaming eyes. "I'm sorry. It's just so unfair."

With one arm supporting a sleeping Inez, Louise smoothed a lock of hair off of Evie's damp cheek and tucked it behind her ear. "What's unfair, dear?"

Evie's breath came in shuddering gulps. "That after — five years, God has f— finally answered our prayers. I'm going have a b— baby. And now I'll have to raise it alone!" Her tentative grip on composure crumbled and she threw her arms around Kathryn's shoulders and gave into renewed sobs.

Joy for her friend swelled in Kathryn's heart, tempered by the ongoing worry. How tragic for Evie's child to never know what a loving father he had. *Oh, Lord, no! Don't let that happen.*

Louisa gave an exclamation and threw her free arm around both Kathryn and Evie. Letitia stood nearby, patting her back with enthusiasm.

Kathryn hugged Evie tight. "Don't give it another thought. Noah is coming home soon."

"Kathryn's right," insisted Louisa. "Why, any moment they'll burst through the —"

The front door flew open. Startled, Evie raised her head and turned. Kathryn watched a stream of men file through, frantically searching each face. Her pulse thudded as she tried to read the news in their fierce expressions.

Then Evie gave a loud and joyful exclamation. She launched herself across the room and into the arms of her husband. Close behind him, Jason entered at David's side.

Tension fled Kathryn's taut muscles, and she grabbed at a chair to steady herself. She closed her eyes against the sting of relieved tears and forced herself to take several deep breaths as Big Dog's voice boomed in every corner of the room.

"Cox is dead, their house burned, but we found these two safe and sound."

"I'm all right," Noah said over and over, holding Evie close. "We were perfectly safe the whole time."

David was similarly occupied in assuring Louisa and little Inez, who had been awakened by the ruckus and was wetting her daddy's shirt with tears. "We met up with them at William's place. Didn't see any hostile Indians, but they did steal our horse and wagon."

"A small price to pay for your safety." Louisa rested her forehead against her husband's arm.

Though she tried not to show it, Kathryn's gaze strayed to Jason's face. She drank in the sight of him, safe and unharmed. Had she not been watching him covertly she might have missed the tightening of his features when he looked at Louisa. With a mumbled farewell to no one in particular, he turned on his heel and strode out of the restaurant.

It appeared as though Louisa was correct in her complaint. Jason was avoiding her. Or perhaps not. Perhaps it was *Kathryn* he wanted to escape.

Before she could reconsider, she launched after him. When she exited the restaurant, she caught sight of him hastening toward the Faulkner House.

"Jason."

At least he did halt and wait for her to catch up. Standing beside him in the darkness, his face lit by a half moon and a canopy of stars behind his head, her mind went blank. Even if she had been able to think of something to say, her tongue became unresponsive.

"I —" Frantic thoughts whirled in her head. She'd almost blurted out *I love you.* Instead she grasped upon the first thing that arose. "Evie's expecting a baby. Isn't that exciting?"

His face became a mask of pain. A paroxysm clenched the muscles in his throat. An instant later, the expression cleared and a polite smile settled on his lips. "How wonderful for her. Now if you'll excuse me, I've had a long day."

The speed with which he turned away from her resembled an escape more than an exit. In an instant, the reason for his avoidance of Louisa dawned on her.

"Jason." She spoke his name softly this time, and he stopped. "How did Beth die?"

For a moment she thought he wouldn't answer. She watched his rigid back, expecting him to mumble an excuse and hurry away. Finally, his shoulders moved as he heaved a breath, and then he turned to face her.

"In childbirth." His whisper held an agony that wrenched her heart. "She died giving birth to our son. He was stillborn."

Kathryn closed her eyes against his pain. "I'm so sorry."

When she opened her eyes, she found him staring at her with an intensity that set her pulse racing.

"You should leave, Kathryn. Leave on the next ship. Go home to the safety of San Francisco."

The fervor in his words stirred the embers of a fear that had cooled in the hours of worrying for his and Noah's safety. Now the flame burst forth with fury. She pulled her collar close about her neck.

"But what about you?" She blurted the question, and then averted her eyes. "I mean, you and Evie and Louisa and everyone else in Seattle. If this town isn't safe, then we should convince them to desert it. If the Indians want it that badly, let them have it."

He held his head erect, his eyes moving as he scanned the area below them. The *Decatur* floated in the bay, moonlight shimmering in the water all around her. Dim lights shone in irregular patterns on the land that stretched between them and the ship, candles and cook fires in use in the houses and buildings spread throughout the wide cleared town.

"This afternoon Noah told me how they came to this place. They've worked hard to carve out a life in this wilderness, and the

Duwamish natives welcomed them, worked alongside them to build this town. It's a big land, big enough for everyone. We *can* live peacefully together." She realized he was looking at the totem pole. Then he fixed those intense eyes on her. "I want to be part of that, Kathryn. Part of them. Red and white, living together in peace. There's nothing for me in Michigan, but *this* is a future worth living."

The passion in his voice stirred her. Oh, to have such devotion to a cause. No, to a people. To Evie and Noah, Louisa and David, Letitia, Big Dog and Red and Murphy.

But what of Will and his threats to expose her? Would the people whose friendship she had come to cherish turn cold toward her when they learned of her secret? In the days since their encounter, Will seemed to have resolved to ignore her completely. Perhaps he would continue. She certainly would not force another confrontation. If she did as he asked and stayed away from him and John William, they could coexist in the growing town. She could live with an uneasy truce.

She *wanted* to stay. The realization struck her like a slap. What had she in San Francisco? Mama and Papa, of course, but how could she return to her childhood home after having tasted the freedom of independence? Besides, Papa seemed determined to force her from beneath his roof and into the arms of whichever man would take her. Here, she could make her own life among friends and . . .

Her glance flickered toward Jason's face.

Looking quickly away, she rubbed hands that had gone suddenly damp on her skirt. "You speak so eloquently, I find myself convinced."

His head jerked in her direction. "What? No. Leave, Kathryn. Go home."

"But this is my home now." She waved toward the Faulkner House. "I have a job, and friends." With an upward tilt of her chin, she continued. "And I'm taking piano lessons."

He stared at her, his eyes growing harder with every passing moment. "I will never remarry," he ground out between gritted teeth. "No one will ever take Beth's place."

With that surprising announcement, he walked away. Stunned, Kathryn watched him stamp across the hotel's porch, jerk open the door, and slam it behind him. Her ears rang with the force of the banging of wood against the doorjamb.

Why would the mention of her piano lessons result in such a harsh and random pronouncement? They weren't even speaking of marriage. Or of art, which would bring his wife to mind.

Unless Beth also played the piano.

If that were the case, then he must suspect her of trying to imitate his deceased wife in order to win his affections. An uncomfortable flush began at the crown of her head and washed down her body, despite the chilly air. That meant he suspected her feelings and wanted to set her straight in no uncertain terms.

Perhaps going home to San Francisco was her best course of action after all. That way she would be spared the daily agony of seeing the man she loved and knowing he would never love her in return.

Tuesday, January 22, 1856

Now that the major part of the work on the blockhouse had been completed, Noah resumed his duties at the restaurant. Without painting or sandwich making to occupy her time, Kathryn threw herself into practicing the finger exercises Helen showed her. That is, until Madame stomped out of her sitting room complaining about the racket and forbidding her to touch the piano again.

"And I didn't pay all that money to ship this thing here to have hymns played on it, either," the rotund woman told Helen with a pointed stare before slamming the door in their faces.

With Jason's heated response from the previous night still echoing in her mind, Kathryn glumly informed Helen that she had lost the desire to learn anyway. Together they left the hotel and braved a cold Seattle drizzle to pass the time in Evie's cheery company.

Noah greeted them warmly. "Kathryn, just the lady I wanted to see." He cast a quick glance over his shoulder toward the store-room doorway, where Evie could be heard humming a lullaby, and went on in a near-whisper. "Do you think you could see your way clear to continuing to help my wife, at least with supper? Now that the fortress is finished, I need to get started on our home. With the baby coming, I don't want her climbing up and down that ladder any-more."

Kathryn agreed with a relieved sigh. "Of course I will." The prospect of long days with nothing to occupy her time — on top of a dwindling bankroll if she had to start paying for her meals — had weighed on her during the night.

"Thank you. Having you here makes her happy. She's grown fond of you."

She returned his warm smile. "And I've

grown fond of her too."

Moving with the ease of familiarity, Kathryn fetched the beautiful ivy teapot from the shelf, filled the kettle and placed it on the stove, and set the sugar bowl on the table where Helen had taken a seat. Worry over the loss of her job was not the only thing that had robbed her of sleep during the night. Jason's stern announcement played over and over in her head. Why did it fall to her to develop feelings for a man so twisted with grief that he could never return her love?

The water had just begun to steam when the restaurant door opened and a familiar figure ran inside. John William paused barely a second to glance around, and then shot across the room to embrace her with his trademark enthusiastic hug.

"John William, what are you doing here?" Fighting to control her alarm, she glanced toward the door as the little boy awarded a second hug, this time on the surprised Helen. Was the child in the company of his grandfather?

Instead, the sedate figure of Princess Angeline filled the doorway. She stood with her arms folded, the same multicolored shawl draped around her shoulders, and scanned the room with an unreadable expression. Rain had plastered her hair to her head and soaked her clothing.

Evie and Noah emerged from the storeroom. "Princess Angeline, what a surprise." Evie gestured her inside with a wave. "Please sit down. Would you like tea?"

The lady shook her head. "I bring a request from my people."

"What do you need?" Noah asked.

"Shelter. Their camps are no longer safe. An army of warriors gathers, and there have been threats against those who refuse to fight our white friends."

John William returned to Kathryn's side and slipped an arm around her legs. "There are a lot of new people in Princess Angeline's house." His childish voice trembled, and Kathryn placed a calming hand on his back to pull him closer. "They left their beds at home so they had to sleep outside last night."

"In the rain?" Compassionate tears flooded Evie's eyes.

The Indian princess dipped her head.

Noah scrubbed at his chin. "How many people are we talking about?"

In answer, the woman stepped aside and gestured behind her. Kathryn joined Evie and the others to peek out the doorway. Gathered around the totem pole were twenty-five or maybe thirty women, children, and babies. Kathryn's heart twisted at the sight of the little ones shivering in the rain.

"Oh, my." Evie glanced around the dining room. "I suppose they could stay here. We'd have to move the tables outside."

"I have a better idea." Kathryn glanced at Helen, whose eyes widened.

"She'll never agree," the woman whispered.

Kathryn folded her arms across her chest with a determined jerk. "We'll *force* her."

"Absolutely not!"

Madame Garritson drew herself up to her full height, the flesh in her jaws quivering with outrage. "This is a hotel, not a dosshouse for indigent Indians."

Kathryn topped her height by several inches, and made use of the discrepancy to glower down at the woman. "They are not indigent. They are temporarily displaced."

"Well, let them be placed elsewhere. I don't have a spare bed in the whole house, as you well know since you make them up every day."

"You can move the extra bed back into my room," Helen ventured. "If it will keep children out of the rain —"

"I will do no such thing. You paid for private accommodations and that's what you'll get." Madame's glower silenced the timid woman.

"Actually, I'm not suggesting you house them upstairs." Kathryn glanced around the Faulkner House's front room, empty but for the writing desk and the piano against the far wall. "I'm sure the ladies of Seattle can come up with extra blankets and the like. It would be tight in here, but I don't think they'll mind."

"*They* won't mind?" Madame's eyebrows rose so high they disappeared beneath her wiry hair. "I mind. And how long will they stay? Answer me that!"

"It's women and children, Madame. Their men say they will stay elsewhere, but we can't leave the young ones with no place to go. It's only until the threat of war is over."

"A war that may never come, according to some." The woman stalked across the room, flinging her arms wide to encompass the cavernous space. "Which means they might stay forever. What would it look like, letting a bunch of renegade Indians move into the front room of the Faulkner House?"

Kathryn stared at the woman, incredulous. "It will look like you have compassion on women and children who are even now

335

shivering in the cold rain."

Helen broke into their heated exchange with a quiet clearing of her throat. "If I might venture a question, I wonder how Captain Faulkner would answer the request." Madame gave her a sharp look, and she went on with a timorous smile. "I did make some inquiries before selecting Seattle, and my decision to come here was largely due to Captain Faulkner's reputation as a fair and honest gentleman of impeccable character. I was told he viewed this hotel venture not merely as a business pursuit, but hopes to make Seattle his home at some point in the future. I was also told he established strong relationships with the local Indians, whom he regarded as friends."

She lowered her eyes demurely, but not before exchanging a quiet grin with Kathryn.

"That's an excellent question, Helen." Kathryn turned a piercing stare on Madame. "Perhaps we should write to Captain Faulkner and prevail upon his sense of *humanity.*" She emphasized the word, as though to imply that Madame had none. "Of course, in the time it takes a letter to reach him and send a reply, some of those poor, freezing children may die of exposure. I'd hate to have to report that to him."

Madame's considerable bosom gave an indignant heave. "Well. It appears the decision is made. See that they're quiet and don't disturb the paying guests." She turned to stalk away with one final instruction. "And don't let the children touch that piano."

When she had gone Kathryn and Helen exchanged a triumphant smile. A minor battle won. Hopefully that portended well for winning the war.

FIFTEEN

A scream pulled Kathryn from a fitful sleep. She sat up in bed and strained to listen over the loud thudding of her heart. Then a clamor erupted beyond the wall at the foot of her bed — the shrieks of women and cries of children.

Her door flew open with a crash and Madame stood silhouetted in the doorway, hair gyrating wildly about her head. "It's happening! We're under attack!"

The panic in the woman's voice whipped Kathryn's blood to a gallop. Then she was gone.

The children!

Kathryn leaped out of bed and scooped up her heavy cloak on her way through the door. She barely noted that Madame's room was empty and the back door stood open. Instead of following, she dashed in the opposite direction, toward the front room.

She opened the door to pandemonium.

Terrified screams filled her ears as women and children struggled to shed themselves of borrowed blankets and vacate the crowded room. Footsteps pounded on the stairs as guests raced down.

"To the blockhouse," shouted a familiar voice. "Run!"

She spied Jason across the tumult, his arms waving people toward the front door as if he were shooing chickens. Moving like a mob, they poured through the doorway and into the pitch black outside.

In the center of the room stood a frightened native girl wearing a sleeveless cotton dress, sobbing in fright. People swarmed around her, desperate to escape. Kathryn scooped the child up on her way out.

"Hold on tight," she shouted above the chaos. Did the child even speak English? Apparently so, because thin arms clutched her neck and trembling legs wrapped around her waist. Pulling her cloak over the girl's body, Kathryn joined a stream of people who raced down the street for the safety of the fortress.

An Indian woman carrying a baby in one arm and a toddler in the other ran over to her side. She babbled something in her own language and nodded toward the girl, whose face was pressed against Kathryn's chest.

339

The child's mother?

"I've got her," Kathryn shouted. The woman dipped her head repeatedly, matching her step for step as their dash to safety continued.

The muscles in Kathryn's arms screamed from the unaccustomed weight as they ran up the knoll. The door of the blockhouse stood open, and a cluster of men had stationed themselves on either side, hurrying people inside. She recognized David as she ran through.

"Hurry." The urgency in his voice rose above the terrified cries. "Move as far inside as you can. We've got to make room for everyone."

Inside it was dark. Frightened people pressed her on all sides as Kathryn obeyed, plunging forward into the mass. A faint light shone in two rows of narrow windows, evenly spaced in all four walls, and she blinked to adjust her eyes. A narrow platform circled the perimeter, open in the center all the way to the roof and accessible by a crude ladder next to the door. A man's silhouette blocked one of the windows above her as he leaned his head to peer along the barrel of a rifle.

Where were Evie and Louisa? Helen? Impossible to see more than a foot or two in this pitch black. She identified the white, pinched faces of the Moreland girls, who were clinging to each other. Sobs filled the close confines of the building.

"Quiet in there," shouted a commanding voice from the entryway. Relief flooded through her when she identified the owner as Noah. He wouldn't be here without making sure Evie was safe. "We've got to be able to hear them coming."

The sobs became muffled as everyone made an effort to obey. Somewhere off to her right a man's voice carried on in a low drone. After a second she realized he was reciting the Lord's Prayer. He was joined by whispers from all over, and her lips moved in unison with theirs.

The backward press ceased as people stopped running inside.

"I think that's everyone."

That's Jason's voice!

She jerked upright and rose to her tiptoes, edging sideways to see toward the opening, but didn't catch a glimpse of him. The door swung closed, plunging them into near total darkness. What was he doing outside, exposed and vulnerable? Why wasn't he inside, where it was safe?

Minutes ticked past. Tension stretched her nerves to their boundaries. Her arms ached, and she shifted the little girl's weight to one hip. The child did not relax her grip. She'd lost track of the mother somewhere, and dared not set the girl down lest she lose her too. Silence, heavy with the strain of waiting, filled the crowded room. The combined heat of more than a hundred bodies in close confines became uncomfortable, and she wished she dared remove her cloak. But beneath she wore only her nightdress. Why hadn't she thought to pack an emergency bundle and keep it by the door?

A whisper from behind broke the silence. "What's happening?"

"Nothing, that's what." The answer, spoken in normal tones, was full of scorn. "Just as I said all along. There's nothing to fear."

"Oh? Then why are you here, Hillory Butler, instead of home in your bed?"

Kathryn knew that voice, and grinned at the disdain in Louisa's tone. Snickers sounded around the room.

Light broke through the darkness when the door cracked open. Dim and gloomy, but looking bright as the noonday sun to eyes grown accustomed to the blackness. The outline of a man appeared, and David's voice carried to the back of the fortress.

"It looks like this might be a false alarm, everyone. A detachment from the *Decatur* has been sent out to see if they can spot any activity in the area. We're waiting for their report before we know for sure."

Mumbles rose from the confined townspeople, some disgruntled but most of them relieved. Kathryn closed her eyes and whispered a prayer of thanks.

Ten minutes later the doors were thrown wide and David announced the all-clear. Weary people filed out of the blockhouse, their faces strained in the moonlight. Kathryn stepped to one side and scanned the crowd as they passed. She caught sight of the girl's mother and waved her to a halt. Setting the child on the ground, she gave her a final hug and then waved off the woman's profuse thanks. At least, she assumed that's what the string of unintelligible words meant.

When they headed down the slope toward the Faulkner House, she waved farewell. Her muscles ached from the unaccustomed activity. With a fist pressed against the small of her back, she looked around, toward the blockhouse.

And right into Jason's eyes.

Jason spied Kathryn as she filed out of the blockhouse in the midst of the throng. In her arms she carried a dark-haired native child on one hip, the same little girl he'd seen her rescue back at the Faulkner House. The sight of her sent emotions flooding through him. Relief, primarily. He'd lost track of her back at the hotel and searched for her in vain during the madness of people running to safety. During the past hour, as his ears strained for the sound of gunfire and nerves stretched to their taut limits, worry had plagued him. Had she made it to safety? Or fallen somewhere along the way, perhaps trampled by the panicked crowd?

Now his fears seemed groundless. Of course someone would have helped her if she'd suffered a mishap. There were more than two hundred and fifty single men in this town, and any one of them would jump at the opportunity to win her favor.

She turned and looked directly at him. A smile lit her face, visible even in the moonlight. The last time he'd seen such gladness in a woman's eyes had been two years ago. Beth used to look at him exactly that way.

A jolt punched him in the gut and left him reeling. Was Kathryn falling in love with him? When she started toward him, he fought an unreasonable urge to run in the opposite direction. If only his feet would move, but they had become rooted in the dirt.

"I hoped I'd find you," she said when she drew near enough for speech.

"Why?" He didn't mean to bark, and was embarrassed when the word snapped out as though he suspected her of something.

She frowned. "Because I saw you talking with David, and I wanted to ask what happened."

"Oh." He forced a calmer tone and fixed his gaze at a point behind her head. "Seems a boy named Milton Holgate shot a man trying to sneak through his sister's bedroom window."

Her hand flew to her collarbone. "Oh no. Who was it?"

"Nobody David ever heard of. Used to be a sailor, and obviously up to no good. Captain Gansevoort identified him as having deserted his post not long ago."

"Well." She looked out over the road and the townspeople streaming toward their homes, and her shoulders heaved in a weak laugh. "At least we got to practice our escape. Maybe people will be calmer when the real need arises."

She hesitated a moment, as though wondering if she should say something more, and then decided against it. Flashing a quick smile that held little resemblance to the one he'd seen a moment before, she made as though to leave.

"Kathryn, wait."

"Yes?" She turned back quickly, her expression eager.

Moonlight shone on her smooth skin, turning her eyes into orbs as dark as pitch. Strands of hair wisped around her face, freed from the confines of a long braid that hung over one shoulder. Standing there with the lace collar of her nightdress brushing against the fine line of her jaw, she looked like a young girl. He fought an almost irresistible urge to reach out and give her braid a tug.

Instead he shoved his hand in his pocket. "Are you sure you won't reconsider leaving? I'm told a ship is due in port Friday. Noah intends to pressure Evie into leaving on it."

"She won't go." Kathryn stated it as fact.

"She might if you go with her. You and Louisa, and as many of the women as can fit on board. Just until this blows over."

"And how long will that be?" She waited for an answer. When he gave none, she shook her head. "You said it yourself. They've worked hard to build this town, the women no less than the men. They won't leave." Her lower lip disappeared behind her teeth. "And neither will I."

A grudging respect for her devotion to her

friends blossomed in him. Was this the same arrogant, self-focused woman who rode through town with her nose in the air just two weeks ago? What had happened to soften her attitude?

"You will take care, though? Don't do anything rash or careless."

"Such as?" She tilted her head to fix him with a curious look that held a trace of humor.

"I don't know. Go for a walk in the forest, or" — he hardened his voice — "incite a riot, or anything."

Instead of taking offense, she laughed. "I promise."

She left, but not before giving him a teasing grin that left him staring after her with a distinctly unpleasant tickle in his stomach.

SIXTEEN

"I don't know about anyone else," announced Letitia, "but I intend to sleep in my skirts from now on. Traipsing through town in my nightdress was most humiliating."

Though it was not yet Thursday, a small contingent of ladies had gathered at the café at tea time to comfort one another and share their observations of the previous night's excitement.

Roberta Blaine tugged at her narrow waistband. "How terribly uncomfortable. I'm sure I wouldn't sleep a wink."

Kathryn noticed her empty cup and pushed the teapot across the table within reach. "A modern form of dress may be more appropriate for running. Back East women wear trousers."

Jaws went slack on a dozen shocked faces.

"It's true." She nodded eagerly. "I read an

348

article in a magazine called *The Lily* by Amelia Bloomer, who is a dear friend of Elizabeth Cady Stanton. Mrs. Bloomer insisted that a woman's tight waist and long, trailing skirts deprive her of all freedom. Trousers for ladies are a new fashion in New York."

From the next table, thirteen-year-old Sarah Moreland broke into the conversation with an enthusiastic exclamation. "I want to wear trousers! Mama, may I?"

"You most certainly may not!" Mrs. Moreland turned a scandalized stare on Kathryn. "The very idea. It's indecent, that's what it is."

Kathryn lifted her cup and hid her discomfiture behind the rim. She would have liked to turn in her chair to see how Evie and Louisa reacted to mention of the well-known reformers from New York, but she dared not. A display of too much interest would certainly focus attention on her liberal leanings, something she felt uncomfortable making known here in this traditional community.

"I'm not prepared to go all the way to trousers," said Letitia, "but I do intend to leave a pair of sturdy shoes by the bedside."

"Do you think we should send over some foodstuffs to be kept there?" Roberta extended her neck and pitched her voice to be heard on the other side of the room. "Louisa, what do you think?"

Louisa answered in a confident tone. "It's being seen to. But I think all of us should consider keeping a small supply of rations within easy access. I hope we'll have some warning when the real attack comes, but if not I don't relish the idea of starving in that fortress."

Tense nods of agreement met that suggestion, and the ladies began listing the items they would pack for an emergency.

Kathryn had barely fallen into an exhausted sleep when she was awakened by her door being thrown open. Madame's shriek filled her little room like a claxon.

"They've attacked! The war is upon us!"

It's a nightmare. I'm dreaming of last night.

But shouts from the front room pierced the walls like a rain of spears, and with her heart thudding, she threw off her bed linens. Thrusting her feet into the shoes she'd laid in readiness beside the bed, she grabbed her cloak in one hand and her emergency bundle in the other. Thank the Lord she'd taken the time to throw together a few things, though she'd intended to make a more thorough plan on the morrow. Now she might not have the chance.

The women and children in the front room were slightly less panicked than the previous night, but fear still showed starkly in their eyes. The cries of young ones echoed off the walls as mothers scooped them up and dashed out into the night.

With a quick, sweeping glance Kathryn searched for unattended children. Though chaos reigned, everyone seemed to be under an adult's charge. She spied Helen hurrying down the stairs, clutching her small valise to her chest with both hands, and she ran to her side.

"Is it another false alarm?" the woman asked as they joined the exodus together.

"I hope so," Kathryn replied, and then she had no more breath for words. Together they ran as fast as they could.

A crowd had amassed at the door of the fortress as people tried to squeeze themselves inside. Panting from the exertion, Kathryn stepped to one side to wait her turn. Some of the millworkers were stationed on either side of the door, urging the people to hurry. Where were David and Noah? And — she swallowed down a swiftly rising panic — Jason? A tide of townsfolk streamed up the hill, and she scanned them for a familiar face.

"Thank heavens I've found you." Letitia approached her and Helen from behind and looped a hand through each of their arms. "I thought earlier that we should arrange a meeting place so we can be sure of everyone's safe arrival. Evie and Louisa are already inside. Come with me."

She started toward the blockhouse with a determined stride, skirts swirling around booted feet. Apparently she had made good on her promise to sleep in her clothing.

"Wait." Kathryn pulled her to a stop. "I haven't seen Jason. What if he didn't hear?"

"He's a capable man, my dear. I'm certain he can take care of himself." Letitia started to continue, but something behind Kathryn caught her eye. Her lips twitched. "Now there's a sight I never hoped to see."

On the road below a trio of stragglers raced toward them. In the front ran Madame Garritson clutching a giant bundle, her fleshy figure bouncing with every step. As they watched, a tall man overtook her, white hair flying around his head and the tail of his short nightshirt flapping in the breeze behind him.

"Hillory, wait! Don't leave me!" The shout came from the third figure, a woman Kathryn recognized as Mrs. Butler.

Her husband either did not hear or chose

to ignore her plea. He overtook Madame at the foot of the knoll and passed her, arms and skinny legs pumping with renewed vigor as he dashed upward. Color flashed around his knobby knees.

"What is he wearing?" Kathryn asked, pointing.

Letitia squinted her eyes in his direction, and then burst out with a laugh. "Why, it's his wife's petticoat. I sold her the red flannel myself not three months past."

Despite the tension, or perhaps because of it, Helen and Kathryn shared a chuckle while Letitia stepped in front of the man, ending his flight. "Hillory Butler, I'm surprised you have the nerve to show yourself. You declared more than once that this blockhouse was an effort in futility undertaken by foolish men."

He drew himself up, gaunt chest heaving. "I have always been an ardent supporter of preparedness in any form."

Then he darted around her and dove through the crowd and into the fort, leaving his wife to follow at her own pace.

Letitia grabbed Kathryn's arm then and tugged her forward. Reluctantly, she allowed herself to be pulled along, craning her neck to search the area. Where was Jason?

The tension inside was no less than the

previous night as the people waited in the dark, straining their ears for sounds of fighting from beyond the safety of the sturdy walls. The crowd seemed bigger tonight. Maybe more people were becoming convinced of the danger. Kathryn clutched Helen's arm, and her thoughts formed a constant prayer.

Lord, keep us safe.

Keep Jason safe.

Time ceased to have meaning as anxiety stretched the seconds into agonizing minutes. Finally, when she feared her legs might collapse from the strain, a crack of moonlight appeared and the door was opened. A man's shape stepped into view.

"Another false alarm," came David's familiar voice. "Sorry, folks. We can all go home."

The frightened people filed into the night at a much more sedate pace, murmuring to their neighbors. Though they might have grumbled about a second interrupted night's sleep, or even voiced doubts of the necessity for another midnight flight, Kathryn heard only exclamations of relief. Judging by the number of people who had flown to safety, there were none left in Seattle who doubted that an attack was coming, and that it was imminent.

Outside the crowd spread out. She moved to the edge, letting people surge past her. At the far corner of the fort a small group of men stood watching the evacuation. Among them was Jason.

With a cry of relief, she started toward him, but then caught sight of the man standing at his side. Will Townsend, with a sleeping John William draped across one shoulder. She came to a stop.

Letitia, who had started down the hill with Helen at her side, stopped and turned an inquisitive look her way. "Are you coming, dear?"

"Yes." With a last look at Jason, she turned away. At least he was safe. "Yes, I'm coming."

She joined her friends for the journey home.

Thursday, January 24, 1856

Jason trudged up the hill, exhaustion weighing on his legs like there were anchors attached to his boots. Two nights in a row with no sleep, and the feverish pace at the mill to make up for the last two weeks when the men's attention had been distracted by construction of the blockhouse were finally catching up with him. He dug at burning eyes with his finger and thumb. He was only thirty-five, but tonight he felt like an old man. When he was younger he used to go days on a few hours of sleep.

The light shining through the curtains in the restaurant's front window created a pleasant picture in the swiftly deepening twilight. The sound of voices in casual conversation drifted through, along with the deep rumble of a man's laughter. The sounds, along with the scent of roasting meat, combined to create such a homey, comfortable ambience that the tension started to seep out of his muscles. With luck he'd enjoy a good meal, pleasant company, and a solid night's sleep. The thought cheered him, and with renewed energy he entered the café.

"There you are, Jason." Noah waved him over to the corner table, where the chair that had become regarded as his sat empty. "We were beginning to wonder if Henry chained you to the desk down there."

A contented sigh escaped his lungs as he doffed his coat. Something about this place appealed to him. Part of it was the story Noah had told him of its building. It represented tenacity and determination that were a trademark of Seattle's founders and, indeed, of the town. His coat deposited on a peg, he turned and looked around the room. Men lifted hands to wave or called greetings, which he returned as he made his way to his chair.

His gaze swept toward a familiar pair of green eyes that locked onto his, and his step faltered. Kathryn looked different. In place of the typical severe knot at the back of her head, she had arranged her hair into a pair of braids and fixed them in loops that dangled behind her ears. He'd seen similar styles on ladies back East, but none of them wore the arrangement to such effect. She looked . . . well, she looked lovely.

"You've met Captain Gansevoort, haven't you, Jason?"

He tore his eyes from her and focused on the uniformed man who had risen from his chair at Noah's introduction.

"Not formally." He shook the extended hand. "Jason Gates."

The captain nodded as he lowered himself into his chair. "You were with Denny the other night outside the fort."

"Yes, sir, I was."

"Jason's the mill manager down at Yesler's, and has been very involved in building the blockhouse." Noah turned his head toward Jason. "Captain Gansevoort came ashore to assure us of the *Decatur*'s support." He lowered his voice and glanced around to make sure no one could overhear. "Even though his superiors think we're a bunch of alarmists."

Jason looked at the man with interest. "They don't believe an attack is imminent?"

"They do not. I've received word from the governor informing me that such an attack was virtually impossible, but that I am to do what I can to, ahem, pacify the locals." With an apologetic glance at Noah, he lowered his gaze to his plate.

An empty mug was plopped down on the table in front of him, and Jason looked up into Kathryn's smiling face. His heart beat an uneven pattern.

"Would you like coffee?" She held up a pot invitingly. "Seattle's best."

"Sure." He slid the mug forward and watched as she poured dark, steaming liquid from the pot. "You've done something new to your hair," he blurted.

"Yes, I have." She lifted a hand and fingered one braided loop. Another wide smile, and then she said, "I'll be right back with your supper."

The hem of her skirt fluttered when she twisted sideways to slip between two tables. He tore his gaze away and focused on the man across from him.

"The governor said an attack is impossible?" He shook his head. "What is he basing his opinion on?"

"Well I can tell you one thing." Noah picked up his own mug and grimaced over the rim. "He's not listening to Arthur Denny. David had a letter from his brother in the last post assuring us that he was doing everything in his power to make sure the threat is taken seriously in Olympia. You'd think the governor would pay attention to the head of the territorial legislature."

The captain speared a piece of meat on the end of his knife. "No doubt that is why I haven't received orders to leave."

"That's something to be thankful for." Jason took a long sip from his mug.

Kathryn returned then. The plate she set in front of him held enough food for three men. Flashing another of those sweet smiles around the table, she left.

Gansevoort waited until she'd moved out of earshot. "How many hostiles do we estimate?"

Jason tore his eyes from her and looked at Noah, whose expression grew grim. "We had a report just this morning. Indian man by the name of Yoke-Yakeman, a friend of the Dennys who's proven to be a trustworthy source of information." He leaned forward and lowered his voice. "Close to two thousand, according to him, and more arriving from the north every day."

Jason sat back in his chair, his appetite gone in an instant. Even if every man in Seattle took up arms, the enemy outnumbered them eight to one. How could they possibly withstand an attack by an army of that magnitude?

"How many fighting men can we count on from your ship, Captain?"

The man answered without hesitation. "One hundred fourteen. We'll be on shore within minutes, and leave only a few on board the *Decatur*."

"And don't forget that howitzer," Noah reminded Jason. "That cannon nearly scared the stuffing out of me the other day. Let's hope it has the same effect on the hostiles."

Evie approached the table and slid into the empty seat on the other side of her husband. "What are you three talking about so seriously?"

Noah's expression cleared. "Nothing." He draped an arm casually across the top of her chair. "The restaurant looks extra fine tonight. Those pine boughs add a nice touch, I think."

For the first time Jason noticed the decorations hanging on the walls. Bundles of multicolored greenery had been artfully arranged and tied with bright-colored gingham. Small bouquets of decorative grasses strewn with tiny white flowers sat in the center of each table. The containers appeared to be jam jars, but each had been decorated with gay bows made from strips of fabric. No wonder the café looked extra homey tonight.

"I can't take the credit. Kathryn did it."

Evie beamed across the room, where Kathryn circled a table with her coffeepot, refilling the mugs the men held toward her. Red must have said something funny, because she threw back her head and laughed and gave his arm a playful slap.

Seeing that casual touch, the oddest feeling erupted deep in Jason's gut. He identified it immediately, and his stomach soured.

He was jealous.

With an abrupt gesture he pushed the plate away from him and stood. "I think I'll go back to the hotel now."

Evie eyed his full plate with dismay. "But you haven't eaten a bite."

"I'm sure it's delicious." He gave her an apologetic glance. "To be honest, I'm too tired to eat. I think I'll try to get some sleep before tonight's midnight dash through the streets."

361

With an apologetic shrug for the lame attempt at humor, he made a hasty exit. He did not look toward Kathryn as he left the restaurant.

Kathryn pulled her cloak around her shoulders and crossed the short distance between the restaurant and the Faulkner House in the dark. The supper crowd had lingered far longer than usual over their pie and coffee, talking of inconsequential things like the unusually mild winter and the hopes that it portended an early spring. Beneath the surface, tensions ran high. No one mentioned the blockhouse or the looming threat of attack, but she saw it in every face.

Clouds obscured both moon and stars, and she hurried through the grass, eager for the now-familiar confines of her little room where the light of a single candle could chase away every inch of darkness. Hopefully she would enjoy an entire uninterrupted night there.

As she mounted the first step, a dark form emerged from the shadows on the far end of the porch. She drew back, a scream gathering in her throat.

"Kathryn. Do you have a moment?"

Jason's voice reached her in the second before she screamed, and she swallowed her terror. Wilting against the post, she released a loud breath. "You scared me."

"I'm sorry. I didn't mean to."

"That's all right. We're all jumpy tonight, I think." A quiet laugh forced its way from her lungs. "Imagine the reaction if I shouted out that I was being attacked."

His chuckle joined hers. "I'm not sure the town can handle another night like the last two. I've been sitting here the past hour, enjoying the solitude. Won't you join me?"

He gestured toward the edge of the porch, and she seated herself with her feet dangling inches above the ground. He slid into place at her side, leaving a few inches between them. His nearness drew her like a warm campfire on a frosty night, and she had to force herself not to lean sideways to feel the touch of his arm against hers.

"You did a good job in the café tonight."

Did she imagine the quiver in his voice? Did nerves plague him the way they did everyone else in town? He always seemed so calm. "Evie is the cook, not me. And trust me, the entire town should be glad of that."

"No, I meant on the decorations. The wall hangings and flowers on the table. They gave the place a homey feel."

"Ah." She waved a hand vaguely in the air. "That's nothing but a few scraps of

363

leftover cloth and winter blossoms."

"No, really." He drew a foot up on the porch and rested an arm across his knee. Though dark with shadows, his eyes bore into hers. "That's a talent not everyone has, being able to arrange things in a way that puts people at ease."

"Imagine that." She turned away with a self-deprecating shrug. "I finally found my talent. I so hoped I would be an artist or a musician."

His hand rose, and he gently turned her face back toward his with the feather-light touch of a finger beneath her chin. Warmth spread from the place where he touched her.

"Allaying people's fears is a gift we desperately need right now, Kathryn. I . . . appreciate your ability to do that."

He spoke her name in a low, husky tone that sent a ripple racing across her skin. She answered in a near whisper. "Do you really?"

Unconsciously she leaned toward him, her gaze searching the dark pools of his eyes. The world around her faded, refocused, and narrowed to the few inches that separated her mouth from his. Her heart performed a crazy dance inside her ribcage. The only thing between her and Jason's kiss was a puff of frosty breath that seeped between her lips on a warm sigh.

He jerked upright, breaking the moment. "Uh, I wanted to talk to you about the ship due to arrive on Friday."

Disappointment washed over her, and she sagged back. "Oh?"

"I want you to leave on it, Kathryn."

That again? "We've already discussed this."

"Yes, but I urge you to reconsider." His head turned toward the hotel's window behind them and he lowered his voice. "The situation is far more desperate than I realized." He paused to wet his lips. "I'm praying for your safety. Every day."

"You are?" If he were praying for her, surely that meant . . .

He nodded. "But I'd rest a lot easier if you were safely back in San Francisco when this war breaks out."

She perked upright, the dance in her chest revived. Did she dare to hope? "Why, Jason? Why is my safety so important to you?"

In the quick pause that followed, she felt his mood shift. He hopped off the porch and took a backward step. Alarm stiffened his posture, and he answered in a loud voice.

"Because you're a woman. I'd recommend the same for every woman. In fact, I intend to. First thing tomorrow, I will speak to

Evie, and to David's wife, and to Mrs. Coffinger." His head jerked toward the hotel. "And Helen, and even Madame. Yes, you should all leave."

Kathryn observed his vehement declarations with blossoming hope. Of course he might be entirely sincere in his concern for the entire female population of Seattle. He probably was, and those fears were not unfounded. But was there, perhaps, one lady whose safety he desired above the others?

"I'm going to my room now," he announced as he dashed up the porch stairs. "I bid you goodnight."

Without another word, he snatched at the door handle, jerked it open, and disappeared inside.

Kathryn lingered in the cold, dark night, staring at the place where he'd sat a moment before. What would cause a reserved, solitary man like Jason Gates to babble in that manner? Could it be . . . love?

A giggle threatened, and she clasped her hands to her mouth to smother it. If Jason was truly praying to the Lord for her safety as he said, that meant at least once every day his thoughts were fixed on her. In the next moment the giddy sensation dimmed, and she wilted back against the porch post.

Wouldn't it be her luck to finally fall in love . . . just in time for a war that might very well end their lives?

SEVENTEEN

Friday, January 25, 1856

The day passed with agonizing slowness.
Kathryn hurried through her hotel duties
and returned to the café to spend the
afternoon in the company of her friends.
One didn't want to be alone at a time like
this, ears straining for the warning sound of
gunshots and nerves jumping at every creaking board or calling bird.

Apparently she was not alone in her need
for companionship. Throughout the long
afternoon the restaurant played host to a
dozen ladies who showed up with knitting,
mending, and other busywork. Afraid to let
the children play outside, they set up a table
for the little ones on one side of the room
and clustered together on the other. Their
talk centered on mundane matters like
recipes for cooking salmon and the rising
price of cotton wool. No one mentioned
Indians or the blockhouse or the war that

loomed over their heads like storm clouds.

In the afternoon the now-familiar call rang out, relayed over and over throughout the town until it reached their ears.

"Ship in the bay!"

Kathryn looked up from the frayed hem on a shirt she was mending, a gift for one of the Indian children. "Shall we go down to the harbor and meet the ship?"

The suggestion met with a lackluster response. No one, it seemed, wanted to stray that far from the blockhouse. With a sigh she returned to her busywork.

When she finished mending the garment she piled it in a stack of others that had been worked on by the ladies during the afternoon and left the restaurant to deliver the gifts. In the hotel's front room the Indian women greeted her with silent nods. On a less stressful day she would have been amused to see that they had arranged themselves almost exactly as their white neighbors, with the women sitting cross-legged together while the children played a game involving small piles of stones. Today she could not muster even a smile. The tension here was every bit as thick as next door. She delivered the stack of garments and went to her room. Perhaps she could read a bit of poetry to the children next door. The older ones might appreciate it.

Ten minutes later she headed back toward Evie's carrying four books. Keats would probably be a bit much for them, but perhaps they would enjoy Coleridge.

She approached the open doorway to find a woman standing just inside. She could only see her from behind, but her attention was drawn to an elaborately decorated bonnet. It perched atop a mass of dark curls that fell in deliberate disarray over a bright yellow shawl. Beneath the loose-knit wool blazed a dress of silky crimson, thick layers of yellow ruffles cascading downward from a bustle to dance around the hem. Her eyebrows crept upward at the short length of the hem and the pair of shapely ankles that clearly showed below the yellow lace. No lady in Seattle would possess such a garment. In fact, no *lady* would wear a garment like that in public, especially in a respectable establishment like Evangeline's Café. This woman must have arrived on the ship, though why she would parade through town dressed like that, Kathryn couldn't imagine.

She stepped into a shocked silence. A dozen pairs of eyes fixed on her. Their astonishment was so apparent she took an involuntary step away from the newcomer.

From where she was seated in a chair at the nearest table, Louisa's mouth fell open, her jaw slack.

"Oh. My. Word." Moving in slow motion, Evie pulled out a chair and sank into it.

The stranger let out a laugh. "Well I have to say, I'm used to drawing folks' attention, but you gals take the cake."

Wait. Kathryn knew that voice.

She turned and let her gaze sweep over the woman. The dress's hem rose to a risqué height in the front while the neckline plunged in a scandalous *V*. A liberal amount of rouge colored two smooth cheeks, and her lips had been painted the same bright red hue as her dress. A beauty mark rode high on her left cheekbone.

But it was her eyes that gave her away. Thickly lined lashes blinked over eyes the same shade of green as her own.

The painted lips spread into a delighted grin and the woman exclaimed, "Katie! What in the world are you doing here?"

Stunned, Kathryn reeled backward and managed to lean her weight on the doorjamb before her weak legs dumped her on the floor. She narrowed her eyes and peered again, trying to see through the thick face paint.

In a tone of utter disbelief, Letitia asked,

"Kathryn, do you know this . . . woman?"

The familiar stranger in front of her swept forward in a rustle of silk and lace to gather her in a hug. "Of course she knows her own sister. Right, Katie?"

Numbly, Kathryn nodded. "This is Susan," she managed to mumble. "She's my twin."

The café emptied in a hurry. Seattle's ladies hustled their children out of the restaurant with many a scandalized stare in Susan's direction. From her position near the window, Kathryn heard snatches of their hushed whispers as they hastened away.

"Did you see . . ."

". . . never in my life thought . . ."

". . . exactly alike . . ."

Kathryn's face burned, and an alarming buzz in her ears threatened to rob her of consciousness. Could it really be Susan, dressed like a . . . like a . . .

She couldn't finish the thought and stumbled on shaky legs across the room. She needed tea, and the stronger the better.

Louisa sent a protesting Inez home with Mrs. Moreland. Finally only Evie, Letitia, and Louisa remained. They seated themselves in a row opposite Susan, who was forced to perch sideways on a chair to accommodate her bustle. Their stares volleyed back and forth between the sisters.

"The resemblance is really quite remarkable." Evie's voice held a note of fascination.

Louisa, hands resting on top of her round belly, glanced up at Kathryn's face as she approached the table with a tray of empty teacups. "Except for the, uh, obvious differences, I doubt I could tell the two of you apart."

Kathryn set a cup and saucer in front of her sister. The "obvious differences" were embarrassingly visible, and she was torn between humiliation and stunned curiosity. What had happened to Susan to turn her into this . . . this . . . she couldn't come up with a word to describe her twin. Her tongue caught in a fit of paralysis, she couldn't muster a comment.

Susan had no trouble answering in an easy, familiar manner. But then again, she had always been the more talkative of the two.

"When we were real little sometimes even our parents couldn't tell us apart. Mama dressed us in different colors to keep us straight." The ruby lips parted to release a giggle. " 'Course, when we were older we switched clothes to fool them." She leaned over the table and lowered her voice to a conspiratorial whisper. "The only way to tell for sure is the mole on Katie's —"

"Who wants tea?" Kathryn asked in a near-shout, horror buzzing in her head like a bee. She most certainly did not want her anatomy discussed, even among her friends.

Susan sat back, a knowing grin twitching her painted lips. "I do."

Kathryn filled both their cups and then slid into a chair opposite Louisa. She pushed the sugar bowl sideways, within her sister's reach.

"No, thank you." Susan pushed it away, picked up her cup, and blew into the steam.

"You always sweetened your tea before," Kathryn remarked. Inconsequential, but her numb brain refused to focus on anything of import.

"Not anymore. Gotta watch this girlish figure."

"I can't imagine why." Letitia broke her unusual silence in a dry voice. "In that dress I'm sure there are a lot of others watching it for you."

Susan gave another giggle and winked broadly. "You know it."

An embarrassed pause followed the remark.

Evie broke her fascinated stare with a little

shake of her head. "Did you come to Seattle to find your sister?"

"I assume Papa told you where to find me," Kathryn said. Susan had been absent from the family for five years. What did their parents think when she showed up looking like . . . well, like this? She tried to imagine their reaction and failed.

"No. I haven't talked to him." For the first time, Susan looked uncomfortable. She fidgeted on the chair and fingered a ruffle on her skirt. Then she straightened her shoulders and the cheerful smile returned. "I heard Seattle has a whole bunch of men and they're just dying for a little social-izing." Her eyebrows waggled. "I heard some of the gals back in Yuba City talking. Seems there's a woman here who's open to giving a girl a chance. So I decided to see if there's any truth to what they said." She straightened and tossed her head with a flounce of curls. "I'm aiming to work at a place called the Faulkner House."

Kathryn exchanged a surprised glance with Evie. What were the odds that Susan and she, who had obviously traveled very different roads over the past five years, would both end up in Seattle working for Madame?

"What an extraordinary coincidence," she

375

said. "I work at the Faulkner House. Papa arranged it."

Now it was Susan's turn to look shocked. "*Our* Papa fixed it up for you to come to Seattle?"

Kathryn nodded. "The hotel manager is a distant cousin. Papa wrote to her several months ago and arranged for me to be her . . ." She cleared her throat. "Her assistant manager."

"This really is quite extraordinary." Letitia turned an excited expression toward Louisa. "I've heard of the peculiar connection between twins. This is proof. Somehow the two of them have come to the same place with the same purpose. It's remarkable, when you think about it."

Susan's eyes flitted down to Kathryn's dress and then up to her hair, a look of disbelief settling over her features. "What does an assistant manager do, exactly?"

Kathryn picked up her spoon and gave her tea an unnecessary stir. "Exactly what it sounds like. I help Madame in managing the hotel. I make sure the guests are comfortable, and their rooms are clean and —"

She was interrupted by a harsh laugh. "Trust me, honey. I'm not planning on cleaning any rooms."

"Well I wasn't either," Kathryn admitted.

"But when I arrived, Madame explained that a manager's first job is to keep the customers happy."

"Oh, I'll keep them happy all right." She extended a foot. "These shoes might look stylish and uncomfortable, but I can dance in them all night long. And if there's a piano I can sing like a bird." She gave another of those embarrassingly suggestive winks. "The more whiskey gets poured, the better I sound. 'Course some of my songs aren't exactly fit for Sundays, if you know what I mean."

Four mouths dropped open. Kathryn's breath had become trapped in her lungs, which threatened to explode with the pressure. Her twin sister was a *saloon girl.*

Susan's glance traveled around the table, and a chuckle sent her curls rippling around her head. "I can see by the looks on your faces you don't approve. That's all right. I'm used to that reaction from ladies like yourselves, but according to what I heard, this Madame Garritson understands that lonely men see things different."

"Oh?" Evie shot to her feet, her spine rigid and her face splotched. "We'll see about that!" She pushed her chair out of the way with enough force to send it crashing to the floor.

377

"I'll go with you." Letitia rose with a little more composure, though her expression was no less choleric than Evie's.

Mumbling something about retrieving Inez from the Morelands, Louisa hefted herself out of her chair and, with a sympathetic look toward Kathryn, followed the other two from the restaurant.

"Well." Susan picked up her teacup with measured nonchalance. "I guess Madame Garritson hasn't told those three about her plans for a dance hall, huh?"

A thousand questions burned in Kathryn's mind. What had happened to Susan to turn her from the daughter of successful financier into a saloon dancer? She glanced at the door. A dozen ladies had witnessed her arrival. No doubt word had already begun to spread through Seattle. At any moment, inquisitive townspeople might come to see Kathryn Bergert's twin sister for themselves.

She pushed her teacup away and stood. This was not the place to question Susan. "Let's go next door. My room is small, but at least it's private. We can talk there."

And perhaps then she could convince her sister to put on a decent dress.

"Goodnight, Jason."

Jason looked up from the ledger to find

Don standing in the doorway of the office. Was it quitting time for the second shift already? The evening had snuck up on him.

He tossed the pencil on the page and rubbed the indentation in his middle finger with the other hand. "I lost track of time. Did we get that shipment wrapped up?"

"Sure did." The man's chest swelled with justified pried. "We ain't never missed a deadline yet in all the years this mill's been cutting timber."

"Good job." He gave the man a congratulatory smile. "This is the smoothest mill operation I've ever seen, thanks mostly to you and Will."

"And to the best crew anywhere." Don's head jerked in a final farewell and he left.

Jason leaned back in the chair and watched through the window as the men filed out of the shed to disappear in the night. He stretched his back, which had been hunched over the desk since his supper of strong coffee, bread, and cheese left over from lunch. He eyed a stack of correspondence on the corner. Three more letters to answer. Problem was, now that he'd been interrupted, he'd become aware that his muscles were stiff — and his brain too. Probably couldn't put two words together that would make sense.

No, better head on up to the hotel and call it a night early. Of course he could stop by the café and grab a bite.

He rejected that idea. After last night's disturbing conversation with Kathryn, he wasn't ready to talk to her yet. Not until he'd had a chance to sort through the jumble of thoughts that crowded him every time her image rose unbidden in his mind's eye. And that was far more often than he was comfortable with.

Dousing the lantern, he left the office in time to join the last group of workers as they left the shed. He fell in beside them for the walk up the street. They acknowledged him with nods and continued their conversation.

"Yeah, Leonard said she was all get up like a fancy lady, full of smiles and such. Said she looked mighty purty."

Jason half listened to the man. What was his name? Bailey . . . or something like that. He didn't know the men on the second shift as well as the first since he'd spent so much time working on the blockhouse. Now that it was finished he was finally becoming familiar with them.

"I heard she even had feathers sticking up out of her hat," said another. Jason eyed him sideways. Harris. That was his name.

"No kidding?" Dorsey, one of the log setters, gave a low whistle. "Wish I coulda seen that."

"Think she'd still be at the restaurant? She stays kind of late, don't she?"

Jason jerked his head toward the man. The restaurant?

"Not this late," answered Harris. "But I'm gonna get up early and head over there for breakfast. Maybe she'll get all gussied up tomorrow too. Start a man's day right, it will, seeing a purty girl serving up flapjacks and eggs."

"Are you talking about Evie Hughes?" Jason asked. He couldn't imagine Evie wearing a feathered hat, but she'd certainly been more emotional lately. Some women were when they were expecting.

"Nah, not Miz Hughes. The new gal. Miz Bergert."

He came to a halt and stared at the man. "Kathryn?"

"Yeah," said Bailey. "Some of the guys said she came to town this afternoon all dressed up in a frilly red dress and with her hair all fancy. Smiling big as all get-out and cutting jokes with fellas. Said she invited them to come visit her up at the Faulkner House in a couple of days."

"Are you sure?" He shook his head, trying

to picture Kathryn in frills.

Harris shrugged. "Leonard's seen her at the restaurant enough to recognize her. Said she was acting friendlier than usual, though. He wondered if maybe she'd been . . . you know." He tipped an imaginary bottle to his lips.

They reached the crossroad then. The men bid him farewell and turned toward the row of small cabins that housed many of the mill-workers. Jason continued up the hill, more confused than ever.

What had come over Kathryn? She *had* been acting differently the past few days. Her new hairstyle, for instance. But a red frilly dress? And coming to town by herself after what had happened with the sailors a week ago? She knew better.

Her image loomed clearly in his mind, leaning toward him in the dark. On the porch last night he'd had the most disturbing urge to kiss her. But that was his idea, right? Or had he fallen victim to an accomplished coquette? Suspicions hammered at him. When he first saw her on board the *Fair Lady,* he'd pegged her for a flirt who'd come to Seattle with one goal in mind. To trap a husband.

Had he been right about her all along?

EIGHTEEN

Saturday, January 26, 1856

The restaurant was full to overflowing on Saturday morning. It seemed like every man in town had picked that day to have breakfast at Evangeline's Café. A steady stream of customers filed into the restaurant, filling every available chair. They even lined up outside, waiting for a seat to empty.

Kathryn hurried from table to table, filling plates and mugs and returning so many wide smiles her cheeks ached from the strain. Evie worked at a frantic pace, flipping hundreds of flapjacks. At the rate they were going they would run out of butter before they ran out of customers. To make matters worse, everywhere Kathryn looked she found herself the subject of dozens of wolfish stares such as she had not seen since the week of her arrival.

"What is going on today?" Evie asked as she slid a stack of cakes onto yet another empty platter. "Is the entire town suddenly starving?"

Kathryn held the platter steady and glanced uncomfortably around the room. "Maybe it's the strain of waiting for an attack." She made a face. "Though it's having the opposite effect on me. My stomach is so upset I don't think I could eat a bite."

Evie turned to her giant skillet and scooped up a mound of crispy bacon to add to the platter. "I hope things calm down soon so we can talk." She lifted a sympathetic glance and lowered her voice. "I want to hear about your talk with your sister."

Heaving a sigh, Kathryn nodded. Her talk with Susan had not been very satisfactory. Or enlightening, either. When they were girls they had talked about everything, had shared every thought, every detail of their lives. Many a time Mama had come into their room in the early morning hours and sternly informed them that their voices were carrying through the walls and that they were keeping the house awake.

But that had been a different Susan. This one delivered a tale of an exciting life working a series of saloons, most recently in Yuba City, which she declared she enjoyed to the fullest. Then, pronouncing herself exhausted from the journey, she had taken possession of the narrow bed and fallen into a deep sleep. Kathryn had begged a spare blanket from Madame — who was much subdued after her conversation with Evie, Louisa, and Letitia — and spent a fitful night on the hard floor, listening to her twin snore. Susan had still been sound asleep when she left this morning.

Speaking of Madame.

She leaned over the platter and whispered to Evie. "And I want to hear about *your* talk too."

Evie opened her mouth to reply.

The door flew open with a crash. A vaguely familiar Indian woman stood in the doorway. Kathryn barely had time to recognize her as Princess Angeline's friend, the one who'd delivered the news of the disaster at the Cox's cabin.

"The Klickitats are coming!" Her scream filled the dining room, an edge of hysteria making her voice shrill. "*Hiu Klickitat copa Tom Pepper's house!*" She turned and fled, her squat legs pumping as fast as she could make them go.

"What'd she say?" someone asked in the stunned silence.

"I think she said there's a bunch of Klickitats around Tom Pepper's house. That's down on the eastern edge of town."

At that moment, an explosion blasted through the air. It vibrated in Kathryn's ears, and she felt the rumble through the soles of her feet.

The room erupted in chaos. Chairs flew as men leaped out of them. Noah descended the ladder leading to the living quarters on the second floor. He leaped to the ground from halfway up and crossed the distance to his wife in two paces.

"Evie, let's go." Grabbing her hand, he jerked her forward.

As she was pulled toward the door, Evie reached a hand toward Kathryn. "This is it. Come on."

Kathryn's mind raced. Her emergency bundle was in her room. No time for that now, but —

"Susan!"

Her sister would have no idea what was happening or where to go. She whirled in the opposite direction and dashed out the back door, heading for the hotel.

Jason finished his tally of the stacked milled lumber and turned to Will. "That's it. Every last board counted and ready for loading."

Will opened his mouth to reply, but then shut it. His gaze fixed on something behind Jason. "What's he doing —"

386

"They're here!"

The urgency in the shout left no doubt about who "they" were. Jason whirled to see a man tearing through the sawmill shed, leather-clad arms waving wildly at the men. He barely had time to recognize David's Duwamish friend, Yoke-Yakeman, before the man completed his circuit and raced through the far end, still shouting, "They're here! They're here!"

The workers sprang into action. Men dropped what they were doing and ran for the road, feet pounding and unintelligible shouts filling the air.

"Somebody's got to send word to Captain Gansevoort," shouted Will.

An answer was yelled from the midst of the crowd. "They already did!"

Jason ran to the bay side of the shed. The water between the *Decatur* and the shore was dotted with rowboats filled with sailors, pulling against the oars with astounding speed as they headed for the dock. A flash and an explosion erupted on board the warship's deck. The howitzer. A few seconds later an answering blast sounded from somewhere beyond the town as the missile found a target. A cloud of black smoke exploded into the sky in the east.

Pulse racing and thoughts racing faster,

Jason bounded toward the office where his rifle lay in readiness beside the door. Then he joined the throng in a mad sprint for the blockhouse.

Lord, help us!

The ground flew beneath his feet. All around him grim-faced men gave their all to the race for safety. Sounds reached his ears, the retort of gunshot echoing off the clapboard buildings. Gunfire. And the shrilling whoops of Indians at battle that chilled his blood. The noise came from the direction of the blockhouse. Hands clasped around the rifle's stock, he pushed his legs to greater effort.

When they reached the knoll, people were already streaming through the door. Flashes ignited in the upper and lower windows, and in a glance he saw the thin, deadly barrels of rifles protruding through the loopholes. Screams filled the air, women and children and more than a few deep male voices, as bullets whipped over the heads of the people who scampered for the doorway, stark terror apparent in their faces.

Was Kathryn already inside? Was she safe? If only he had some way of knowing . . . but there was no time. He caught sight of a familiar face and sprinted the last few feet, screeching to a halt at David's side.

"Get these people inside," the man yelled, and, leaving Jason in charge, darted around to the other side of the fortress.

Jason waved his hand above his head, shouting to be heard over the people's cries. "Hurry. Make room in there."

A little boy fell and his panicked mother shrieked. Intent on getting to safety, people swarmed around him, and the terrified child curled into a knot on the dirt, head buried in his arms. Jason dashed through the crowd and snatched the boy up. Thrusting him toward his mother, he gripped her arm and propelled her forward, releasing her only when she was safely inside.

The blockhouse was nearly full, the running stream of people reduced to a frenzied few. Noah and Evie ran up together. Her face was white as paste.

"Have you seen Kathryn?" he shouted as a gunfire crackled from somewhere behind him.

They all ducked instinctively.

"I don't know where she went," Evie yelled back. "She was right beside us, and then she was gone."

They turned to scan the road, and then Evie let out a screech. "Louisa!"

Jason looked where she pointed. Louisa Denny ran down the center of the street.

She held her daughter tight over her swollen belly, clutching a pouch of her apron in one hand. Another volley of shots rang out and she bent over in a crouch, but did not slow. A blur from the corner of the blockhouse caught the corner of Jason's eye, and then David dashed down the hill toward his wife.

Breath slammed in his lungs when Jason's gaze fixed on a pair behind them. Two women were running all-out toward him, arms locked together at the elbows. A mass of dark hair flew out behind one like a mane, while the other —

Panic blurred his vision.

The other's hair flopped in twin braided loops dangling around her ears.

Shots cracked. A dozen mini-explosions flashed from the forest to his left. A barrage of bullets and arrows flew through the air.

One of the women stumbled.

"Kathryn!"

The scream ripped from his throat, while horror spread over him. Kathryn tumbled to the ground and lay there, unmoving.

Jerked to a stop by Kathryn's fall, the other woman looked down on her prone body. And then she too collapsed.

Jason flung himself down the hill before he could think about it. Brain numb, thoughts frozen, he flew toward the prostrate pair and reached them a split second before Noah. Dirt sprayed when his boots skidded to a halt.

"Kathryn, are you —" He stopped, words arrested by a tongue dazed with shock. He looked from one unconscious face to the other.

There were *two* Kathryns.

"I've got this one," shouted Noah, and grabbed up the one in the nightgown.

A bullet whipped through the air above Jason's head. Forcing his dead limbs to move, he grabbed the other. When he hefted her in his arms, something tumbled to the ground. A dark brown braid. He couldn't make sense of that now. Snatching it out of the dirt, he whirled and carried the inert form to safety.

Kathryn swam to consciousness, the air around her thick with the smell of gunpowder. The crack of gunshots ricocheted off the walls, fired from every direction around her. The noise was deafening. Even worse were the high-pitched whoops that penetrated the fort from outside, ferocious battle cries echoing toward them from the forest. The savage screeches chilled the blood in her veins.

"You're all right. You're safe now." Evie's voice, soothing and comforting, was accompanied by something cool and wet pressing against her forehead. She opened her eyes to find her friend's face hovering over hers.

"What happened?" Her memory was a foggy jumble. The battle had begun, that much she remembered. She'd rushed to the hotel, jerked Susan out of a deep sleep, and dragged her, protesting, outside.

"You fainted, that's all." Evie picked up her hand and pushed her fingers in place to hold the compress to her own forehead.

"Again?" How utterly embarrassing. When had she turned into one of those fluttery women who swooned?

"Apparently it's a family trait," her friend said drily. "Your sister fainted too."

She pointed to a place a few feet away, where Susan sat propped against a post, her hand trembling as she held a cup to her lips. People huddled all around her, most of them seated on the dirt floor, faces pale in the glow that shone through the slitted windows. Dust motes danced in the light, whirling around the heads of the men who stood at every opening, upstairs and down, rifles pointed outward.

Another battery of shots volleyed around

them, and nearby a child's crying took on a fevered pitch. The import of her situation struck her, and she jerked upright. The war had begun.

Evie tried to push her back down, but she waved her friend off.

"I'm fine. Let me help someone who needs it. Are there many wounded?" She hesitated, almost afraid to ask. "Or . . . killed?"

Amazement stole over Evie's features. "None so far. A few gunshot wounds, none of them too serious."

A child near the far corner stood from where he had been sitting with a group of other youngsters. He dashed around the perimeter of the crowd in her direction.

"Miss Kathryn!"

The poor boy's face crumpled as he drew near, and she opened her arms. Sobbing with fear, John William threw himself into them. Forget what his grandfather might say. For now, the child needed comfort. She hugged him close.

"It's okay," she whispered. "Everything's going to be okay."

When his wretched shivers stopped, he pulled back to look up at her with round eyes. He lifted a hand and tugged at her hair. "You look funny, Miss Kathryn."

"I do?"

She reached up to feel her braid, and her fingers grasped ragged ends. It all came back in a rush. The mad dash down the street with Susan. Louisa running ahead of her. The blockhouse looming in the distance. The fear, the stark *terror* as a bullet blasted into the dirt not two yards away. She'd spotted a familiar figure standing at the top of the hill, tall and beckoning, and her heart had leaped into her throat. Jason! She'd wanted to sob her relief, but she couldn't waste the energy.

And then something whizzed by her head. A bullet! She heard it whoosh past her ear like a tornado. A pungent, burning smell. Her hair was on fire. She'd reached up, grabbed her braid, and it came off in her hand, the edges singed. And then everything went black.

"They shot straight through my braid." She looked up at Evie for verification.

Her friend nodded and pulled something out of her apron pocket. She tossed it into Kathryn's lap. "Jason picked it up when he went after you."

"Jason came after me?" Tears leaped into her eyes, blurring Evie's nod. Furiously, she blinked them away. "Where is he?"

Evie's head lifted to scan the upper perimeter. "There." She pointed to the platform above them.

Kathryn twisted around to look, and her gaze locked with his. Jason! She saw his lips move, saw them form her name. Emotion rose up in her, so thick for a moment she couldn't breathe. His eyes blazed with an intensity she could see even in the dim light, even across the distance, and it wrapped around her like an embrace.

Then he turned back to the window and lifted his rifle back into place.

Another torrent of shots pounded against the thick wall behind her. A new chorus of screams arose from the terrified people in that vicinity, and the ones seated closest to the wall scurried toward the center. Susan yelped and closed the space between them on her hands and knees, where she hovered beside Kathryn, trembling.

"What kind of place have I come to?" She squeezed her eyes shut and buried her face in Kathryn's shoulder. "I shoulda stayed in California, where it's safe."

John William leaned back in her lap to look at the newcomer, and surprise flashed onto his features. Tears forgotten, he lifted a hand to stroke Susan's cheek.

"There's two Miss Kathryns," he said to Evie, his eyes full of wonder. "Only that one still gots all her hair."

A wild desire to laugh seized Kathryn. She swallowed it back. A ferocious fear hovered over her, and she was afraid if she started laughing she would give in to hysteria. Instead she forced her tone into a semblance of normalcy for the boy's sake.

"There aren't two of me, sweetheart. This is my sister, Miss Susan. Susan, this is John William."

Susan lifted her face to peer at the child. A quick, nervous smile flashed onto her lips. "Hello. Aren't you a cute little . . ."

Her voice trailed off, and her mouth inched open. She stared at the child, jaw dangling. A look of utter disbelief stole over her features.

In a flash, everything fell together. Will's accusation rang in Kathryn's ears even louder than the retort of the rifles.

"Does your father know what you really are, or have you fooled him along with everyone else?"

"I don't know what game you're playing but I will not let you ruin everything. We're happy here."

All the time she thought he knew her secret. That he would expose her for being a criminal. But she was wrong.

He thinks I'm Susan.

And that meant he knew Susan from somewhere. With eyes that felt like they were finally open for the first time, she looked at John William. The time she'd seen him biting the tip of his tongue, he'd looked so much like Papa. The round green eyes, so very similar to her own. The same color as hers . . . and Susan's.

From his vantage point on the upper deck, Jason counted the pillars of smoke visible through the loophole. Eight, and that was only on the east side of town. How many homesteads had been ransacked and burned? How many lives lost? He turned to scan the people crowded below him. Nowhere near the three hundred souls who called Seattle home. Had their senses of danger dulled with the repeated false alarms, or had they been too terrified by the actual attack to escape?

The gunfire from the forest had slowed to a few scattered shots twenty minutes ago, and then ceased completely. One of Captain Gansevoort's scouts reported that he'd heard a squaw shout *hyas muckamuck,* which David translated as *lots of food.*

"Do you smell that?" Beside him, Noah pointed his nose in the direction of the window and sniffed. "They've butchered our livestock for sure and roasted them for lunch."

Beyond Noah, Big Dog turned a wry scowl on him. "It'd be nice if they'd share. My belly's as empty as a rain bucket with a hole in the bottom."

"Here." Noah scooped a bulging scrap of linen off the floor near his feet. "It's only a biscuit, but it's better than nothing."

"Where'd you get that?"

His shoulders shook with a quick laugh. "Louisa Denny. She said she was pulling them out of the oven when the alarm came, so she dumped them in her apron, grabbed her daughter, and left."

Jason looked down to find Louisa, but his gaze stole once again to the place below him where Kathryn and her sister sat in a small cluster of women. Twins. With a hand that smelled of sulfur he scrubbed at his scalp, as if he could force his thoughts into something that made sense. The frenzy of the past eight hours had left him too bone-tired to think straight.

To his right, Will had claimed a seat on a half-empty gunpowder keg. He, too, stared at the pair, his expression one of stunned disbelief.

"All this time, I thought it was her." His head shook back and forth. "I thought she'd given a false name to deceive me until she could make arrangements to take him."

"I can see why you'd think so." Though he had not yet seen Kathryn's sister up close, the resemblance from this distance was so striking as to be uncanny. "I couldn't understand why you hated her so."

"I can't bear the thought of losing him." The agony in his voice snatched at Jason's heart, and he followed his gaze to the boy, John William, who was seated between Kathryn and her sister. "She didn't want him. John told me so. He met her in a saloon in El Dorado and fell for her. I went and saw her dance there once. Didn't tell her who I was." His glance slid sideways to Jason's face. "He would have married her when he found out there was a baby coming, but she wouldn't have him. Said she was too young to be tied down to a husband and child. When the boy was born she gave him to John. A month later she left town. My son brought my grandson home. To me. And then he was killed." He closed his eyes, pain etched in the creases on his face. "I made inquiries about her, found out her father was a wealthy man. I was afraid he'd come for his grandson. My grandson."

"So you came here, to Seattle."

"I never thought she'd find us here." He

turned sideways on the keg and fixed an intense gaze on Jason. "I can't lose him, Jason. John William is all I have left of my son. And I — I love the boy."

Jason clasped his shoulder with a sympathetic grip. He had no answers. Did a grandfather have rights in this situation? It was a question for legal minds, not his. Perhaps David would write to his brother Arthur in Olympia. With the Dennys vouching for Will's character, he might have a chance.

Unless Kathryn's sister could claim that he was unsuitable to raise a child. Another answer fell into place in his mind.

"You stole the oil of turpentine from Kathryn, didn't you?" He pitched his voice low.

Will gave a miserable nod. "I thought if I discredited her, people would discount her claim when she finally made it. I wouldn't have struck a match, Jason. I wouldn't do that."

He squeezed the man's shoulder. "I know."

A movement below them drew their attention. A woman moved slowly among the frightened people, bending here and there to whisper a word of comfort. Jason recognized Miss Everett — Helen — as she ran a hand across the forehead of a crying child.

The gesture calmed the child, and his mother squeezed Helen's hand gratefully. As she moved away, Helen lifted her gaze to the platform where they sat. For a moment Jason thought she was looking at him. Her expression softened into one of compassion, and beside him, a soft moan escaped Will's throat.

"How will I ever face the people of this town?" The man lowered his head and covered his eyes with a hand.

Jason was still searching for an answer when the crack of gunfire sounded from the direction of the forest. Within a few breaths, a second followed, and then a third. The men stationed around the perimeter of the blockhouse leaped into action. Jason snatched the rifle from where he'd leaned it against the wall during the lull. Apparently their attackers had finished lunch and were ready to fight again.

Nineteen

The afternoon stretched into evening, and the tension inside the blockhouse approached unbearable proportions. As evening fell, Kathryn joined those gathered around Reverend Blaine for a time of prayer, a sleeping John William draped over her shoulder. He had attached himself to her and refused to leave her side all day.

The worst part, Kathryn thought as the minister concluded his prayer, was the silence. Though she would have never dreamed that anything could be more terrifying than the sounds of battle, the absence of those sounds stretched her nerves taut. After the fierce morning's battle, the fighting had never regained momentum. Throughout the afternoon the men protecting them had exchanged a few shots with their enemy, firing blindly into the forest, but nothing that approached the frenzied fighting of before.

She left the prayer circle and returned to the corner in which she and her friends had gathered all day.

"Do you think it's over?" Louisa clung to Evie's arm for support as she lowered herself to the ground.

"I hope so." Evie settled beside her and arranged her skirts around her legs. She lifted a worried face toward her husband, who stood watch on the platform. "Do you suppose there's anything left of our town?"

Susan roused out of the solemn silence she'd maintained for most of the day. "I sure hope they didn't get in the hotel. Everything I have in the world is in there."

Kathryn hugged the sleeping child in her arms and said nothing. The story of John William's birth had come out slowly, in snatches whispered between volleys of gunfire. All afternoon her thoughts had circled around a single question. How could her own sister, her *twin,* walk away from her baby? In fact, how could she do any of the things she described? The woman seated beside her, once the closest person in the world to her, had become a complete stranger.

The sound of men's voices reached them from outside. Not the urgent, intense whispers they'd strained to hear all day, but men

403

speaking in normal tones.

Louisa jerked upright. "Something's happening."

A moment later, the blockhouse door opened. Twilight flooded the gloomy interior, along with crisp, cool air scented with that distinct blend of the sea and forest that was uniquely Seattle. Kathryn drew deep draughts of it into her lungs.

David stepped into the center of the doorway. "It's over, folks."

A cheer rose from every throat, male and female. Kathryn's gaze flew upward, where Jason stood between Noah and Will, his fist raised in victory. The triumphant grin he fixed on her sent her heart soaring.

"You can come out," David told them. "Captain Gansevoort's men have scoured the whole area. No sign of an Indian warrior within five miles of here. We'll post a watch throughout the night, but it looks like the hostiles have lost their thirst for white men's blood."

Holding tight to a still-slumbering John William, Kathryn filed outside, where she stepped to one side and drank in the sight of the swiftly darkening sky. She scanned the relieved faces of the steady stream of people exiting the fort. Not until the last of the townspeople had exited did her gaze light on the one she longed to see.

Jason's head turned as he searched the area. When he caught sight of her, his face lit and he hurried to her side.

"Kathryn." He spoke her name in a husky whisper that sent her heart into a wild dance.

In a moment they were surrounded by their friends. Noah's arm circled Evie's waist protectively, while David gently lifted Inez from Louisa's arms and then wiped a tear from her face.

"We're safe." He tore his gaze from hers and looked at Evie. "Our homes are un-harmed, and the restaurant. I'm afraid the dry goods store was ransacked."

"Oh, no." Kathryn scanned the crowd. "Poor Letitia."

"One of Gansevoort's lieutenants is al-ready accompanying her there to assess the damage. At least it's still standing." His expression became grim. "Most of the outlying homes have been burned."

Evie tightened her arms around her hus-band's waist and asked in a fearful voice, "How many people were killed?"

Wonder crept over David's features, and his lips softened into a wide smile. "Not a single one, as far as we can tell."

"It's a miracle," Kathryn whispered.

Jason nodded, a look of fierce wonder on his face. "It truly is. With all those bullets and arrows flying, that's the only explanation."

Kathryn smiled at him. "God heard your prayers."

"Well, we didn't all escape unscathed." Jason reached toward her face, and her heart slammed to a stop as she anticipated the touch of his finger against her skin. Instead he grasped a ragged lock of short hair and tugged on the burned end. Everyone laughed.

"There's no way to tell if our attackers will come back, but Captain Gansevoort thinks they've run out of ammunition for the time being." He grew serious. "I think it would be a good idea to build another blockhouse, and maybe even a stockade."

After the day just past, confined in close quarters in a dark building, Kathryn couldn't agree more. A noise behind her alerted her to someone's approach. She turned . . .

. . . and looked directly into the face of Will Townsend.

He looked miserable. For a second he fixed a tortured gaze on her, and then his head dropped forward as though he could not bear looking at her.

"I owe you an apology."

Kathryn glanced at her sister, who stood a little apart from the others, watching him through narrowed eyes. Pity for him stirred in her. Imagine the fear the man had lived with since her arrival. How horrible to have the threat of losing his grandson hanging over him.

"You don't owe me anything," she told him softly.

"Yes, I do." He stared at his boots, but spoke loud enough for everyone to hear. "I thought you were — her. I took your bottle from the hotel's back porch and planted it in the blockhouse to incriminate you. I hoped that if the townspeople suspected you — or her — of a terrible crime you would be forced to leave Seattle." He looked up at her. "I spoke badly of you, both behind your back and to your face. Then I threatened you, accused you of deception." His glance flickered sideways, toward Susan, and then settled back on her. "I was wrong. I truly hope you can forgive me."

Those around them remained silent, waiting for her answer. In the faces of Evie and Louisa, who had become her friends, she saw that they would staunchly support her no matter what she answered.

But of course there was no question of

withholding her forgiveness. "If my father was in your position, I hope he would be just as staunch in his support of his grandson. Of course I forgive you. I hope we can be friends." She stepped forward and transferred John William into his arms. The boy tossed his head, eyes still closed, and then nestled into the soft skin of his grandfather's neck.

He gave her a grateful look, and then his forehead creased. "One thing I don't understand. Why didn't you speak out when I accused you that day at my house?"

Now it was her turn to avert her eyes. Her secret would come out one day. Why not today? She couldn't live with the threat hanging over her head any longer.

"I mistook your accusation for something else. I thought you were threatening to tell everyone" — she clasped her hands together in front of her apron and looked up at Jason — "of my arrest in San Francisco six months ago."

Jason's eyes widened. "You were *arrested*? For what?"

She swallowed hard. "For chaining myself to a flagpole along with two dozen other demonstrators protesting the unfair treatment of women. I spent an afternoon in jail."

Evie stepped forward, eyes alight. "You're a suffragette?"

"How exciting!" Louisa actually clapped her hands. "As soon as the baby is born, let's all make ourselves trousers and parade down Mill Street."

"What?"

The look of consternation on David's face elicited peals of laughter from his wife. "Come on, dear. We'll talk about it on the way home."

She looped her arm through his and they wandered off, Evie and Noah right behind them. With an unreadable look in her direction, Jason followed, but did not leave the knoll. Instead he joined a group of millworkers talking with some sailors, but his eyes strayed continually in Kathryn's direction. What did he think of her now? Before the night was over, she would find an opportunity to pull him aside. After all, she had yet to thank him for carrying her to safety. The idea sent her pulse into an acrobatic tumble.

For a few seconds after they left, an uncomfortable silence fell between the remaining trio. Will shifted his weight from one foot to another so often he almost appeared to be dancing with the sleeping boy.

Finally, he blurted to Susan, who had

maintained a distance of several feet from the others. "I'll pay you."

Susan's head jerked toward him. "What?"

"To leave Seattle and never come back. Leave John William with me. I've got some money saved up, and I'll give it to you."

A scornful snort blew through her lips. "You can't buy a baby."

He took a forward step. "I wouldn't be. I'd be paying your expenses to start a new life somewhere else. Somewhere far away." When she would have said something else, he cut her off. "Don't turn me down outright. Think about it. The ship you came in on leaves tomorrow."

Before she could answer he hurried away, clutching the boy close. Kathryn and Susan stood watching as he strode through the small number of townspeople who remained in the vicinity. At the top of the knoll, a waiting figure separated herself from the crowd and joined him. After exchanging a brief word, he and Helen disappeared down the hill together.

"Huh. I never thought I'd see my kid again." Susan's chest heaved with a silent laugh. "Or you. Imagine you spending a day in the hoosegow. Never would have guessed."

Kathryn bit down on her lip. "Papa would

have conniptions if he ever found out."

A smirk twisted the lips so like her own. "Honey, Papa would have conniptions about a lot of things if he ever found out."

Since that was blatantly obvious, she had no answer. They stood a minute, a marked strain between them. It made Kathryn sad. In their younger days they had been so close. But Susan was a different person. And so was she.

"What will you do?"

Susan cocked her head, her expression thoughtful as she stared in the direction Will had gone. "Do you think I'd make a good mother?"

"No." Kathryn suppressed a shudder. "I don't."

"Thanks for the support." Her lips twisted again, and then she shrugged. "You're right. I'd make a lousy mother."

Susan's shoulders sagged, and the sass seemed to drain away. For the first time since her arrival Kathryn glimpsed the sister she remembered. "But you would. You could raise him. It would almost be like having his real mother, only better."

"Will is a good grandfather, and he loves John William more than anything. They have a happy life together." She spoke as gently as she could. "I could never interfere with that."

Susan's teeth appeared and clamped down on her lower lip. "But you'll watch out for him, won't you? You know, stick around here and make sure the kid's taken care of."

Stay in Seattle permanently? Kathryn's gaze slid over her sister's shoulder to the other side of the knoll, where Jason stood watching them. "Yes. I think I will."

With a deep breath, Susan nodded. "All right then. I can leave him in Aunt Katie's capable care."

Relief washed over her. "I knew you'd do the right thing."

The cocky grin returned. "I'm taking the money, of course. Been thinking about heading south. I hear those boys down in Texas really know how to have a good time."

With a toss of dark curls, she sauntered off in the direction of the Faulkner House.

Kathryn watched her go. Who knew? Maybe Susan would find herself a cowboy and settle down.

Miracles did happen.

Heads turned to watch Susan flounce down the hill, but Jason couldn't tear his eyes from the other twin. Finally, an opportunity to speak with her alone. He excused himself

412

and crossed the space between them before she could get away.

Problem was, his tongue felt as though someone had jerked a knot in it, and all he could do was stand there, looking down at her. How could he ever have thought they looked alike? There was no hint of her sister's cocksure conceit in the guileless green eyes fixed on his, only an open and genuine intelligence and a lovely spirit that reached straight into his chest and squeezed his heart to a halt.

Her lips parted, and she spoke in a soft voice. "I was hoping I'd have a chance to thank you." A blush colored her cheeks. "I can't believe I fainted again."

An automatic reply rose to his lips, a dismissal that he'd done nothing more than any one of the men in Seattle would have done. But a light breeze stirred her hair, and the words would not come. He reached up to brush his fingers across the fizzled ends, the realization of how close that bullet had come slamming into him.

"It's a miracle you weren't killed," he said.

She gave a little laugh. "This has been a day of miracles."

"I didn't know you had a twin," he blurted. "Or that you'd been arrested."

Her smile faded. "Does it matter? Do you

think badly of me?"

The concern on her face softened the edges of the awkwardness that held his tongue hostage. She cared about his opinion. Did that mean she cared for him?

"I could never think badly of you," he said gently. The smile returned, tinted with relief. Swallowing against a lump, he went on. "Beth was an ardent supporter of Susan Anthony. She always wanted to go to New York to attend a rally."

Her eyes softened. "I'm sure you miss her very much."

He didn't answer. Yes, of course he missed Beth. He couldn't imagine a time when the memory of her death wouldn't twist his soul with grief.

And yet . . .

Anger crept over him. What was happening to him? He'd come to Seattle to find a place where he could live in peace with his grief. To find solace in the company of other lonely men, without constantly being reminded of his loss. To escape the presence of women.

Lord, what's happening to me?

"What's wrong?" Kathryn laid a hand on his arm, alert to the sudden change in his mood.

His pulse beat like a drum in his ears.

Even her touch had the power to cloud his thoughts. The impact of that realization struck him.

"Wrong? Nothing's wrong." He had to say it, had to get it out before his brain had a chance to catch up with his heart and stop him. The words spilled out, tumbling over a tongue that refused to be still. "I've only just realized that . . . I'm in love with you."

She nodded sympathetically. "Frightening realization, isn't it?"

"It scares me to death."

A slow grin spread over her lips and crept upward to ignite sparkles in her eyes. "I know how you feel, Jason. Today really is a day of miracles, because I love you too."

A day of miracles. Yes, the Lord had heard his prayers. A battle with no loss of life? How could anyone attribute that to anything but the hand of the Almighty? But the biggest miracle was an answer to a prayer he had not even voiced. Something in his heart had changed. A wound had healed. He loved Kathryn. And she loved him.

The world around them disappeared. He pulled her toward him, and her arms slid up around his neck. Men's voices faded and the lingering smell of smoke dissolved. All that was left was the woman before him and the emotion that washed over his heart like a wave at high tide.

He loved her.

He lowered his lips to hers, determined to prove it with his kiss.

EPILOGUE

Saturday, June 15, 1856
The front room of the Faulkner House was no longer empty. On this rainy Saturday afternoon people filled the chairs set up in two rows facing the fireplace. The cozy furniture had been moved into Madame's sitting room temporarily in anticipation of the wedding guests. It seemed everyone in Seattle wanted to be a part of the bride and groom's happy day.

When all was ready, Reverend Blaine nodded toward the piano and his wife placed her hands upon the ivory keys. Stately music filled the room and echoed up the stairs, a cue to the bride that it was time to meet her groom. He stood beside the minister, fidgeting nervously with the string tie around his neck. That is, until he caught sight of his bride, and then he went still, his eyes alive with a quiet joy.

She descended slowly at first, each step

placed in time with the music. Delicate pink flowers circled the hem and sleeves of her simple wedding gown, each one lovingly embroidered to match the bouquet of sweetbriar that bloomed so plentifully throughout Seattle in June. When she saw her groom across the heads of the guests, a smile lit her face. Her pace sped, and the bride nearly ran down the center aisle.

"That's my new grandma," declared John William from the first row. "Ain't she a beaut?"

An indulgent chuckle rose from the assembled. Seated beside him, Kathryn leaned down to gather him in a hug.

"Yes, she is, sweetheart. She's a beautiful bride." She combed her fingers through his hair with a quick gesture, ending with a finger on his lips. "We must be quiet now and listen."

"Okay," he answered in a loud whisper, and then climbed up into her lap and settled himself comfortably, his attention fixed on the two who stood in front of him hand in hand, beaming into each other's faces.

Jason slid sideways into the place John William vacated and draped an arm across the back of her chair. A giddy delight swept over her at his nearness, and she missed the first few sentences of the minister's ceremony. How could she concentrate when every bit of her was focused on the man whose very presence robbed her of breath?

Well aware of the effect he had on her, a teasing grin tugged at one corner of his lips. He leaned close and whispered, "Two more weeks and that will be us up there."

As if she could forget. Mama and Papa would arrive on the *Fair Lady* next week, bringing with them a cargo hold full of wedding presents that Papa insisted on bestowing. She could not muster much interest in gifts. How could she, when the best gift of all was already hers? And he was sitting right beside her, distracting her with the memory of his embrace when he left her at her door last night, of his lips nuzzling her neck and whispering "I love you" in her ear.

Outside the rain began to fall, huge, fat drops that quickly became a downpour the likes of which she had not seen since the day she arrived in Seattle. They beat on the porch roof so loudly through the open windows that they nearly drowned out Reverend Blaine. Kathryn watched them fall, a silvery curtain that hid the town from view. She'd heard somewhere that rain on a wedding day was good luck. She prayed that omen would hold true for Helen and Will. And for her and Jason.

Turning to face the front of the room, she settled herself comfortably in the curve of Jason's arm and rested her chin on her nephew's silky head. They had love, and that portended a happy marriage far more than a silly omen.

A NOTE FROM LORI
& VIRGINIA

We're sure you've read this disclaimer in almost every novel you pick up: "The characters and events in this book are fictitious. Any resemblance to real people or events is purely coincidental." That statement is true of *Rainy Day Dreams,* with a few exceptions. We created a completely fictitious story and then put it in an actual historical setting during a time when something interesting was going on, and tossed the names of a few real people into the mix as well. We think the combination makes for a delightful reading experience, and we hope you enjoyed the results.

Among the actual historical people featured in *Rainy Day Dreams* are Henry Yesler, David and Louisa Denny, and their daughter, Emily Inez. Henry built the first steam-powered sawmill on the Puget Sound in Seattle. David and Louisa were two of the original settlers in Seattle, and Emily Inez was born there. Quite a bit is known about the Dennys, so we had a lot of material to rely on as we researched this and the previous book in the Seattle Brides series, *A Bride for Noah*. Two sources proved invaluable, and if you're interested in reading actual accounts of the founding of Seattle and the Battle of Seattle, we recommend them to you: *Westward to Alki: The Story of David and Louisa Denny* by Gordon R. Newell, and *Blazing the Way: True Stories, Songs and Sketches of the Puget Sound* by Emily Inez Denny.

If you read those books, you'll discover that many of the events we fictionalized in *Rainy Day Dreams* did happen, though we have taken a bit of literary license — sometimes quite a bit. For instance, there really was a woman running with Louisa Denny on that fearful dash to the blockhouse on January 26, 1856. She wore her hair in fashionable braided loops, and a bullet really did pass through one of the loops. We hope you'll forgive us for inching that bullet a tad to the left and having it chop that braid right off so Kathryn (our fictional heroine) could have another fainting spell that put her in need of rescuing by our dashing hero. We loved Jason and wanted to see him spring heroically into action.

The bare facts of the Battle of Seattle are represented in our account, woven throughout the fiction. The white settlers of Seattle were befriended by the Duwamish Indians under the leadership of Chief Seattle, but many other tribes didn't take kindly to being crowded off of their ancestral lands. They were particularly insulted by a series of treaties initiated by the governor of Washington Territory, Isaac Stevens, beginning in late 1854. These treaties offered trinkets and a little cash for land, plus the requirement that the Indian tribes move onto several small reservation areas. Interracial hostilities escalated, and then the word came that the tribes most offended — which included the Nisqually, Muckleshoot, and Klickitat — had begun amassing an army of braves to force the settlers off of Native American land. Word of an impending attack began to leak to the residents of Seattle through their Indian friends, who were also the targets of hostility because of their friendship with the white settlers.

The construction of the blockhouse from David Denny's personal stock of milled lumber did take place, as did the false alarms that sent the terrified citizens of Seattle dashing for the safety of that small fort in the middle of the night. The *U.S.S.*

Decatur, a U.S. sloop of war under the command of Captain Guert Gansevoort, was stationed in the bay even though the governmental authorities insisted that the people of Seattle were alarmists and that there was no danger of an attack by hostile Indians.

When the attack finally came, the settlers were ready. They huddled inside the blockhouse while a small group of their own, along with one hundred fourteen sailors and marines, defended them. Bullets and arrows and cannonballs flew at a fevered pitch for half a day, and then slacked off when the attackers broke for lunch. Later in the afternoon the fighting began again, but not with the same furious pace. A few volleys of gunshots were exchanged, but by nightfall the hostile Indians gave up and left. The settlers were amazed to discover that though most of the outlying buildings and homes had been ransacked and burned, miraculously there was only one reported death that day. The Battle of Seattle was over almost as soon as it had begun.

That's not to say life became peaceful. Tension hung over Seattle as the citizens worried that more attacks were imminent. They built a second blockhouse and a stockade around the entire central town, and all winter everyone slept inside the fort.

They were tense times, but in the end the pioneering spirit prevailed, the settlers persevered, and Seattle's future remained secure.

Sadly, the Indian war chiefs' hopes that they might one day drive the interlopers from their lands dwindled. We found it interesting to note that in her book, Emily Inez Denny expressed a huge amount of compassion and sympathy for those who had been displaced. The citizens of Seattle truly hoped for a peaceful coexistence with their Native American friends. In the cases of some, like Yoke-Yakeman and Princess Angeline (whose Duwamish name was Kikisoblu), they were successful. But as for the rest of the displaced peoples of that area . . . well, those accounts are well documented in history books.

Beyond those bare facts, almost everything else in *Rainy Day Dreams* was created out of our imaginations for your reading enjoyment. And, to be honest, for our own enjoyment. We fell in love with Kathryn, Jason, Evie, Noah, Helen, John William, and the others. We hope you have too.

To learn more about us and our books, we invite you to visit our websites — www.LoriCopelandandVirginia

Smith.com, www.LoriCopeland.com, and
www.VirginiaSmith.org

Lori & Virginia

DISCUSSION QUESTIONS

1. With which character did you most identify, and why?
2. When she arrives, Kathryn is unhappy to discover that she will be a hotel maid. Why? What happens to change her attitude?
3. Half the town scoffs at the idea of an Indian attack, while the others take the warnings seriously. Discuss the reasons for each viewpoint.
4. What was the main cause of the conflict between the northern Indian tribes and the settlers? Between the northern tribes and the peaceful Duwamish?
5. Why does Jason take an instant dislike to Kathryn?
6. Several friendships develop quickly after Kathryn and Jason arrive in Seattle. Discuss the basis of the friendship between Evie and Kathryn. Between Jason and Will.

7. In a town where the men outnumber the eligible women a hundred to one, how do the ladies handle their position of minority?

8. How did Susan's absence affect Kathryn back home in San Francisco? How does her arrival in Seattle affect Kathryn?

9. For those who read *A Bride for Noah,* how has Evie changed? How has Seattle changed?

10. Jason has not prayed since his wife died. Why? What makes him start praying again?

11. In what ways does Kathryn change from the beginning of the book to the end?

12. Will's dislike of Kathryn was obvious to everyone. What was the true basis of that dislike? How did he let his fears control him against his better judgment?

13. Did Susan choose correctly in her decision regarding John William? Why or why not?

14. Identify all of the happy endings in *Rainy Day Dreams.*

ABOUT THE AUTHORS

Lori Copeland is the author of more than 90 titles, both historical and contemporary fiction. With more than 3 million copies of her books in print, she has developed a loyal following among her rapidly growing fans in the inspirational market. She has been honored with the Romantic Times Reviewer's Choice Award, The Holt Medallion, and Walden Books' Best Seller award. In 2000, Lori was inducted into the Missouri Writers Hall of Fame. She lives in the beautiful Ozarks with her husband, Lance, and their three children and five grandchildren.

Virginia Smith is the author of two dozen inspirational novels and more than fifty articles and short stories. An avid reader with eclectic tastes in fiction, Ginny writes in a variety of styles, from lighthearted relationship stories to breath-snatching suspense.

To learn more about books by Lori Copeland and Virginia Smith or to read sample chapters, log on to
www.harvesthousepublishers.com

The employees of Thorndike Press hope you have enjoyed this Large Print book. All our Thorndike, Wheeler, and Kennebec Large Print titles are designed for easy reading, and all our books are made to last. Other Thorndike Press Large Print books are available at your library, through selected bookstores, or directly from us.

For information about titles, please call:
  (800) 223-1244

or visit our Web site at:
  http://gale.cengage.com/thorndike

To share your comments, please write:
  Publisher
  Thorndike Press
  10 Water St., Suite 310
  Waterville, ME 04901